Praise for Ethan Hawke's

A Bright Ray of Darkness

"[*A Bright Ray of Darkness*] reads like a crackling debut: ruminative, raw, and seemingly pretty personal. . . . Divided, like a work of drama, into acts and scenes, the book wrestles with love, lust, fatherhood, and fame, but what it's mostly about is the occasionally life-threatening but ultimately redemptive hard work of making art."
—*Vogue*

"Ethan Hawke, successful actor, writer, director, producer, has written a very good novel. . . . Hawke, the artist, is one of the more interesting figures we have working today."
—*Chicago Tribune*

"Hawke explores the personal and moral costs of fame and celebrity."
—*The Boston Globe*

"Lovers of theatre will delight in actor and author Ethan Hawke's first book in twenty years. . . . Hawke examines the meaning of marriage and fatherhood across themes of guilt and redemption."
—*Reader's Digest*

"An impressive adventure of the mind. . . . [Hawke's] gripping novel is a meaningful and well-written look at the many ingredients of life in the theater."
—*The Florida Times-Union*

Ethan Hawke

A Bright Ray of Darkness

A four-time Academy Award nominee, twice for writing and twice for acting, Ethan Hawke has starred in the films *Dead Poets Society*, *Reality Bites*, *Gattaca*, and *Training Day*, as well as Richard Linklater's Before Trilogy and *Boyhood*. He is the author of *Rules for a Knight*, *The Hottest State*, and *Ash Wednesday*. He lives in Brooklyn with his four children and his wife.

A Bright Ray
of Darkness

Ethan Hawke

A Bright Ray
of Darkness

VINTAGE CONTEMPORARIES

VINTAGE BOOKS

A Division of Penguin Random House LLC

New York

FIRST VINTAGE CONTEMPORARIES EDITION, JANUARY 2022

The Library of Congress has cataloged the Knopf edition as follows:
Names: Hawke, Ethan, author.
Title: A bright ray of darkness / Ethan Hawke.
Description: First edition. | New York : Alfred A. Knopf, 2021.
Identifiers: LCCN 2020019918 (print) | LCCN 2020019919 (ebook)
Classification: LCC PS3558.A8165 B75 2021 (print) | LCC PS3558.A8165 (ebook) |
DDC 813/.54—dc23
LC record available at https://lccn.loc.gov/2020019918
LC ebook record available at https://lccn.loc.gov/2020019919

Vintage Contemporaries Trade Paperback ISBN: 978-0-8041-7052-9
eBook ISBN: 978-0-385-35239-0

Book design by Cassandra J. Pappas

www.vintagebooks.com

Printed in the United States of America
10   9   8   7   6   5   4   3   2   1

To Jack

A Bright Ray
of Darkness

So Shaken as We Are

When you finish a movie, they always forget to call you a car. When you are starting a movie, everything runs perfectly—town cars, hotel rooms, per diem—but once the film ends they couldn't give a shit. I arrived home late in the afternoon on the first Sunday of September. Rehearsal for *Henry IV* would start the next day. I should say I arrived in New York. I didn't go home. I got into a taxi outside JFK international arrivals and told the guy to take me to the Mercury Hotel.

The driver stared at me through the rearview mirror.

"William Harding?" he asked, in a slight Indian accent.

"Yup," I answered.

"Is what they are saying about you and your wife true?"

I had been in Cape Town, South Africa, and wasn't yet aware of the media buzz around my collapsing life.

For my driver, my silence was an admission of guilt.

"People of your kind, they make me feel upset where I breathe." He spoke to the mirror. "You have everything, but . . . that is not enough. You are greedy, my friend, am I right? Driven by greed?"

We entered the highway.

"You don't even know me," I said quietly.

"Pardon me?" he shouted.

"You don't even know me," I said again, louder.

"I know you. I used to like your movies very much."

I could see his brown eyes bounce up from the road and scour my face and my clothes.

"I am a large fan of the cinema. I thought you were different than the shiny fake ones. I liked the futuristic movie—with the music. Ahhh . . . great music. And the one you did with the young Russian girl, very sexy movie, but good, smart. I liked that one. People like you are spoiled so it is difficult for you to live a meaningful life. You do what you love for a living; you get paid well to do it; you get awards. Do you think I have any awards at home? Do you think that's because I am undeserving?"

"Keep your eyes on the road, pal," I said.

"Remember this next time you are complaining," my taxi driver continued. *"No one wants to be hearing you!* I have a seventeen-year-old who is giving me hell all day long. I am paying bills, always. I work two jobs and if you want me to listen to you whimpering— you are speaking with the wrong taxi driver. You are hearing me? I am not crying salty tears for you, my friend."

I did my first movie when I was eighteen and now at thirty-two I'd been sort of famous for the entirety of my adult life. So, I've been dealing with being recognized by strangers for a good long while. Usually I am adept at ignoring it. My powers of denial are formidable. They have to be. If someone told you that everywhere they went they hear people behind them whispering their name and details about their life and ex-lovers, you might assume they were a delusional paranoid schizophrenic. But this was my reality.

"Why don't we celebrate goodness, honesty, substance? Why not?" my cabdriver said. "Why don't we find somebody who's not a self-satisfied plastic pod person and put them on the cover of *People* magazine and sell twenty million copies of that? What if a person of humility could have twenty million Google hits? Why are we not having awards show full of adult people, who are talking about grown-up-person ideas? Like for why are we born? It's not all your fault," he reassured me. "If they put me on *Entertainment Tonight* would I be as big an asshole as you? That's the valuable question."

"I don't know," I said.

I didn't want to go home. If it weren't for my kids I wouldn't have come back to this city for twenty or thirty years. Coming back to New York was like placing my head into the center of a well-made noose.

My driver took me to Thirty-second Street and First Avenue. He quoted the Bhagavad Gita, talked about Eli Manning and the New York Giants, and told me that sex wasn't relevant. He'd been faithful eighteen years and his wife was a lesbian.

I didn't say anything. I just looked him in the eyes through the mirror and nodded.

"If your wife leaves you, it's OK," he lectured. "You violated a sacred trust, the covenant of your marriage, and you must respect her decision, my friend. We must respect each other's freedom and everybody agrees with that idea until that freedom causes us pain. Then, when they hurt us, we resent their freedom and talk about how our ex-person is a crazy, or looney tunes, or that *'they have problems.'* They are not a crazy person; they don't have problems— they just have their own will." He laughed and stopped in front of the Mercury Hotel, an old building covering half a city block, mysterious, gothic, like a place where one goes mad and shoots himself, as many had. I'd romanticized the hotel since I was a kid; famous writers, poets, musicians, and painters had lived and worked there. Built just after the Civil War, it was now run-down and seedy, full of tourists from Tokyo and Germany, and operating on reputation alone.

"If you respect your woman, you will let her grow her own course. She is not the important person right now. You have children. Your son needs you. Your daughter needs you. Please take a shower and smell more-better. You dress like a hobo and stink of piss and cigarettes! Get to rehab!"

"Cut me a little slack, will ya?" I shook my head. "It was a long flight."

I shoveled the money through the bulletproof slot.

"One more thing," he added. "Can I get a photo?"

I WALKED THROUGH the doors of the hotel and up to the front desk. The lobby was paneled in a dark, rich chocolate wood. The place smelled like soft moss around an old tree. The ceiling had a mural of cherubs riding clouds as if they were horses. They were friendly angels but it was unclear if they were welcoming the living or the dead.

"Wow, look who it is, Hester Prynne herself," said the owner, Bart Asher. Even at seventy-four, he still manned the front desk. "When I read about you in the *Post* and saw how you fucked it all up, I got excited, figured we might see you."

"You got a room?" I asked.

"Best room in New York City," he said proudly.

BART SHOWED ME to room 714, which was lightly furnished with a living room set from the Eisenhower era. The space was dark but warm and comfortable, with high ceilings and large thick wood moldings. Dirty yellow light seeped in from the cloudy windows.

There was a kitchen, a den, and two bedrooms; one for me, and one for my children.

"How much?" I asked.

"How long will you be staying?"

"What kind of chances did the *Post* give my marriage?"

Glancing to my bags, he studied the stuffed animals and African coloring books. He looked up with a warm smile.

"I'm a romantic. I'll give you the place for free for one month. Till you get back together."

"What happens if we don't get back together?"

"You gotta get back together," he said simply.

Rebellious Liquor in My Blood

Scene 1

R ehearsal for Shakespeare's *Henry IV* began promptly at 10:00 a.m. I hadn't slept at all and the back of my throat still burned from puking. My first night at the Mercury had not ended well. I worried people could smell the alcohol seeping through my pores as I stepped off the elevator and into the rehearsal hall.

I like old theaters or sweaty church basements, places where you can smell some history on the walls. This place was antiseptic. Spread over half of the twenty-seventh floor of a corporate office building, our rehearsal area was roughly the size of a baseball diamond. The lengths of the far two walls were floor-to-ceiling windows. The lights, cops, and chaos of Times Square screamed mutely through the glass. It was distracting as hell.

Earlier that morning I had taken my daughter to school. We paused in front of her Upper East Side kindergarten. She asked me, "Are you living in a hotel because it's closer to rehearsal?"

I stood there, hungover and silent.

"That's the only reason I can think of," she added.

"Well, that's one of the reasons."

"Are you gonna keep living there?"

I stared at her in silence.

"'Cause I was thinking," she continued, "if you and Mommy aren't going to live together anymore, that would be great! I can get a puppy and Mommy wouldn't be allergic."

"This afternoon, when school and rehearsal are finished, we'll go to the pound and rescue a puppy. Deal?"

"I get to name her."

I nodded and we shook hands.

Promising a child a puppy. Pathetic.

INSIDE THE REHEARSAL HALL, tables were set into a large square with folding chairs arranged all around the outside edges. The first day of rehearsal for a play is always the same: bagels, coffee, orange juice, pencils, Actors' Equity forms, nervous chatter, people who haven't seen each other since that boring production of *The Iceman Cometh* back in '04, the election of a union deputy, the stage manager's speeches about promptness and work-related injuries.

This morning was a little different only because there were so many people, thirty-nine in the cast and about twenty-five designers and assistants and producer types. The "Star" was already there when I arrived. That's how you know you're late: when a movie star like Virgil Smith is there before you. To his credit, he had about four scripts with him, all different versions of the play—and the play was damn long, so he was surrounded by piles of papers. A massive white beard, which he must've been growing for a year, covered his face. He looked like Orson Welles; or, I guess, in truth, he looked like Falstaff, which was the idea. Virgil stood up when he saw me and walked over to the table where I was standing. He gave me a big bear hug. I know he meant it to be nice, but it felt embarrassing, like pity. I was so hungover and dizzy I could've cried in his arms or punched him in the face. He was probably the only legitimate American film star who was also a universally celebrated and respected theater actor. He was everything I'd ever wanted to be, since I was old enough to want. In England, it's common I guess, but in America, Virgil Smith is one of a kind. He's a Rhodes Scholar, a Yale Drama School graduate, who won his first Oscar playing a gangster in what is arguably considered the finest American film since *Citizen Kane*. He'd won the Tony three times, once for his Macbeth, and two other times for his performances in original plays. We had never met before, but since I was kind of famous and he was superfamous, I guess he figured we should hug.

"Is it true?" he asked with his big, wet Academy Award–winning eyes.

"Is what true?" I asked.

"What I read in the papers."

"Depends on what you read."

"Well"—he paused and smiled; I'd seen him give this same look in a hundred movies—"I read you cheated on your wife and that she's demanding a divorce."

"Yeah, that's pretty much it. That's the story," I said and left him there. This was not the conversation of my dreams.

Next, I went and sat down at my assigned seat, took out my script, and tried to be nervous about the read-through that was to begin soon. There were many things in my life about which it made sense to be nervous, and this was the gentlest one.

The previous night had been worse than I expected. I left the hotel, went home to see the kids and talk to my wife. She didn't come downstairs to say hello, but I could hear her clomping around above us. She told the nanny to inform me I could take the kids out to dinner and put them to bed. She would meet me at the bar across the street at 10:00 p.m. The kids and I went to the park. We had a pretty great time seeing each other. I sat in the sandbox over at Union Square Park with the two of them pushing sand around and watching the sunset.

"It's darking again!" my three-year-old son shouted, pointing at the sun drifting below the buildings, the last gold light of the day hitting our faces.

"It does that every day, silly," said my daughter.

"But it's darking *again*!" he said, tugging on my shirt and looking me square in the eyes only an inch from my face.

"I know, buddy. It does that every day."

"No, it doesn't. This morning it didn't," he said.

"The sun goes down at *night*," my daughter responded.

"It's a miracle," he said.

"No," my daughter corrected, "it's a miracle when it comes up."

"I like it when it goes down," he said.

My love for these two young people was easy, uncomplicated, and unceasing, like a love for water, stars, light, breathing, or food. For me, marriage had been misshapen but parenthood had been a spontaneous pleasing reflex. Making a peanut butter and jelly sandwich, watercoloring, listening to Woody Guthrie and Elizabeth Cotten, playing crazy eights, throwing a ball, playing pickle, putting on shoes, treasure hunts, walking through puddles, singing songs, paper airplanes, I could do all that. Meeting my responsibility to these two was more nourishing than sleep.

After I put the kids to bed, read them stories, and scratched their backs, I went to the bar across the street to wait for my wife. Mary didn't show and I sat there alone for over three hours, waiting, dousing myself with whiskey, until I was blind drunk and angry about being stood up. I don't think it was the alcohol, I think it was the rancid gazpacho I ate; regardless, I finished my first night back in NYC violently vomiting my guts out, crying in spastic fits and spurts at the base of the Mercury toilet. Turns out I was at the wrong bar. Mary had been waiting down the block. The strange thing was neither of us had even tried to call the other.

It was darking indeed.

A MUSCULAR MAN in his late forties took his seat next to me at the rehearsal table. His name was Ezekiel. He wore a crocheted Rastafarian beanie, about five or six gold bracelets, and an olive green U.S. Army jacket. All of which, on him, radiated a masculine vitality. We sat there for the next couple hours with the rest of the cast going over all the necessary Actors' Equity information you need to sort through before you're allowed to begin any production. The fluorescent lights above us hummed in a frequency that made you want to murder someone. There was the unspeakable boredom of being guided through the contracts. How many weeks you must work to qualify for Equity coverage. The Equity rep giving his long speech about workers' compensation and the future of the union. These guys are always out-of-work actors and give each union address with a sincere attempt at flair, like it's an audition. Then the company was allotted a fifteen-minute break before rehearsal would officially commence. Time alone with myself was the last thing I wanted.

I rode the elevator down the twenty-seven floors to Forty-second Street and stood in the middle of Times Square to smoke. Waves of people moved past me, bumping and shaking with their shopping bags, off to see some tourist attraction. Madame Tussauds wax museum, the Disney Store—it was all there. My son once asked me, "Mommy has two figures in the wax museum and you don't have any. Why is that?"

I lit my cigarette. A few other cast members were lurking around as well, smoking or buying a slice of pizza, but I didn't want to talk to them.

Two days earlier I had been in Cape Town filming a movie. The shoot should have been a meaningful, eye-opening experience. I saw South African townships with soul-racking poverty: a nine-year-old boy climbing an electrical wire on the side of a highway to siphon electricity for his family; a little girl dividing her ice cream sandwich into thirds for her brothers when it looked like none of them had eaten in a month. I went on a safari and stared into the eyes of a lion three feet from my face; I saw a leopard eat an impala and drag the carcass up into a tree for her cubs while hyenas tried to snatch it away; I spent four days at sea looking at wild penguins, whales, and dolphins; I saw the prison cell where Nelson Mandela spent eighteen of his twenty-seven years in prison and quietly transformed a nation. But all the while, I could only think about the dissolution of my marriage.

Mary and I had first met six years earlier backstage after one of her concerts during the largest blizzard in living memory. Watching her dance and sing, I was transfixed by the idea that someone of my own generation could be so confident. The whole of Irving Plaza felt warm from her light. Onstage, she was fierce and blistering with intensity. In the greenroom, she was the same. I shook her hand. She was sweaty, fresh from the performance. Our attraction was immediate and uncomfortable. This was in the days that followed my first major studio film release. She complimented me on the movie. I praised her latest album. She understood everything that had been happening to me. We were both inside the hurly-burly of fame, and we felt known by the other. The connection we shared was simple and unavoidable, like gravity. I was grateful to have a friend. After hours of conversation, I looked around and realized we were the only ones left in the greenroom. Her bandmates and manager were waiting in her bus. We shook hands goodbye, but it was actual work not to strip down naked and fuck right there on the tables full of snacks and beer. It was as if I could already smell our kids. I went home to my East Village apartment and looked out the window. In the light of the streetlamps I could see the still falling snow. I prayed:

Whoever created that woman, I worship you.
I dedicate my life to you. Please, Lord Creator,
Let me be that woman's husband. I will care for your
     creation.
I will honor every step she takes.

The sky seemed to unlock all the snow in the world.

"YO, DUDE, aren't you that guy from that fuckin' movie?" An acne-riddled young man came up to me. Then he shouted over to a couple of his friends across the mind-blasting noise of Times Square.

"Don't worry about it, man. I'm nobody."

"Yes you are. Come on, dude, let me take a picture of you." He was wearing a bright red Adidas sweat suit and had an aggressiveness about him that was unsettling.

"You don't want my picture," I said, trying to keep him moving with the current of people around us.

"Yeah, I do," he said simply, taking out his phone and continuing to try and wave his buddies over to us.

"You don't even know my name," I said.

"You're from that movie," he said excitedly, "I know you."

"Yeah, well, I don't like to do photo ops, you know? It makes me feel like a freak, you know what I mean?" I asked, trying to briskly move away.

"Don't be an asshole, bro." He grabbed my shoulder and turned me around. "It's the least you can do for your fans."

"Yeah well . . ." I tried to meander away.

"Just let us take your picture," said his larger, more powerful friend, who had shuffled over.

"You rocked in that fuckin' movie, dude. '*Yo, Jackie,* give me the kiss-ash!'" Another buddy stepped close and imitated me from one of my least favorite films. There's a direct inverse relationship between the quality of a film and how much you get paid. The dumber the movie the more they pay. That film was my most lucrative.

"Yeah, thanks a lot, guys," I said, offering out my hand to shake theirs. "I appreciate it. I'm happy to meet you all. I just don't want a shitty photo of me stuck on the Internet forever, ya understand?" I smiled.

They stared at me blankly.

I went on, "But, thanks anyway."

This dude in the red Adidas sweats, the two buddies, and now two of their girlfriends would have none of it. They all wrapped their arms around me. Somebody else, an older guy, grabbed a cell phone to take the photo.

As a kid, I confess, I fantasized about signing autographs or people taking my picture. I generally imagined all the people being admiring. I never imagined hate mail.

This dude in the red Adidas sweats whispered in my ear, "Man, you are a fuckin' idiot." With his arm draped over my shoulders as our photo was taken, he continued, "You should be grateful. Just fucking smile."

TAKING THE ELEVATOR back up to rehearsal, I leaned against the wall and cried. Now, usually in life whenever I've cried, I've felt better afterwards, but these days I couldn't stop crying and nothing ever changed. As soon as I pulled myself together and wiped my eyes, the elevator doors opened and my blood ran with anxiety about being late. I was letting my director down. I imagined him humiliating me, using my lateness to set an example for the rest of the cast. Sometime in the last few days I had forgotten completely that I was a thirty-two-year-old grown man.

When I got out at the twenty-seventh floor, everyone was still just milling around drinking coffee. No one noticed I was late. A gentle hand touched my shoulder. I turned.

"I'll be playing your wife." An attractive young woman looked up at me from underneath meticulously groomed red hair. This woman's translucent skin, expensive clothes, and bright green eyes were so intoxicating that she looked as if she had stepped out of a Renaissance painting. She even smelled classy. *So, this is Lady Percy,* I thought to myself. *I must stay away from her at all costs.*

"Who abandoned you?" she asked in a warm theater-trained voice.

"What do you mean?"

"Your mother or your father? I've never met an actor who was any good at all, who wasn't left by one or the other." She winked and walked away. I tried not to stare.

I turned awkwardly and walked to the "welcome" table, poured myself another cup of coffee, and stood next to Ezekiel.

"What's going on?" I asked.

"The diva's in there complaining some more," he said, referring to our Falstaff. All morning, our "star" had been sifting through various copies of the folio, arguing minute textual discrepancies with the dramaturge.

"He better be as good as advertised." Ezekiel sighed.

I nodded.

"You get any of them Danishes?" he asked.

"Nah, I'm not hungry," I said, trying to keep my distance.

"How you holding up?" he asked me, taking on a more serious tone.

"Barely," I mumbled, as I sipped my coffee.

"You look skinny." He smiled. "Don't forget to eat."

There was a long silence as we stood and watched the rest of the cast mill listlessly around. Ezekiel seemed to be studying my situation. Finally, he leaned over and whispered conspiratorially, "Did she have a shaved pussy?"

I looked at him and absorbed his warm, smiling brown eyes. "Yeah." I nodded.

"Jesus wept," he lamented. "They all shave these days." He nodded in amazement. "It's sad really . . . I grew up with bush. These girls today, they grow up on porn. They have dirty little potty mouths and send nasty little text messages that'd make a sailor blush. Tattoos?"

"Yup." I nodded, remembering.

"Of course," he said, scolding himself. "Well, let me be among the first to say: good for you."

MY YOUNG MISTRESS had been delightful, like a hot-air balloon; the sound of water falling; the scent of cherry blossoms—all that simple, ancient, cliché shit. Within moments of being introduced to this young South African woman in a Cape Town nightclub, I knew exactly what I was going to do. And don't think I don't understand that every second of this tawdry adulterous high jinks isn't horribly pat. I realize that there is no way to present my infidelity now that would give it substance, but that's not how it felt. It felt like the stuff of Tolstoy—grand, sweeping, epic. She was a time machine. I was young again; I was mysterious; I smelled good. Life was vibrant, dangerous, unknown, and I lit cigarettes in a cool way. This young woman handed me my life back and she loved doing it. And let me be very clear: I was overflowing with gratitude. Her father was an ANC member who owned a local independent bookstore and she ran the place. Together they published a literary journal and organized a variety of political events. She was badass. Her older sister was nine months pregnant, and in labor. She kept checking her phone. She was thrilled about becoming an aunt. I asked her to dance, listened to her breathe, bided my time, and counted the seconds until I would kiss her. Like a sophomore getting hard at the high school sock hop, I pulled her close to avoid public embarrassment. She looked up at me with knowing, wet brown eyes as she felt me press against her.

"Aren't you a married man?" she asked.

I snuck my dance partner safely out a back door of the bar. I wasn't aware of the photos people took of us dancing at the club until they were all over the Internet. We skulked down a fire escape into a parking lot and kissed as soon as we were out of sight. I'd forgotten what a kiss was like; I'd forgotten what it was like to hold someone who *wanted* to be held; someone who dissolved upon your touch; who wanted you to launch your hand up under her skirt; who was hoping you would reach a little bit further; push a little harder; someone who made little noises. Now, I'm smart enough to know that blind pursuit of these kinds of shenanigans doesn't lead you to any kind of authentic, substantive, enlightened existence. I guess I know that. I mean, maybe I know that. Or I should say I had long held that to be true, but in that moment, I would have rather died—had a bullet zip right through my cerebral cortex and my blood splash out onto the asphalt—than let go of that girl's hand. She felt like an instrument of the Divine. She was escorting me through a door. A door that would close abruptly behind me, end my life as I knew it; break apart my family and decimate the life I had been building for years. I would be left despondent, suicidal, and having done permanent damage to my children's lives. I pretty much knew all that would happen and still, I wanted this young woman so badly I was without anything resembling conflict.

"You're married to that rock star, right?" she asked simply.

"We're doing a 'trial separation,'" I answered with no expression.

"You're still wearing a ring?"

"That's true," I said quietly. "Because our marriage counselor suggested we not move too fast, so we are not supposed to sleep with anyone else, just live separately. I'm still hoping maybe our marriage can be salvaged. But, I also keep hoping that I accidentally die so I don't have to live through the storm that I know is coming. My wife hates my guts. She told me the word 'wife' is like a fork stuck between her shoulder blades. I have two kids that I love more than anything, and starting this family has been the most important thing I ever tried to do—the only thing that matters to me. I promised myself I would never be as stupid and selfish as my own parents . . . I know I want to stay married but I don't love my wife anymore, and I am scared shitless. And I don't know what I'm going to do without that love."

She agreed to drive me home.

WE STOPPED IN FRONT of my apartment. I was still hoping she might refuse my invitation and save me from what I was trying to do.

"If I come up, will you dance with me again?"

My Cape Town apartment was a three-story walk-up and it took us twenty minutes to climb the stairs. We made out on each step. Once inside, I put on music that she thought was "sad and sexy." My wife hated this music; hell, she flinched any time I reached for the radio.

"Melancholy," this young woman whispered into my ear.

"What do you mean?"

"You know," she said with a slight smile.

She stood on my feet as I danced her around the room. I wanted to be inside her lungs, to swim in her. I picked her up and carried her to my bedroom. I know if my confidence were stronger, my sense of self more secure, I would have been less moved. This was not lust; it was not as simple as that. For the first time in years, I felt like a human being—born of this world and passing—but here, present and alive. I laid her down on my bed and lifted her light cotton skirt up, pulled down her underwear, and unveiled an entirely shaved pussy with a little tattoo of an old-fashioned key right below her hipbone. I kissed her key, slipped my shirt off, and started snaking out of my jeans.

"Do you have a rubber?" she whispered sweetly, taking off her skirt.

"No," I said, hoping this would be the bell saving me from adultery or whatever the hell you call what I was doing.

"Hold on a second, I have one in the car." She hopped up and ran out and down the stairs, then onto the street in only a T-shirt that she was pulling down to cover her bare bottom. I lay there in bed, anxiety seizing its moment—*What am I doing? what am I doing? what am I doing?* But I knew exactly what I was doing.

When my young lover came back up the stairs to my Cape Town loft with a condom in her hand, she was thrilled her sister had safely given birth to a healthy baby girl. I was a disaster. My erection was gone and I knew it wasn't coming back. That made me hate my wife even more than I had hours earlier. This girl looked so adorable naked in her bright blue T-shirt against her dark skin. I was miserable that I would disappoint her. Moments before I'd felt large and masculine. Now I was diminished, and fragile. Trying to will my body to function, I lay on top of her pretending to be domineering and assertive, but my penis betrayed me. It was shrinking smaller with each phony kiss. This was ridiculous, I thought. I *wanted* to cheat on my wife, to throw my family to the wind, but I wasn't man enough to do it. A failure on all fronts.

"Are you OK?" she asked.

"I think I'm about to die," I said.

"Your heart is beating so fast," she whispered.

I looked down and saw my chest rattling like a washing machine in an old cartoon.

"I think I'm going to die," I repeated.

"Let me hold you," she said into my ear. I buried my face in her chest and cried and cried and cried. It was the first winds in what would become an absolute hurricane. I don't know how long tears fell down my face, but when I returned to consciousness hours later, she was writhing underneath me and we were fucking.

"Let me get those rubbers," I said.

"Don't worry about it," she breathed into my ear. "Just come on my belly."

I lay there in the darkness absorbing the faint image of her deep brown eyes, so caring and passionate. Her young breasts, her shimmering skin, her arms holding mine—the smell of her—the smell of sex. Why hadn't I smelled that in so long? I rubbed my face in her hair, pulled out, and came on her belly as she had so politely requested. Then I buried my head in between her legs, holding her ass as she wriggled and came. I hugged her tight and she purred in my ear. We held each other for an hour or so. Then we were at it again.

"Where do you want me to come now?" I whispered.

"On my breasts," she said. "Come on my breasts, sweetheart."
And I did.

Immediately, before I grew soft, I slipped inside her again. I couldn't stop. It's not like I am some gonzo dynamo Casanova. It was more like I was having a manic episode or seizure. I knew that as soon as I stopped making love to this young woman, an ugly new reality would rain down. So, I kept fucking.

"Come on my face now," she said. "On my lips and on my neck."

And I did. And I wasn't done.

"I am going to come on your ass now," I said.

And in the silent space between us, some deeply underground realm we had entered together, she asked sincerely, "Do you want to hurt me?"

"Yes," I answered, quick as thought.

"I am so scared," she said.

"Me too," I said.

And I came for the last time. She was bathed in me.

"Melancholy," she whispered again into my ear. "You are like a memory already."

THE STAGE MANAGER ANNOUNCED that work would begin momentarily. We all walked back into the rehearsal hall and sat with our open scripts, freshly sharpened pencils, coffee, and bottled water in front of us. The thirty-nine members of the cast waited quietly as the stage manager shuffled around showing the producers where to sit. We stared at one another from across this large square around which we, the cast, were seated, each assessing the others in our own fashion. *Who will be my friend? Who will try to stop me from getting what I want?* Many were anxiously flipping through their texts with highlighters. The designers and the assistant stage managers were the last to take their seats along the perimeter of the room. In the center of everything, as if in spotlight, sat Virgil Smith, his beard, and his piles of paper.

My first exposure to the Bard was when I was near thirteen. I stayed up late one night and watched Laurence Olivier's *King Lear* on public television. The production was cheap and I spent the first hour stupefied in boredom. I didn't understand a word, couldn't fathom what all the fuss was about. Then, somehow, the play's spell was cast. Three hours went by and I found myself sobbing as the credits rolled. I didn't understand Shakespeare, but I loved it. I loved the mystery of not knowing something that was so clearly masterfully created. It seemed to promise that answers might exist, for those hungry enough to pay attention. Christmas that year, my mom gave me a copy of Laurence Olivier's *On Acting*. Somewhere near the end, Olivier challenged young actors, asserting he was the reigning king . . . and that if any young actor was serious, they would get to work and take the crown from his head. He would not give it away freely. Well, Laurence Olivier was long dead and behind all those papers his golden crown lay squarely on the head of Virgil Smith.

OUR DIRECTOR, J. C. CALLAHAN, stood up in front of us. He was in his early sixties with a shaved, balding head, a bow tie, and a custom-made tweed suit. He was an elegant and powerful man with large, kind, teary blue eyes. His formidable confidence was a mystery. He stood before us, five feet, six inches tall, like an Irish Buddha. Underneath his feet and sprawling out beneath all our tables, chairs, and shoes were reams of tape, probably ten different colors laid out in odd geometric designs of the various floor plans of the set. Red for scene one; yellow for scene two; green marked the battle; et cetera. It looked like a map of our future.

Times Square loomed silently, blinking its mad lights through the immaculately clean windows around us.

"All right, here we are," J.C. began, taking an extraordinarily long and uncomfortable pause before he continued. "I know what you all are expecting—the generic 'Let's get started' speech." He barely moved as he spoke. "But I don't have time to tell you all to take it easy. I don't have time to say, 'Let's get to know each other'; 'Let's get more comfortable.' I simply don't have time." He reminded me of a lion with its eyes fixed, body completely still, but its tail swishing back and forth behind him.

"I have six weeks to prepare this play. I don't want you to take it easy. I don't want you to relax. Today we are going to read through the play . . . and I know what good directors say: 'Let's familiarize ourselves with the text'; 'If you stumble . . . just take it back.' But I am not a 'good' director. I say, *Do not stumble*. I say you should already be 'familiar with the text.' Six weeks. That is nothing. I want us to begin today by grabbing this play by its very significant balls and squeezing them so tight that the world hears its cry. You understand me?" His cadence was unadorned and clear.

"There are only two kinds of Shakespeare productions: ones that change your life, and ones that suck shit. That's it. Because if it doesn't change the audience's life . . . the production has failed." He paused for effect, surveying the room. He was not scared, not overconfident, just tremendously alert. I had met him only once before, over coffee to discuss my playing Hotspur. I told him I was a film actor. I couldn't "afford" to do the play. I lacked the training. I gave him a bunch of excuses. Then he spoke for a half an hour about the value of scaling the great roles, pitching ourselves against the past, measuring our mettle against the generations that came before, inspiring ourselves to be our best, meeting the wall of our talent. Until abruptly I said, "I'm in." I shook his hand right then and there.

"Shakespeare isn't beautiful," he continued. "It isn't poetic. Shakespeare is the greatest mind of the theater, ever. Shakespeare is nature, like the Niagara Falls, or the aurora borealis. The Grand Canyon. Shakespeare is life, and life—if it is to be a great life—is not meek. Life is full of blood, piss, sweat, cum, vaginal fluid, tears, and I want to see that all onstage." Some people kind of half-chuckled. "Don't laugh. We will do it. I want the audience to smell you. When your friend dies, I want to hear your tears smack the floor. When you fight, I want to feel adrenaline slip through my bloodstream. Violence electrifies a room. I want our fights to be so real that people think about leaving the theater *and*"—he stressed—"I want no one to get hurt. That is the razor's edge that we will walk. We can do it because we are serious craftsmen and artists and our life is dedicated to something larger than ourselves."

He smiled for the first time. The room was dead still.

"For a few short months we will be monks and nuns dedicated in totality to our calling. We will care only about beauty. Beauty defined as complete honesty. We will celebrate what is best in each other; bring it out and plant it onstage; let it grow and then we will die."

He glanced over at an older actor sitting directly to his right. In the look exchanged between them, it was clear they had known one another for many years. This actor was playing King Henry the Fourth. He'd won a few hundred thousand theater awards. If I looked at him too long I got nervous. He wasn't the biggest star in the company (as mentioned, that slot was reserved for the A-list movie star playing Falstaff), but he was our finest actor.

"Some of you may be thinking, *Ahhh, he's talking to the folks with the big parts* . . . Let me assure you, I am not. We are a company. Nothing makes me want to slap myself on the head with a concrete block more than a production of the Scottish play where everyone sits around and watches the Thane act. Laughing it up at jokes no one else gets. It makes me physically *sick*. Our goal is a company goal. To put life onstage. Shakespeare and his poetry will lead us—like an incantation—but *we,* each one of us, need to be present. If we do not believe that art and beauty are important, who will?"

We sat silent.

"The play is designed for the ear, not the eye. The eye can look ahead; it can look behind. It can be distracted. It can close. But the ear is always only in the present. It hears what is. The actor needs to make our author's intentions 'visible' to the listener. The way to do that is clarity of utterance, and to breathe—at the end—never in middle of each line. Are you listening?"

We were.

"We will become Shakespeare's voice. I have been doing this my whole life. I directed my first production of this play with my youth group in the basement of my Methodist church in Minneapolis when I was fourteen years old. I was born to do this, and I'm telling you: it takes a *company*. We need to inspire each other. This shit is not for students. It is for grown-ups. That's why it's always done so badly. And we, with this group of people sitting in this room, have the chance to excel. Like a melting snowball flying through the fires of hell, we have a chance to be part of the solution. We are going to come down on this city like God's fucking fist and do the *greatest American Shakespeare ever.* That is our goal. And we will begin today. With Act One, scene one."

Nothing in the room moved.

THOUGH MY WHOLE WORLD was collapsing around me, there was one thing I still possessed. I don't think it's important; I don't think it will get me past St. Peter or through the pearly gates of heaven; most of time I mock it—but I have always been a good actor.

There was always someplace in the world where my body knew what to do. I was good at something and having that place to go had been enough. And now more than ever, I needed my profession. I needed to lean on it, to be held by it. It isn't much and I've often been embarrassed by it (as pretending to be someone else seemed a dubious thing to excel at), but somehow my life as a performer is at the absolute core of my sense of self-worth. And I have never misplaced a gratitude for this love in my life. I've done nothing to deserve it and little to nurture it. It was a gift that had been given to me and, with this in my pocket, I have always thought of myself as lucky. So, this little fighting Irish oddball director didn't need to say all that to rile me up—my pencil had broken in my hand two sentences into his speech. I couldn't wait to act. If I could do it well, I might reach back and drag my pride out of the dark, cavernous well into which it seemed to have fallen. This was going to be the one thing in my life I would not fuck up.

J.C. sat down, glanced around our sprawling rehearsal room, seemed to look each one of us in the eyes, closed his script, and, as if preparing to submerge himself in a dream, closed his eyes. Virgil Smith fiddled with his big white beard and the wrinkled pages of his manically underlined script. The King opened his notebook and found his place with an absolute minimum of movement. Ezekiel took a sip of coffee and checked out the young redheaded woman playing my wife as she dabbed her lips with gloss. Everyone was still quiet.

Directly across from me was the actor playing Prince Hal. We had met a thousand times at auditions and openings over the years. We were the same age and physical build. The path of his career had been humble and hardworking; Juilliard, London, Broadway. For casting calls, we were constantly up for the same roles. He had won an Obie and been nominated for two Tonys already, but was still as poor as Job's turkey. I was rich as a ragman and had made an absolute donkey's ass of myself on the global tabloid page.

I smiled at him. He smiled back. The stage manager began.

"*King Henry the Fourth, Parts One and Two* by William Shake-speare . . ."

AS THE RUN-THROUGH BEGAN I discovered that by reciting these lines of this warrior, Hotspur, I could feel a breeze blowing through me ventilating the seething anger that was scalding my organs and literally hurting me. My stomach was twisted in pain all the time but there was a rhythm in the words that soothed. Long speeches fell out of my mouth without thought. The beat of the play sunk into my guts and surged like cool water splashing against my fury, easing the burning of my stomach. When a performance is going well there is no thought, you are not amused at how well you might be "acting"—there is no *you*—you don't remember how it went. You have no discerning mind. When my scenes finished, I would sit alert in my chair and listen to the text, watching the other actors—but still there was no thought, no opinion. Then like lucidly stepping into a hallucination I would be inside the play again. Sometimes another actor's nervousness, a glint in their eye, a self-conscious hand gesture, would almost break the spell. Or I would distract myself and remember the director staring at me with his hard, unflinching beam and I would fall out for a second noticing "the real" world, but quickly the beat of the words would carry me off again. The first two and a half hours of the play went by like a subway train that forgot to stop.

We arrived at my death scene and I was foaming at the mouth challenging "Prince Hal" to meet his doom. The heat and energy of Shakespeare's language was filling me with strength. I could feel *hate* and for the first time in my life understood how an all-encompassing rage could feel good. It was clear and unconflicted. In those moments, I was living deep inside the metaphor of the play, intuiting the text instinctively—for a moment there was no Mercury Hotel, no divorce, no children, no shame; there were only the ideas, the rhythm, the language, and my breath all happening spontaneously.

The outside world tends to celebrate the most trivial superficial aspects of an actor's life, lifting their personality to a plastic God-like status, but the actual joy of acting lies in the absence of personality. In taking on and inhabiting the accoutrements of another's being—where they are from, their accent, their clothes, their background—you realize that every element of your own personality is malleable. You can do it, you can wear the skin of another human being—and yet still you are *you*. This, in its own small way, feels profound because it illustrates that none of the things you point to as *identity* are intrinsic. *You* are something far more mysterious than a person who is funny, who is angry, who is hurt, who likes Marlboro cigarettes, who is Presbyterian, who is a playboy, who is Nigerian, who is a Real Madrid fan—all of that is dressing. Of course, acting felt good to me, inside the play it felt possible that I was not a person defined by his adultery, or his unloving parents, or his lies, his failure as a father. It is possible that I could be defined by something else.

When I was younger and first started performing professionally, all I wanted was to be "true" and "genuine," but now, having passed thirty, I wasn't sure what those words meant. I'd turned down a fantastic role once, because I felt I would be phony if I spoke with an English accent, as if the cadence of my "natural" voice was not an affectation. As if there was anything at all about me—the casual unbrushed hair, the old blue jeans, the T-shirt worn thin, all deftly presenting the impression of a person who was not concerned with his "appearance"—that was not affected. And it was real. Affectation is very *real*. My big break in the movies came with the role of a stuttering seventeen-year-old delinquent in a 1920s juvenile home. Everyone thought that *was* me. But the real (so to speak) me was obviously an actor who practiced a "stutter," stepped into the makeup trailer, and then walked back out again. The real me was kicked out of drama school because he missed too many voice and speech classes. Later, I did a film adaptation of Chekhov's *The Seagull*. Fans of the film would come up to me and kiss my face—so grateful I did not actually shoot myself. I learned quickly of the power, the absolute nuclear power, of the deceit attached to any kind of storytelling.

Scene 2

After rehearsal, I picked up my kids from their mother's (still no sign of her) and went out to buy a puppy. There was a vet around the corner that gave away rescues and in a little cage was a small black and white puppy who had just been delivered from a farm upstate. Immediately, it was unanimous, she was ours. The first time my kids saw my new apartment in the Mercury, they couldn't have cared less why we there; they just chased the newly named Night Snow around the hotel room as the little puppy pissed, shit, yapped, and chewed her way into their hearts. They loved their room and even agreed as to who got the top bunk. My son feared the ladder. When I took the kids back to their mother's, we left little Night Snow in the bathroom. I bought them ice cream and for a moment felt confident someone loved me. However cheaply that love may have been bought, I was happy to have it. Back at their mom's house, I put my kids to bed again, scratched their backs and read them stories. My old apartment had the witch hazel scent of their mom—that was starting to give me the creeps. Already I was drifting so far away. I was distracted and kept wondering when *she* was going to come home. When my oldest was finally knocked out, I came to the kitchen and *she* was there, my wife. We looked one another in the eyes for the first time in five weeks, for the first time since I told her the smut gossip about my antics in Cape Town on the cover of the *Post* was true, and this was the first time our gaze held absolutely no veil of loving mystery. We were naked now. We knew each other better than anyone else on the planet, better than our mothers, and we hated one another.

"Want to go get some dinner?" I asked.

MARY AND I SAT and talked for a long time, in a restaurant that's not there anymore, both our hands trembling, and said all the normal hateful shit that husbands and wives say when they forget how to be friends. I walked her home to the front steps of our apartment. We were unsure how to say goodbye. I knew I wasn't going up. It was like the end of a terrible first date.

"I want to tell you one thing," I said as she walked away, up towards the front door. "I don't know what 'love' means but I do know that you can't get anywhere serious in this life without suffering. And love and suffering may have a lot to do with one another. And if there is a heaven or any life after we die, I know that you and I will be there together. We are family."

She looked at me, her eyes under the shadow of her hat, turned around, and stepped inside our old apartment building.

I NEEDED A DRINK. I needed ten. My hands were still shaking. There is a bar right next door to the Mercury. An old shitty Mexican cantina named Lucy's El Adobe. At least it was there; I bet it's gone now, but I didn't want to be alone. I went inside Lucy's, ordered a margarita and some chips and salsa, and sat there with a paperback copy of *Henry IV,* trying to memorize Hotspur's opening soliloquy.

Believe it or not—sitting at the bar about five or six stools over was Eugene R. Whitman. He was at that moment, to my mind, the greatest living playwright. American anyway. It was strange to see him. Here I was, as mislaid as I have ever felt in my entire life, and six stools away—as if brought by the hand of the *Divine*— was my ultimate father figure, America's father figure. I saw one of his plays when I was sixteen, and read it probably twenty times in the next two years. His picture on the back jacket was, to me, a snapshot of John Wayne, James Baldwin, Johnny Cash, Samuel Beckett, the Buddha, Baudelaire, and Billy the Kid—all rolled up into one. The pure artist, no education, no bullshit, an irascible maverick, a rodeo riding rebel. I had acted in three of his plays. He came to one performance, apparently, but got drunk at intermission and disappeared, to the great sorrow of the whole cast. We were sure he hated us.

He was sucking down a beer and chatting up some girl in her early twenties. Then in a wild spontaneous gesture I heard him say, "Ahhhh for fuck's sake!" and watched him storm outside. The young girl—who was attractive in a Dallas Cowboys T-shirt kinda way, turned to me and said, "Do you know who that guy was?"

"Yeah," I said, trying to be cool.

"Do you think he really won a Pulitzer Prize?" she asked, struggling to pronounce the words.

"He won two," I said.

"Gosh, wow, I thought he was totally lying," she said to me apologetically. Then she checked her cell phone and then ran over and joined a gaggle of young people who were just arriving.

Moments later, stinking of smoke as bad as I probably did, he walked back into the bar and sat a couple of stools away from me. He ordered a shot of tequila on the rocks and another Tecate. After a moment, he casually spoke to me.

"So, I hear you're having woman troubles?" he said.

"Woman troubles?" I laughed; this guy was my absolute hero. "You could say that."

"Is your heart like fish when they're fryin'? Like you just

can't breathe without knowing she's there? Is it like missing your hands?" he asked, bearing down on me hard with a stare that made me laugh. My hero was blitzkrieged drunk.

"Nah," I said. "It's not like that."

"Good," he said sharply and sucked back half his Tecate in one quick slug. "That's good. I was worried we were gonna have to have a different, dumber conversation."

There was a long silence. He was charismatic and handsome as hell. Even at seventy there was something hypnotic about his movements. I imitated him, drinking my margarita in a slow-motion way I imagined he would find manly.

"So, tell me the story," he demanded, moving two stools closer to me. "The hard dirt. The nitty-gritty. Huh? Give me the skinny." He was smiling as if my trials and tribulations were sure to be hilarious.

"I got caught cheating on my wife and she's pissed off about it," I stated simply.

"Yeah, I read all that."

"You shouldn't read them papers," I said, trying to adapt his tough guy cowboy talk.

"Everybody's gotta buy groceries, right? Everybody's gotta get a tooth capped."

"I guess," I said to my drink.

"You're an idiot for letting those rags get ahold of you."

"Tough to avoid."

"I don't envy your position," he said, shifting to a different posture as if he were instantaneously sober. "So you cheated on her. Big deal. You gotta pair, don't cha? She knows that. How old are you? Thirty?"

"Thirty-two," I mumbled.

"Well, what did she think? She think you were gonna keep it tucked away till you were in the grave?"

"I don't know what she thought."

"Well, she'll get over it." He spoke authoritatively.

"She's a proud woman," I said.

"She's got to be, you're not alone, right?"

"What do you mean?"

"I mean, you two are not just making decisions for the two of you. There's other people you're responsible for, right? Little people."

"The kids?" I asked, like an idiot.

"Yeah, the kids. They need you guys to work this out. You gotta teach them with your actions right now. You gotta love each other, forgive each other, you gotta be humble."

"I am so unhappy living with her. I feel like I'd rather cut off my head," I stated. I would tell my problems to anybody who'd listen.

"Of course you're unhappy. You married a rock star." He laughed. "I fucked a couple rock stars. You're always just material." He kept playing with his empty shot glass, moving it around the bar top.

"So, what do you want to do, get a *div-or-ce*?" He said the word in a mocking tone.

"Nahhh, I don't want a divorce, but I don't think I can live with her anymore. That's my trouble. Let me tell you"—I just launched into the details—"when I fucked this other girl I felt like somebody pulled a long dirty sock out of my trachea, and I don't want to put it back in. It's like I can breathe, like oxygen is getting to my brain."

"You're growing up, son." He slapped me on the shoulder. "You're growing up. People think unrequited love is heartbreak, but it isn't. Unrequited love is a blissful state of melancholy. Watching love die: that's an ornery armor-piercing bullet. When taking the kids to school, the laundry, and the dishes rain down on the last remaining coals of your romance like piss on a morning campfire. When all you're left with is enough smoke to choke on. Then your heart is dead. And if that happens to you at thirty-two I am sad for you."

He ordered us both a beer and a shot of tequila on the rocks.

"I just always believed that ultimately *love* was a decision you made, you know?" I said. "Feelings come and go, right? I just always wanted to provide a home for my kids."

"I gather you're talking about your own old man?"

"I wanted this marriage to work more than anything I've ever wanted."

"Why?" he asked.

I looked at him dumbly. I didn't know.

"Just go get her back, can't cha?" he asked like a kid. "Start there."

"If I do it just for the kids she'll smell it, and it won't go over."

"Take a break for a year," he said, considering my situation deeply. "Just take a break."

"She says she can't live like that. She wants me to get a lawyer."

"Then you got to get radical," he said.

"What do you mean?"

"You got to disappear." He waved for another drink. We hadn't been seated there ten minutes and he was on his third.

"Keep 'em comin'," he said to the waitress. "Don't make me ask again. It makes me feel like an alcoholic. Now, listen to me," he said, locking eyes. "You disappear for a week: you're an irresponsible child. You disappear for a month: you're a bum. You disappear for a year: she'll be glad you're *alive*. You disappear for a year and nobody will be asking you to get a lawyer, nobody will tell you when you can and cannot see your kids. She'll be beggin' you to take 'em. You disappear for a year and you will get your dick sucked upon arrival. I guaran-goddamn-tee it. I shit you not, my friend. Do you even know how to disappear?"

"No," I said.

"Montana, Idaho, Nova Scotia, the Dakotas, ten grand cash, a fishing pole, some decent tackle, a pickup truck, and you will turn this year on its ass. Have the best time of your life, you'll come back and all this shit will have sorted itself out."

"What about my kids?" I asked. He gave me a look that made me feel like my dick was barely an inch in length.

"How old are they?"

"Five and three," I answered.

"No problem. They won't even notice you're gone. They don't take note of their old man till they're eight. She's a good mom, right? She loves 'em. They'll be fine. Let her know you're a man. Let yourself know. Start being judged by your gifts, not your faults. Let everybody know what they're missin.' And for God's sake don't start pussyfooting around with lawyers and timetables and meaningless details."

Mr. Whitman took a long look at me and then waved me off. "You're not going to do it. But you should. Sometimes life asks you to get radical."

He played with the ice in his glass.

"It's like this," he told me, his drunk snake stare going cross-eyed. "You're driving a car, tryin' to get cross-country, or someplace, you don't even know where you're going, you just know you gotta *move,* but something's buggin' you. Something's not right. Maybe it's the car, there's a noise you don't like. You look at the engine but you're not a mechanic. Fuck! you think, if I touch one thing in that contraption it'll all come apart. I don't know what I'm doin'. So, you hit the road again. Pressing on. Rambling. Hopin' for the best. And you crank up the stereo to try and cover the noise with pop tunes. It doesn't work. Every time there's a slight pause in the melody—you hear that same sickly sound. It makes you twitchy, and anyway, you hate pop music. You stop and pick up a woman. You think maybe chattering and smooching with her will cover up the rattling noise. Her lips are hypnotizing. But shit, she's annoying, *wrong woman*. So, ya get rid of her. You get another more distinguished female, but she's *boring* . . . And damn it, you still hear that damn sound of change falling out of your pockets. And now you're getting spooked. Maybe it's not her that's boring. It might be you? You wanna suck back a fifth of Wild Turkey, but someone has absconded with your bottle. Good news, you got a secret stash! But you know soon you're gonna sober up, and now there's no more hooch. You think ah . . . maybe I should get radical and get a new car! You can't see that to get radical—you gotta lose the car entirely. Walk. Better yet, where the hell you think you are going anyway? Sit down." He stared at me as if he had said something insightful I should remember forever. "Every time you lose something, you should scream—*Thank God*. You are now a little bit lighter, you are a little bit more *you*. 'Cause if you can lose it—a car, an idea, a belief, a woman—it wasn't yours."

After about an hour of sitting with him I was stumbling drunk, again. Old Eugene just kept spilling out more old-man howls of disappointment about the cold and holy night. I finished my second evening back in New York City alone in the Mercury Hotel, just as I had finished the first, puking up what felt like a few feet of my intestines. My arms were literally wrapped around the commode as I tried to sleep. Only this time there was a starving black and white puppy, barely the size of my palm, chewing on my boots. The cool tiles of the bathroom floor felt kind against my cheek. I remember thinking what a mistake it was to meet your heroes.

Crush Collision March

Scene 1

I was going to let this motherfucking teetotaling altar boy have it. Adrenaline was shooting through my fists. With a sword twirling in my right hand and a dagger poised in the other, the blood of my fingers throbbed against the leather handles of each blade. I was going to slice this punk Prince's head right off his body with two heavy, hacking blows. Anger lifted from some ancient cavern inside my heart was coming up in heaves. I stared at this Prince as sweat dripped into his nervous eyes. The others around us, thirty or so people standing hypnotized by the violence, approved of my every gesture—I could sense it. They loved me, and their approval felt good, like water on a hot brand: not cold enough to dampen the heat, just enough to release a touch of steam and alchemize my hatred into a red-hot, razor-like edge.

Oh Jesus. Oh my lord God.

How did I get so fucking angry?

And why did it feel so goddamn grand?

"Easy, easy," I heard my friend call out from the crowd.

Fuck easy, man. I was going to show everybody the ancestral line from which I descended. You don't think I have a warrior's heart? Why don't I rip open my rib cage so you can watch the ventricles pound? My heart is old, my bones are strong, and my blood is fresh. *Believe me, boys, there's plenty to go around. Try me.*

"*My name is Harry Percy,*" I announced for anyone within miles to hear. There is a formality to the universe, and it respects you if you honor its code: always introduce yourself. It's the right thing to do, even if it's the last thing you do before you chop into some sucker's spine and sever their head from their shoulders. He spit some nonsense at me, this puny Prince with his weak voice and his rehearsed lines.

I didn't care what he said. I wasn't listening. I was staring at the artery frantically pumping fear from inside the soft delicate skin of his throat. That's the spot. The first hack will be placed right there. I imagined how good it would feel.

"*The hour has come to end the one of us,*" I shouted at this pissant, "*and would to God thy name in arms were now as great as mine!*"

I like talking like that—old school. Let everybody know you've got a brain in your head and a pair in your pants. My voice was strong and sure as I made my move, screaming towards him. He flew backwards, as I knew he would. Feeling the others slink out of my way in silent fear, I charged. Everyone was trembling and cowering, but stealing secret glances. They didn't *want* to see. They *needed* to see. Time slowed; each move for me was easy— I could observe where he would be retreating before he'd even had the idea. I knocked him left and stayed on top of him as he scurried away. The men flanking us were begging me to kill him. I don't know why they loved me, but they did. Men are weak and silly and they admire strength and goddamn it, I had it.

The final stroke—I swing at him—right for that magic open spot—certain I will lop his head halfway off his body. But I don't.

The pussy punk ducks and I miss him entirely and up from the ground the Prince snags some mislaid spear from a fallen soldier and thrusts the spike directly into my chest plate.

"*AHHHRRRGGGHHH,*" I scream.

The blade at the tip of this lance was supposed to be retractable—that's how the fight had been choreographed—but, of course, this being the dress rehearsal, the first time we are performing the play onstage, in costume, the damn lance gets jammed and pummels me directly in my solar plexus.

Worse than the white-hot pain rocketing out from my breast was the tear I heard in my throat. I just blew out my vocal cords.

I fought my way forward through my death monologue. I had to.

I could hear the tear. I had to dig deep into the lowest part of my register to get through the last few lines. The empty theater was cavernous.

> *But thought is the slave of life.*
> *And life, time's fool.*
> *And time, that takes survey of all the world,*
> *Must have a stop.*

I fell down dead. Our first preview would be the following evening, with eighty-one performances lined up after that. I lay there, a bag of nerves, eyes closed, face smashed against the hard wood. The play continued around me: voices above me; feet stomping to the left and right of my head. Six months of *Henry IV, Parts One and Two,* eight times a week, coming straight at me, and I blew out my voice during the fucking dress rehearsal. Quietly, with my eyes closed, still lying dead in center stage, I hummed to myself, hoping that I might be overreacting.

No, my voice was shattered. How could I lose my voice? I felt like I'd just walked into a moving propeller. This play was everything to me; it was the only thing keeping me alive. I was still living in the Mercury Hotel; my wife loathed me and wasn't speaking to me. My son and daughter seemed disoriented around me and sobbed every time we parted. Weight was falling off me like off a turkey being carved on Thanksgiving. I'd lost fifteen pounds in the last four weeks and was scared to get on the scale again. I couldn't eat. I was never hungry. My cheekbones were jutting out of my face. Anxiety surged through my bloodstream. No, not anxiety: heart-pounding terror. I'd failed as a husband, as a father, and now, in the dress rehearsal, I had failed my art. My art was the best aspect of me.

I could not lose my voice.

Other actors continued with the play, their dialogue sparkling above me. My eyes remained furiously clenched shut. Some characters mourned my death, others sounded pleased.

That morning I had watched my wife on a television program, as I brushed my teeth and got dressed. She was dutifully promoting her new "chart-topping" album, while this talk show host sweetly and mournfully told the nation about all my disreputable actions. The facts are not always friendly. The court of public opinion was finding me unequivocally guilty. There is so much they don't teach you in acting class.

Playing dead was the best I was going to feel all day.

THIS WAS THE LAST NIGHT of the long week of tech rehearsals, which is the most tedious section of the rehearsal process, where you basically live in the theater for a time (usually about three or four days) while they set the lights, costumes, and sound, and fine-tune all the technical elements. We had worked until midnight, so by the time I changed out of my costume and was heading home it was almost 1:00 a.m. I had shaved my head earlier that day (Hotspur didn't brush his damn hair), and now my scalp was freezing. When my phone rang, I was dead tired, with bandannas coiled around my throat and no hat. It was Dean.

Now, I don't give a shit what anybody else says; for my money, Dean Deadwilder is a great actor. Of course, he had a terrible reputation for throwing random shit at paparazzi and hotel employees; punching producers; all that kind of celebrity antics. The last time I'd talked to him, he'd just had a nervous breakdown on set, probably drug related, and was hospitalized. I read about it in the paper and called his cell, thinking I would leave a message. He picked up.

"I left the studio unconscious in an ambulance after five months of shooting and no one from the cast, the crew, or production has called yet to see if I'm alive . . . that should give you some idea what kind of giant asshole I have become."

This time, however, he called me, saying he was worrying about me (we'd done a movie together about five years before). He would pick me up in three minutes outside the theater. So, after an epic day of tech, destroying my voice in the final dress rehearsal, I stepped into his limo. His driver was hidden behind a black screen. Dean dipped a key into a very large bag of cocaine while he talked, casually offering it to me. I had tried cocaine several times before but have never been drawn to drugs. Not so this night. This night I began to snort cocaine like it was magical healing fairy powder.

It was not.

The inside of the limo was dark, but the lights moving outside lit Dean's face. He's not model handsome. He looks like a man, the man every fifteen-year-old boy wants to see himself as: large, powerful, with deep, expressive, soulful eyes.

"William, you think you got it bad? I buried my old man three nights ago, I've been in this limo for three fuckin' days. We put my pop into the ground in Alberta and since then I've just been driving around. I had to get away from my mom and my sisters and my daughter, my ex-wife . . . Without my old man they're all nuts."

He stared mournfully out at New York City. Lights passed by out the window, red, green, blue. His face seemed to move erratically, lit by the glow of the storefronts and moving with the speed of the limo.

"Here's the deal," he continued in his famous, almost high-pitched lisp. "The great thing about being a man is that as you get older you get more masculine. Unfortunately, so do the women." He laughed at his own joke. "There's a gender war out there and don't pretend there isn't. The way everyone's reacting to your cocksmanship. It's the matriarchal society trying to make sure that you are shamed significantly enough that their lousy husbands keep their pricks in their pants."

I jammed the key in the bag and slid it to my nose.

"Here's what I know: I fucked Ida Hayes, this is when she was only twenty-four, in an elevator at the Oscars. I had my finger on the door close button till I came. Then I let go of the button, zipped up my prick, walked into the house, and sat my bum on national TV. OK, that's a great story, right?" Dean grinned at me as we blazed uptown. "I've won Best Actor at Cannes, which was my life goal; I have fished while discussing the enlightenment of the individual soul with Victor Chavez at dawn over a lake in Venezuela. I have prayed with survivors in the gas chambers at Auschwitz, I've handed out rice cakes in Rwanda, I sat in a cave in silent meditation by myself for a month in Mongolia, I smoked peyote, I did all that, and guess what? It's all without meaning. Everything. Everything real is happening inside the self. I know that scares you, 'cause no matter what you say, I can see in your eyes that you still believe in God."

The coke was shining a bright light up my nose and through

the top of my empty skull. I wasn't thinking about anything—much less the concept of God. I wondered what it was about my face that made him think I was a believer.

"You can't handle the fact of nothing," he said, tossing his head like a horse. "There is nothing. There is no such thing as an individual. As William Harding or Dean Deadwilder. Thirty-five years from now you are not going to mourn the dissolution of your marriage—you will only wonder why you gave a fuck. You'll think about it the same way you remember the feelings you had when your mom took you on a trip to your grandma's but forgot your favorite blankie—and you cried and cried. You kicked and hollered. You considered it unjust. You throttled your car seat, people tried to console you, but you were despondent. Now, years later, you can laugh about the little blue blankie because you can see how trivial that was. It's a blanket. Get along without it. It did not define you any more than that sweet wife of yours did. You get it? Everything that's happening, is happening inside the self. And whatever the self is, it is not William Harding the movie actor or the adulterer. Whatever the self is will not die when your body has worms crawling through your eye sockets."

We were racing across town; one second his face was lit a bright friendly yellow, the next a sickly green, then a terrifying red.

"I can see by the way your cheekbones are trying to fight their way out of your skin that you are still in love with the idea of being married. You want your 'woman' back. You want to be normal. A family man. You want people to respect you, to think you are a good person. But let me tell you something, you are trying to use your ears to walk and crying 'cause it ain't working."

At this point my brain was fully hijacked by the cocaine.

"Let me tell you about the Gender War," Dean continued. "He vs. She. Man vs. Woman. Venus vs. Mars. Men do, women are. It's a battle. It happens in our relationships and it happens inside ourselves. This is the real struggle. The male says, I want to *do*! And the female says, I want to *be*! Both desires exist in all of us. They are in conflict. I want to enjoy the river vs. I want to catch all the fish and dam the fucking bitch so it never floods my crops. And everybody's looking to make peace. Marry me. Let's be *one*. We can unite. The masculine and the feminine, we can heal the great split, the original chasm. Ever since the first cell split, illusion was created and the war commenced. But here's the thing: The illusion is that we are, will be, or ever were anything but *one* cell. We don't get it. The things that separate us, be they our bodies, our countries, our genders, they are not *real*. It doesn't matter if you and your wife split up. Because it's a false perception that you are even separate beings."

I guess I had a stupid look on my face because he leapt up in his seat and almost shouted at me excitedly.

"Listen, it's a like a wave who thinks it's different from the wave next to him . . . he doesn't even notice that they are both, always have been, and always will be water. Get it? Look at you— you don't understand a word I'm saying."

He was right. I had the key up my nose again and was staring blankly.

"Let me ask you this," he proposed. "What is the point of your life? Why do you wake up, why do you go to the bathroom, ride the subway, smoke cigarettes, go put on your costume, recite some lines, bow, call a friend, go home, eat dinner, watch a movie and jerk off and go to bed? Why do you do that? You've already done it all before? See, what I mean is, some people have never reached their goals—so they still think their goals will have meaning and create *change*. Some people never try—so they still secretly think when and if they do try, their goals will have meaning. But those few of us who have achieved our goals, or those people who are racked with the disappointment of failing to meet their goals after a lifetime of *real* effort, both know that the fuckin' goal was pointless—like the winner of a 1919 minor league baseball game. It's a shared fantasy that any of this crap ever mattered in the first place. People love to apply themselves to games, jobs, relationships, politics, to create the illusion of meaning . . . If I can just heal my shoulder, then I could be quarterback! If only I could finish this documentary and tell the story of my great-uncle to the world; then I would *matter*. If I was a movie star, then I would *exist*. People will light a crack pipe or steal a television just to try and *feel* that they exist—to ramp up the idea that something is in fact *happening*—or others just turn on a video game and go to sleep—they don't want to look square in the eyes that there is nothing to *do*. Maybe people think that if they confront the meaninglessness, the utter worthlessness of life they will buckle under the weight of the emptiness, and they are afraid. Maybe . . ."

He took a deep breath, trying to settle his coke-fueled brain, and continued, "What if I say, wait a goddamn second here, I am not going to buy into it all—I know my life is transitory and that my whole existence is at play in this galaxy no more and no less than a beaver in the backwoods of Ontario, *I know that!* I can see the Milky Way. So, I don't want my life to depend on what I achieve, what some asshole movie critic thinks of me, what Ingmar Bergman thinks of me . . . But, then, where will my sense of self come from? I need some sense of identity, right? I am a great *actor*. I have won numerous prizes! That is my identity. But that's obviously pretense, right?" he asked me with that famous odd, almost feminine, lisp.

"We all know that—an award, success, has no intrinsic meaning. Vincent van Gogh never won an award. So, then I say, OK, I get it, I want to live for the simple *joy* of living. What about that? Like a kid who just enjoys a game—doesn't look for an identity as a great *game player*. She just plays! See, if we allow ourselves to be totally fucking intimate with nothingness; to embrace the great nothing—without defending it at all—without getting caught in the gender war of being or doing. When you recognize that you are an insecure macho pretentious asshole without trying to change it, then we can be still long enough to see that there is a hole—a shotgun-blasted hole—right there in the center of our chest, that we imagined that was our identity, but now we can see there is nothing there. And if we embrace that emptiness and stare down inside it—we might see that down this dark never-ending well is peace. And it's not scary to have no self, it's a relief. Like telling the truth instead of defending a lie . . . Stop defending a reality that doesn't exist: *you*."

He stopped for a moment and shoveled two more heaping keys of coke up his nose.

There was a silence. He stared at me, waiting for a response.

"I'm supposed to be on vocal rest"—I smiled—"and I think I lost you pretty soon after you gave me the coke."

He laughed a big warm laugh that shook the car.

Dean knew some media-mogul type who was having a party in a suite on top of the Pierre hotel. There were giant glass chandeliers in the lobby and the doormen wore snazzy suits. We went to the penthouse floor, talking a mile a minute—both of us squinting, chewing on our lips, and swirling our tongues like a couple of drug fiends. At least I was; Dean might have been more composed.

WHEN I WALKED into the party, it was like entering a wide-screen film version of a teenager's idea of a movie star's nightlife. I moved in slow motion. I imagined myself photographed elegantly—my hands swaying when I moved, like I was strolling into the Playboy Mansion. My glances were imbued with knowing irony. One lingerie model after another passed me, giggling, or calling to a friend, or singing a pop song. We walked through the cigarette smoke and the thumping music to the faux hotel kitchenette in the back. Dean dumped his coke out on a breakfast table, opened us each a beer, and started talking to a young South American woman standing by the fridge.

This tawdry eighties crap—parties, drugs, models—has always embarrassed me. I find that whole aspect of my profession revolting. Or at least I wanted to, or believed I should. When I was younger and first becoming famous, I would ask myself, in these situations, *What would Jack London think? Would he be here?* And I would usually leave. But I don't think I knew Jack London that well anymore.

I immediately made eye contact with a dead ringer for a twenty-one-year-old Brigitte Bardot. This woman was a stone-cold fox. She was a walking key lime pie—if you *love* key lime pie. She was the type of woman that even heterosexual women would love to see naked. Her tits were huge, gravity-defying. She could drive cross-country for a month, not change her jeans, and her pussy would still smell like crushed roses. Her hair fell softly with each gentle toss of her head, moving like the mane of a unicorn. She walked over to me and, in a dopey midwestern accent, told me that she had had my picture on her locker back in the twelfth grade. Three *whole* years ago!

"That's nothin' to be embarrassed about," I said, smug and cocksure.

"Hey," Dean interrupted us. "I need to tell you one thing, before you two leave." Obviously, I was not aware I was "leaving."

"All right," I said and looked him in the eyes.

He leaned forward and whispered in my ear, "This is one of those moments where I'm not sure how to behave, but I'm gonna risk it—sins of commission are better than sins of omission, right?"

I nodded hesitantly.

He pushed me gently back so he could look me in the eyes one more time, as if to ready us both, then leaned forward again and said, "Your wife. I saw her at six-thirty yesterday morning, making out with that Valentino Calvino in the lobby of the Four Seasons. You don't know her at all anymore. You never understood her anyway. Frankly, I like her and I think I understand a panther like Mary better than you do. But it's over with you two. Let her go. Get a lawyer. I got one that's going to call you tomorrow. Hire him."

He leaned back and looked me in the eyes to see how I was doing, then handed me the giant bag of coke with ten blue pills (to ease the edge), pointed at the blond Brigitte Bardot type, smiled, and said, "Go have a great night."

Now, I didn't know who the hell Valentino Calvino was, but I didn't believe Dean at all. Mary was going to come back to me. I felt sure. She needed me. I wasn't going to back down. Dean was always so dramatic. Also, I wasn't sure where he had this idea that I *wasn't* letting my wife go. This was my plan. I'd let her go, and she would come back. Not to mention, I was still making googly eyes with a twenty-one-year-old Brigitte Bardot.

I did manage to ask Dean before he left, "Who's Valentino Calvino?"

"He's that Italian fashion stud. Come on, you know who he is."

"Isn't he gay?" I asked.

"Well, if he is, he's the fag fuckin' your wife." Dean smiled his world-famous insouciant smile, kissed me on the mouth with his beard scratching my face, and walked away.

Then I was alone with Brigitte; the coke was whipping my mind the way an old-time stagecoach driver might whip some poor sweaty horses. For a moment, a timid voice in my head reminded me that the first preview would be happening later this same day and that I should probably sleep and protect my voice. But as fast as you can say "Free Acting Lessons," I started laying a rap on Brigitte. I didn't care about Valentino Calvino, my voice, or the goddamn play. I finally felt good.

"Are you an actress?" I began.

"No . . . I would like to be, but . . . it's hard to break in when you're a model. I mean, I'm taking some classes at HB, but . . ."

I cut her off. "Don't believe that," I said. "Just because you are stunningly attractive does not mean you should buy into society's fiction that you cannot also be gifted. Have you seen *Frances*?"

She shook her head no.

"The Jessica Lange film?"

Still the movie did not register.

"Well, when Jessica Lange was young, people thought she was a sex kitten sent directly from Zeus to fuck up mankind. And I say this so you understand that she was nearly as sultry a siren as you are, OK? But she didn't let that define her. Her performance in about three to five films will stand strong next to anything Robert De Niro or Gene Hackman has ever done. Brigitte Bardot's early work is sensational. Have you seen *Contempt*?"

She shook her head no again.

"She could actually put on screen, for an audience to understand, how alienating it must be to be placed behind a glass wall the way men do to ravishing women—the way men must do to you. That's the point of acting: to bring about awareness of humanity, to conjure compassion, and to alleviate shame. Your beauty doesn't exclude you from your greater role as a human being. Vanessa Redgrave, Elizabeth Taylor, Catherine Deneuve—you must watch these women's work. Watch it compulsively. And you can have that. Because the uncanny thing about you, the way you look—yeah, you're foxy as hell and you have a sexuality that, I'll be honest, makes it difficult to form sentences in your presence—but more than that, there is a deep fuckin' kindness to you, a kindness that can't be faked." I was on a roll. "Something that people, men and women, are going to try to eat up and destroy, and you can't let them. Your intelligence radiates a kind of crazy-sad nostalgia that I guarantee you, if it hasn't already—this nostalgia, mixed with the way your skin shimmers, is going to make you feel lonely sometimes . . . Do you know what I'm talking about?"

She nodded. I offered her a neatly chopped line of blow.

"See." I paused as if I were feeling awkward. "I want to kiss you right now. But, more than that, I don't want to kiss you, because I don't want you to think this whole conversation we're having is a come-on. Because let's just call a spade a spade—you read *InStyle* magazine and *Us Weekly* and *People,* right?"

Again, she nodded.

"Well, my life is like the goddamn space shuttle exploding right now, being played over and over on folks' television sets, and I'm not going to be anybody's boyfriend—you know that, and I have to try to accept that.

"But I just want you to hear me on this. It's not hard for any two-bit famous actor to get into some girl's panties—I'm not saying yours specifically, I would never be that presumptuous, but you gotta trust me on this. Getting ass is not a struggle for the contemporary film actor, even one who is a bastard-adultering playboy, all right? So, you can relax, and know that I don't want anything from you—except to see you across a room seventeen years from now . . . I'll be in a tuxedo talking to some boring movie executive and you will be glamorous beyond any mortal's imagination, standing next to your husband, and we will make eye contact and you and I will both know that in regard to you—I was a part of the solution, not the problem. I'll be one of those who helped you on your way. You hear me?"

"Yes," she said.

"You want to get out of here?" I asked.

"Yeah, but I think you should stop doing cocaine. I've never seen somebody do so much at one time," she said with sincere concern.

I looked at her completely deadpan. I had no idea I'd even been doing it, but it seems I was cutting up lines for two of us, and then doing them both all by myself. Dean's baggie was beginning to empty.

"Yeah, I think you're right." I looked around and swallowed one of the blue pills with my beer.

THE HOTEL WE WERE IN had a heated pool on the roof. This was not a great idea for my voice, but nothing about this night was on any of my to-do lists. I talked young Brigitte Bardot into going for a swim. She insisted on bringing a friend. By normal standards, this friend was a very attractive young woman, but naked and next to Brigitte, the friend seemed like a small, wet camel.

I sat on the steps, keeping my privates in the water, while the girls splashed and frolicked through the October steam floating above the heated pool. Reciting some of Hotspur's soliloquies for the girls—I was feeling like Errol Flynn. I cannot tell you how exquisite it all was—the 4:00 a.m. Manhattan lights snapping around us were almost musical in the crisp fall air. The stars were bright. I could see Brooklyn, I could see Central Park, and I could see these two young mermaids with their heaving breasts bouncing playfully. I could hear their giggles and squirms. I thought about my children and their laughter. For a moment, with the little blue pill helping, I knew everything with my kids would be OK. Soon the girls began serenading me on the steps of the pool—their nipples wet, cold, and erect; their naked legs clasped tight around their vaginas, beads of heated water dripping from their hair; their melodic, fairylike voices singing:

> *If you want to be happy*
> *For the rest of your life,*
> *Never make a pretty woman your wife,*
> *So from my personal point of view,*
> *Get an ugly girl to marry you!*

Then they would dangle their hair in front of my face and shake their magical young titties by my mouth. Turning up my face to the stars, I thought, *You gotta be kidding.*

Finally, at about 5:00 in the morning, I got Brigitte alone and in a cab hustling back to the Mercury. We made out the whole way downtown. Kissing her was like rubbing my face in a birthday cake.

"Please," she whispered. "This night has been so perfect. I don't want to rush. I don't want you to think I'm a tease, but I really have only slept with two boys and I don't know if I'm ready to move this fast."

"Don't worry," I said. "I don't want anything from you. I just need help to fall asleep. And . . . I'm in love with you." I was out of my mind, and just pleased to have momentarily forgotten my first preview was later that same day.

Back in my hotel room we messed around until the sun was high. Finally, at what felt like 9:00 or 10:00 a.m., she took off her underwear and said, "Let's do it." Immediately I tried to insert my prick inside her. Fucking this girl, I figured, would do worlds for my self-esteem. I needed this. This was important for me, and the show. But I knew if I thought too much about it I would lose my erection—so I had to charge.

"Wait, wait, wait," she said, pushing me away. "One question, I can't help it, but I have to ask," she said tenderly.

"Sure," I said, holding my breath, thinking it would prevent my prick from descending. She sat up naked in bed, the sheet tousled around her elegantly. Then, in the gentle morning light, with her hair over her eyes, she asked sincerely,

"Am I as pretty as your wife?"

Scene 2

For every high, there's a low. After failing to make love to Brigitte Bardot, I walked her out into the morning light to get a taxi. She seemed happy to escape. The ways in which I hated myself seemed to be multiplying, taking the shape of a scorpion living in my nasal cavity. On the elevator, headed back up to my room, I longed for suicide the way I imagine a woman in labor might long for birth.

My mom was flying in that afternoon from Haiti to see the first preview, and to attempt some public damage control. Mary's assistant had called and said Mary was leaving town for some last-minute press obligation for her album release. So, after school the kids were on their way to the Mercury. I was never going to get any sleep.

Mysteriously, my voice was a little better. I went into a deli to buy some lozenges, juice, potato chips, PowerBars, Emergen-C, aspirin, and cigarettes, and there on the magazine rack was the new issue of *Rolling Stone* magazine with the most beatific, inspiring photograph of my estranged wife I had ever seen. She was on the covers of about three other glossies. *Vogue, Elle, Cosmo,* all that crap. But on the *Rolling Stone* cover her face was kind and rested, with sleepy bedroom eyes staring into the lens of the camera. Suddenly, I felt so proud of her. Of course, I hadn't spoken to her in weeks. Her assistant answered all my calls and negotiated the kids' movements, but it was nice to see the magazine cover. My wife was dressed in a little white teddy and seemed genuinely warm, and satiated. In this picture, she looked like the best friend

I remembered. That was the woman I loved, prayed for, promised to honor. I picked up the magazine and flipped to the article. The headline read in bold black ink:

WOULD YOU CHEAT ON THIS WOMAN?

The third time I read the line I vomited on the deli floor.

I ARRIVED AT my dressing room for our first preview early, praying for a nap. I found a piece of paper taped to the door with the inscription "To W," and an Elvis Presley quote explaining how onstage he felt his "heart was going to explode." I knew the feeling. There was no signature. I looked around to see who could have left it, but the halls were empty. Sitting down in my station, I taped the quote to the mirror. Ezekiel wasn't in yet. In a few hours, I would make my Broadway debut, but at that moment I couldn't be positive I was even inside my body. It seemed perhaps I was floating above, a few inches alternately to the left or to the right. I hummed softly to myself. My voice was holding on. Finally, on the small bed in my dressing room, I fell asleep.

I WOKE UP to a knock at my door. It was "Lady Percy" in a pink Clash T-shirt. She was nervous too. Her head wasn't moving right.

"Are you alone?" she asked quietly.

"Yeah," I said, still sleepy. "Come on in."

"I don't think I should." She shifted her weight awkwardly in my doorway. She stared at me for a long, uncomfortable, silent moment. Suddenly, I got a squirrelly feeling, and wondered if she was going to kiss me.

"I feel like I'm in drama school, you know?" She smiled a crooked sexy sort of snarl. "I mean, are you going through this too?"

There was another long weighty pause.

"What do you mean?" I asked.

"Oh fuck you," she said. "Are you really that out to lunch?"

She turned down the hallway and clomped off to her dressing room.

Oh boy, I thought, *here we go.*

BACKSTAGE, 8:02 P.M., approximately three minutes before the first preview, I was dressed in thick black leather, on my knees in the utter darkness of the Lyceum. My head was shaved and cold. My throat was raw and hurting. My hands were shaking so badly that I had to clasp them together and bite my knuckles to pray:

Dear St. Christopher,

Please forgive me. Forgive me for being so irresponsible.

Tonight as the audience takes their seats and the clock spins past eight . . . I give thanks for my life and for this opportunity to contribute.

And I ask for a blessing on this stage in the hours to follow.

In return, I offer my love and my sincere desire to be in service to something larger than myself. I will do better.

I had to remind myself to breathe. Exhaling, I hummed slightly, checking in for the 3,764th time that day to make sure my vocal cords could still produce sound. Why had I done that cocaine? I was so angry at myself, it was work not to punch myself in the face.

I want to do a good job, but I know to do that I must let go of that desire. I must rely on my preparation, on my imagination, and on my breath.

My breath is the connective tissue between my fellow

players, the audience, and myself. My breath is alive. It is not ahead of me or behind me. It is present and immediate.

So am I.

I hummed again quietly to myself. In the last twenty-four hours this odd animal hum had ballooned into a full-blown nervous tic. I couldn't stop. Much of the time I was totally unaware of it. I was either warming up my voice or making sure it was still there. My vocal cords were in tatters, and my eyes would well up with salty tears as I contemplated my own pathetic voice. All day long my throat had ached in some odd muscular way. It was difficult for me to stop imagining the horror I would suffer if I blew my cords out completely when I was onstage. I pictured myself squawking like a frog with its tongue cut out in front of mocking thousands. Everyone hated me so much these days, I was sure a spectacularly humiliating Broadway failure would please the world immensely. The Internet would ignite with joyous derision if I embarrassed myself in some particularly dramatic fashion.

I believe in the theater.

I believe that in dialogue, thought, expression, and communication, a healing can take place—I ask to be a part of that healing.

If I can be of service, I offer up everything. I offer my whole life.

Forgive me. Let me be your voice and be of service.

I was teetering on the edge of what some people might call a stage ten anxiety attack, like a man about to be shot to the moon. *This is why all those British hams are drunks,* I thought: *stage fright.* I yearned for a pint of whiskey. When my nerves go ballistic, they physically obscure my vision. My focus turns hazy and images seem to vibrate red with my pulse. Beyond the blackness of the auditorium around me I could hear the audience sitting down, turning off their cell phones, chatting about trivial things, folding their coats.

> I pray for everyone in the audience, that this night may sit
> inside the larger context of their life as some beautiful piece
> of fabric neatly laying in with the weave—I pray that they
> forgive my deficits, or at least find some value in them.

Oh God, I cannot tell you. I did my first play when I was thirteen goddamn years old and back then I couldn't wait to get onstage. I was light as a feather, happy, shimmering with wonder. Now, at thirty-two, I was supposed to know what I was doing. Acting on the *big* stage with the *best* people. *Broad-Fucking-Way*. Even the guys with two or three lines were trained, and talented. They'd all played King John at Arizona rep or something like that. I was a dopey movie actor. I am a bed swerver! *A cheat!* I wear the scarlet letter! The guy who ran around on *Redbook* magazine's "Mother of the Year"! *Noooooo,* I screamed in my head. *Calm down. Breathe. Pray.*

> I pray for all the writers, living and dead. Shakespeare and
> the guy Shakespeare ripped off. The young playwright with
> his second play, all the writers who feel more nervous and
> more responsible than I, I pray that they know that if their
> play is any good at all—it's not theirs.
>   I pray for the directors, standing in the backs of the
> theaters counting empty seats . . . looking for one last thing to
> control.

When I breathed in and out and prayed, my pulse would return closer to a normal, sustainable beat.

I pray for all the theaters everywhere across the earth—the ones in the war zones, the ones in the basements of mosques, or in the parks of Argentina, the ones on the West End and the ones in Tokyo—for in them lies the possibility for some kind of magic, mystic, holy conjuring.

Just as thought leads action, imagination leads consciousness—and the theater is the living consciousness of the world. There is a healing imaginative dance between the audience, the light, the music, the rhythm of a few carefully chosen words, the spontaneous gesture of a certain actress's left hand. A dance that announces: WE ARE ALIVE TODAY, MAYBE NOT TOMORROW. THIS IS REAL. THIS IS NOW. This is my prayer: that I may be present for this evening.

Standing up, I breathed into my belly and hummed again to myself, checking my voice for the 3,775th time that day. I was feeling a bit better maybe, a small reprieve. I was beginning to be able to see again. There was a spot near the edge of the curtain where I could get an angle and peer out at the audience. I did. I knew I shouldn't look at the jury, but I wanted to know if she was there. My wife, Mary. I knew she was furious with me, kissing some dude named Valentino, but I thought maybe she would show. Maybe she sensed how scared I was and would get a sitter and come see my silly play. Afterwards, she would arrive backstage, come to my dressing room, and we'd both weep and hold each other. The pain and alienation we had been feeling would fall from our shoulders and our friendship would return, ushering in a healing.

I peeked out and scanned all the faces. Somehow I believed that if my wife came to the play, we could get back together. That was my gut instinct. All my hope was placed there. If she came to the play, it would mean she loved me and knew I had been punished enough. It would be a gesture of admission that I was not alone in creating the dissolution of our holy covenant. My shoulders relaxed as I considered how happy my daughter would be at the reconciliation. The thought of that small girl smiling, waking me (getting the words "spring" and "morning" confused as she used to), saying, "Dada, it's springtime, wake up," sent splinters of joy through my body.

I scanned the seats. Mary wasn't there. There are about twelve hundred seats in the Lyceum Theatre, but I could tell my wife wasn't sitting in one of them. I felt the heartbreak fresh. When I was a little boy, I'd always wanted my own parents to get back together, not because it made sense, but because I wanted love to have a logic I could follow. Even at twenty-one or twenty-two I would still have dreams where I'd see my parents kissing in the back of a car. Could love just vanish? Horrible cruel things my wife had said to me replayed through my mind. I remembered sentences that came out of my mouth that I could never take back.

Oh shit, I realized. *I forgot to pray for her or my kids.*

So there, still hidden in the shadows of the offstage props and curtains, I tucked my sword around, and got back on my knees. I continued almost out loud:

Dear St. Christopher,
     Let me not forget my children.
     Help me to remember them. . . . Bless their movements, answer their prayers . . .

Then I tried with my whole being to ask St. Christopher to smile favorably on the mother of my children, to bless Mary's movements, but I couldn't. I could not pray for her. I knew it was in my kids' best interest for their mother to thrive, to be content and fulfilled . . . so I tried again. On my knees, I looked up to heaven, into a ceiling lined with lights that were "leashed in like hounds," about to be set ablaze. I wanted to pray for peace and, in doing so, cool the boiling blood that was screeching in my gut, but I still couldn't. She had tricked me. She said she'd love me forever, and she didn't even like me anymore. Or had I tricked her? Why did she get our children? Our house? Our life? Why was she talking about me all over the world? I didn't want St. Christopher or God or anyone to smile on my wife. I knew what I wanted to ask St. Christopher: I wanted my fucking kids. I couldn't say that— I couldn't say anything. Some mammoth Moloch of hatred was swelling and hooked inside my throat. I couldn't breathe. My veins were engorging against my leather collar, tightening, choking me.

How was I going to go on? I was dizzy.

Someone put a hand on my shoulder. It was Samuel, dressed in chain-mail armor. Big Sam played a nameless character that was Hotspur's main henchman, my right-hand dude. We had some killer battle scenes in the second act. At six foot six and at least three hundred pounds, he had been an all-state middle linebacker in high school and college. He approached acting just as he had approached football: "I just keep my head on a swivel and contain trouble," he would say. He was my friend.

"Come on, man," he said calmly. "Our cue light's on."

WHAT IS IT about standing in front of our fellow men that makes our voices shake, our balls yank up inside our bellies, and our knees quiver? Why do we assume they hate us? Was high school that bad?

Big Sam and I stood in the darkness with a bucket of blood

at our feet. We dipped our swords and arms deep into the warm, thick red syrup until we were the image of dripping violence that our director wanted. Now we waited. Staring at the light, waiting for it to go out. Over the monitor, you could hear the stage manager say, "PLACES FOR ACT ONE."

The houselights dimmed and immediately the audience hushed.

As the announcement asking people to unwrap their candies and turn off their cell phones began, I could hear our Falstaff walk through the backstage door. Virgil was crawling to his position like a homeless madman, muttering to himself, with his dresser following, trying to give the fat man his belt and sword.

"Fuck all you people. Leave your cell phones on, you slimy, sleazy limousine bastards," he called out to the audience. "Think you can stay awake for a four-hour Shakespeare play, do you? Going to go back to college for a night, are you? Taking a break from funneling martinis down your gob to pretend like you have a brain? Want to get a little culture, you old, slave-owning scumbags!" They couldn't hear him, but it was dangerously close.

Everyone backstage deals with nerves a different way.

"Dropped a hundred and fifty bucks so you could tell the friends at the yacht club that you're not a complete *moron*. Or did you come here just so that the old hag would finally shut up? You don't deserve this play. I fart on you. No, my gas is too precious for you elitist scumbags. I'll bet there's not one decent person out there. *AHHH!*" Virgil kicked at the floor of the stage, forcing himself to stand. "Why don't I get a life?" He turned to face one of the stagehands, who move the heavy props around, and asked, "Why do I humiliate myself like this? Why do I perform like a monkey for these corpses?"

The music swelled.

I took a deep breath.

I knew what was next.

My cue light turned off. Samuel and I stepped forward. The five hundred thousand watts lit our faces.

Our production began with a series of portraits of the major characters. Lights up, center stage on Prince Hal and Falstaff, passed out with three half-dressed women; lights down. Lights up, stage right with the King in his isolation; lights down. Lights up, center on Hotspur and his men dripping with fury and war; lights down. On and on like that, as all the major characters were introduced. When the lights were hot on my face I dug deep into my belly and tried to touch with my breath all the spirits inside me, attempting to unleash them as I stared out at the Broadway audience. I absorbed the watchful gaze of twelve hundred people in an instant. Almost immediately, with the follow spot exposing me fully and blood dripping from my ears, boots, and gloves, I heard quietly but clearly the voice of an old woman in the left side of the house whisper, "That's him. That's the one who cheated on his wife."

Then the lights went out.

Stepping offstage, arms still soaked and sticky with blood, I held on to Samuel's shoulder for balance. "I think I'm going crazy, bro. I think I'm losing hold of my mind."

"No, you're not," he said. "You are about to give the greatest performance of your life."

"Will that make me feel better?" I asked him.

He shrugged.

"Did you hear that woman out there?"

He sheepishly nodded his head, patted my shoulder, and sprinted all three hundred pounds to the far stage right door for his next entrance.

I went to my dressing room and closed the door and washed my arms. I had thirteen minutes until my first real scene. My roommate, Ezekiel, was onstage (I could hear his voice over the monitor), and this was my opportunity to be alone, pull myself together, and warm up my voice. The Lyceum Theatre is not small. Pinning your *t*'s to the back wall, as J.C. kept asking me to do, was no easy effort.

First, I had to change clothes into another badass black leather coat. These were easily the best costumes I'd ever had. I lay down on the floor of my dressing room, underneath the mirrors and makeup table, and began my warm-up exercises.

MAW NAW LAW THAW VAW ZAW
MOO NOO LOO THOO VOO ZOO
MAH NAH LAH THAH VAH ZAH

For some reason, this idiotic woman out in the audience had galvanized my energy and I was not nervous anymore; I was angry. Virgil was right, they didn't deserve us. My voice felt good. Strong. I was going to be all right. I became bored of warming up. It's always struck me as a pansy thing to do anyway. I still had nine minutes before I went on. I poked my head out of my dressing room. Down the hall exiting from stage right was "Mistress Quickly," played by a lovely older actress. I liked her. She always brought me cookies and brownies and begged me to eat better. She said I looked like a piece of rope and that she prayed for me every night. Just making eye contact with her made my eyes sting a little. I felt my anger twist and spin into pathetic, self-pitying tears. I couldn't cry right now. I had only eight minutes before I went on.

Through the backstage hallway, the performance could be heard over the monitors, marching through the text like a train deliberately moving down the tracks. If Mistress Quickly didn't touch me I would be able to hold it together. I looked to the ground, to avoid her gaze. She tapped me on the shoulder. I looked at her and let her soft arms fold around me. Why did she have to fucking hug me?

I held myself together long enough to close the door of my dressing room, where I promptly exploded into a *howl*. The sound of which was animal. I had seven minutes before I went onstage and tears were leaping out of my eyes like paratroopers. I started punching the walls, hoping the pain in my fists would stop me from crying, but I couldn't feel anything. For five weeks, all I had been doing was worrying. Worrying about my kids, my voice, my marriage, my useless prick (I was still carrying the humiliation of not being able to fuck Brigitte Bardot), and my performance. I couldn't go onstage without fear of losing my voice. I didn't like going outside for fear of a sore throat—there was less light each evening and it was getting colder every afternoon. I didn't want to see my friends because whenever I did I couldn't stop myself from drinking ridiculous amounts of whiskey and talking nonstop about my ex-wife.

I actually thought Mary would be at this evening's performance. I didn't think she would let our family fall apart. I kept thinking she would show up at my door. I longed for her to make some gesture of reconciliation, yet I couldn't make one myself. I couldn't reach out to her.

In the moments before our wedding, waiting for Mary to walk down the aisle, I was so happy and proud. Nervously, I stood in my tuxedo and looked up into the rafters of the church and saw a five-year-old girl playing up near the organ pipes. It was a hallucination, but still somehow I *felt* this child's realness. The little girl waved at me and smiled a sly, contagious grin. She burst out laughing as the organ began to lurch into its bellyaching wail. It was a visitation. An angel. I knew it. I never told anybody this till right now. Not even my wife; it felt too secret and indefinable to go on yapping like it was a cute anecdote. The significance of this angel's appearance would somehow be diminished in the telling, so I kept it to myself. The little angel girl was teasing me, mocking my formal stance and my bow tie. I laughed too. As Mary began to walk down the aisle, for the first time in my life I knew I was in exactly the right place at exactly the right time. Now, in the dark of my dressing room, I had to wonder what had gone so terribly wrong. Is this the end of the poem? People don't write their own vows, make up poems, and see angels as music chimes, and then have nasty venom-spitting divorces, do they? I had *zero* doubts about my marriage as I said my vows, but where is my angel now? *Oh no,* I thought, *I cheated on my wife, and that is why heaven's cherubim will take away my* voice!

Seven minutes until my entrance and my face was getting more red and blotchy. I was hyperventilating. White spots were swimming around my eyeballs. I couldn't even find my breath. Where was it even supposed to be? My chest was heaving in great giant silent swells, like that of a ten-year-old child who has fallen from a swing.

My dresser, a sweet young guy named Michael, knocked at my door.

"You OK in there? Need some help?"

I couldn't speak. I went to the dressing room toilet and locked myself in there so I couldn't hear his voice.

My chest finally released in loud, convulsing sobs.

I'm aware I don't intimately understand fuck all about true suffering. I see what's happening in the world. I read the paper. The polar caps are melting. I see the poverty and the disease. I comprehend that mankind is immersed in some larger, massive struggle . . . but I thought I was complete, finished, a fully cooked mature adult male human being, I mean before all this happened. At around twenty-eight, twenty-nine, or thirty years old, after my kids were born, I figured I'd hit some plateau that was adulthood—where I believed things would just stay level for about forty years while I would do great work and have interesting experiences—then rather uneventfully I'd begin to decay and die. But this was just not the case. I was not on a plateau. I was descending, tripping, stumbling, and burning. My whole being, or personality or self or whatever is supposed to be the seat of me, or the soul behind my eyes, was being boiled away in a giant iron cauldron like the flavor leaving a carrot.

"Are you trying to kill me?" Michael screamed with keys in his hand as he unlocked the first door. "Clean up and get onstage."

I just wailed from behind the still closed toilet door.

"I know why you're sad," he said, quietly, through the crack, "I read the papers. But this is one of those moments, right now, this moment, when you either grow up or you grow down."

I turned off the bathroom light so I wouldn't be tempted to look at myself in the mirror.

"Stop cryin' and listen"—he paused—"I'm your dresser, and I know everything. I want you to go home tonight and put a sign on your door that says: 'No Narcissistic Bitches Allowed!' Can you hear me?"

In the dark I punched myself hard on one temple to try to stop crying.

"You're sad because you are getting a divorce, but what you don't know is that you were never married. Do you hear me? I don't lie in bed at night and wonder if my husband loves me. I *know* he does! You seem to have this intellectual view that maybe all married people are like you, either living 'unexplored' lives or are secretly unhappy. But that's not true. I love my husband and he loves me."

My head was bruised and throbbing.

"My husband is my best friend. When I was on tour last year with *Bye Bye Birdie,* he took care of everything—laundry, school forms, bathtime for our son, soccer practice, our taxes, everything, and I would do the same for him because we *love* one another. We share the same *beliefs*. Love is not a *feeling*. It's *action*."

I was crying so hard there was no way I was going to stop. This guy needed to just go tell the stage manager or somebody that I couldn't go on.

"You don't even remember this, because you and your wife are so self-centered, but I spent Thanksgiving with you and your hot-shot wife. I've been to your house."

This stopped me. I had no memory of ever meeting this man before. "When my husband, Henry, was dancing in one of her videos, we got invited. Whoop-de-do! I went to your daughter's playhouse and hung out with your wife's assistant and the Guatemalan cleaning lady and that big-titted nanny. And you and your wife acted like it was such a fuckin' privilege to be in your presence but you two didn't even notice that both my husband and I left your house feeling sorry for you guys. I wanted to steal your sweet kids. *Wow!* The cook made a great dinner! *Wow!* The big-titted nanny was great at playing games—the children didn't bother us at all during that air-stifling conversation of a meal! Who cares! I would have rather ordered a pizza and watched TV!"

I started listening, wondering what he was talking about.

"You do not need to be depressed about getting a divorce, cowboy. You may feel like you are dying, but let me tell you, you were dead! But the thing is, dead people don't know they're dead. You're crying 'cause you are getting pushed through some kind of rebirth canal. *Wake up* and serve those children. Get the best custody deal you can—I don't care if it's one stinkin' day a year—it will be one stinkin' day a year they get to have a grown man for a father. You are a good man—go find a good woman—and have a good life. 'Nice' is not a bad word. Nice partner equals nice life. Crazy partner equals crazy life—you get it?"

"Why did I marry her?" I mumbled through the door.

"Are you nuts? Are you a crazy person? She is so fucking beautiful! *I love her!* She is like my favorite! She's *everyone's* favorite, OK. Don't be mad at yourself about that. Come on, she's a frigging *legend*! The real question is why did she marry you?"

I was silent.

"Find your sense of humor, big shot!" he shouted. I looked up at the clock. I had four minutes and twenty seconds before I was due back in front of the audience. Michael was still trying to open my bathroom door.

"I can't go onstage," I muttered, snot pouring out of my nose. "I can't stop fucking crying. Tell somebody I can't do it."

"I know you feel like a failure, and you're right 'cause you did fail. But everybody's gotta lose sometime. Are you going to kick your feet and whine or are you going to go over the game plan and study which plays didn't work and why, so that you can win tomorrow? You don't have to throw out the whole plan; just the marrying a brilliant-smoking-hot-icy-stuck-up princess part. You've always been a smart kid, I've been a fan for years, but you're thirty-two years old now, killer, and it's time to be the best version of you and grow out of the needy I-want-everybody-to-like-me guy. That's what I never like about your profession. It indulges all you actors. I see it every production I work on. What you need right now is to know where you want to be in five years, and a goddamn printout of your to-do list. One step at a time. What do I want to accomplish in this tiny lifetime and how am I gonna do it?"

"I want to stay married," I mumbled with three minutes and ten seconds to go.

"Uh-oh, you're forgetting what the sign on your door says: 'No Narcissistic Bitches Allowed!' Damn. So . . . that means you *cannot* stay married to her. Not if you want to have a nice life. You two built a house on shaky ground. Now go take what you learned, find some firm ground, and build again. Mary should do the same thing, by the way—she deserves someone who will love her for who she is, instead of someone who is always wanting to change her—which is what I imagine you did."

"I did do that!" I said, and I was crying some more. Less than three minutes. Michael was beginning to sound desperate.

"Come on, William," my dresser continued, "show your kids you can handle some adversity. Show them you are making good decisions. You've got deeper roots than the ones you laid down with their mother. Sometimes you gotta fight back in this life. Harvey Milk. Rosa Parks. You want to know why Nelson Mandela went to jail? 'Cause he kicked back hard. That gorgeous young man was stockpiling weapons. People act like he was some kind of preacher. He was trying to buy tanks from Haile Selassie in Ethiopia. Then they wanted to let him out of prison—all he had to do was toe the nonviolence line. He said if they released him from prison and apartheid was still law then the first thing he would do is see if he could get some tanks from the Chinese. He said, 'Fuck you, you Nazi pigs!' He kicked back. You got to find your guts and hire a crackin' lawyer and let this screamin' Judy Garland diva know that these kids have a daddy who loves them and that he is gonna claim them. *Your life will speak for itself.* Go out there and reclaim yourself. When I first saw you act I was like thirteen and you played that stuttering juvenile delinquent. I was so jealous of you. You were beautiful. Make me jealous again."

He paused. One minute, five seconds.

"WILLIAM!" he screamed.

One minute, one second.

"Come on, William," he continued. "You are exactly where you are supposed to be. Trust me, we all are. Most of us don't know ourselves very well, and that's why it's so fucking important to put on plays."

I sobbed. Forty-five seconds.

"*WILLIAM!* If you do not get onstage I will get fired!"

I opened the bathroom door.

"Come on, you asshole, quit crying, we can still make it," he said, putting my costume back together and wiping my face with a wet cloth. It was obvious this guy had experience with this kind of antics. "Be brilliant," he whispered. "It's Broadway, for fuck's sake. Then go home and eat some pasta. You look like a friggin' junkie. OK?"

"OK," I said, finally standing straight up. Twelve seconds.

"What's the sign on your door say?" he asked, pushing me down the hallway.

"I'm exactly where I am supposed to be?" Eight seconds.

"No." He pushed me through the stage left door.

"No narcissistic bitches allowed?" Four seconds.

"You're on," he whispered and everything disappeared.

MY FIRST SCENE BEGAN with a showdown of sorts between the King and Hotspur. When I walked onstage, I put my hands behind my back and tried to act unembarrassed by my red, blotchy face. The King shouts and scolds me until I can take it no longer and then I launch into my defense—a long, beautiful monologue that is often done at auditions for theater schools. It's a cumbersome beast and you can lose the audience entirely by the tenth line; but not so on this night. I just locked eyes with my King and disappeared inside the play.

The King never "acted" at all. The words fell out of him. Deep in his gaze you could see a castle and tapestries, you could even smell the air of a summer afternoon in London six hundred years ago. He spoke with every aspect of his body, motivating my next line with a skeptical glance. He kept trying to interrupt me, guiding me effortlessly, heating my anger and impatience line by line. In my actual life, I'd never been able to access anger. I would twist inside and punch walls, but I have always been uncomfortable with conflict and could never approach anger head-on.

Now, something was changing. My anger at my wife was like a stream coursing down a mountain, gaining in power and speed. Onstage, this fury was free to take full form. I screamed at the King, and after he exited, I screamed about him. I wasn't worried about losing my voice. There was no next show. No tomorrow night. I roared.

That first preview, and during the first four weeks of previews that followed, I would baby my voice all day with green apples, tea, honey, lemons, zinc lozenges, cough drops, and jalapeños by the dozens—any trick I heard, I would try. But then, when I got onstage, I would scream my balls off. I couldn't help it. People talked to me about breathing from my diaphragm, and all kinds of other parlor tricks designed to keep me from hurting myself. They didn't realize I liked hurting myself. My character was a spitfire and that's what I wanted him to do: spit motherfuckin' flaming cannon shot. I would think about my wife and the ways she would dismiss me and scold me, criticize me, make fun of me, demean me. I would meditate on why the fuck she thought our kids should live with her, and before I knew it, I would be up in some other actor's face, ripping his head off. I'd hated being married. I didn't want to be buried with that woman, or anyone. I wanted my own goddamn tombstone.

That first preview I sounded my barbaric *yawp* from center stage in a spotlight surrounded by twelve hundred people. My black leather snapped with every gesture. I was alive. The audience was right where we needed them. It's hard to explain, but you can feel it when over a thousand people are hanging on your every word, and it feels good.

My first scene ends with a pop, in the form of a rhyming couplet:

> *Uncle, adieu: O, let the hours be short*
> *Till fields and blows and groans applaud our sport!*

When I was done, I would go backstage and alternate smoking and steaming my throat.

I was only happy during a performance. I wished the play were ninety-two hours long.

I just prayed I could make it till opening night. I didn't care if I died after that.

When the second intermission came, at hour three, Hotspur was dead and my own life returned. I felt good now, purged, and snuck out into the alley behind the theater to have a cigarette. A bunch of the other "dead" guys were out there, too. We were a unique sight: six bloody knights, in full armor, passing around a lighter and a soft pack of American Spirits, in an alley off Forty-fifth Street, leaning on a dumpster and talking about the "house."

The other guys eventually went back inside—they had more scenes—but I had forty-eight minutes to pass before curtain call. I was almost peaceful. This would become my most relaxed hour in any given day. My voice had made it through the show and it was too early to begin worrying about tomorrow night. That would start soon after the bows. I sat alone underneath the fire escapes listening to the city wind down. I could hear a few people who walked out of our play bad-mouthing us. That would happen almost every night but it never bothered me. A lot of people don't like Shakespeare, there's nothing you can do.

On my dressing room table I had a scatter shot of quarters and loose change. Still in costume, I bought an ice cream sandwich from the vending machine in the back hallway. That's where Lady Percy found me.

"You were great tonight," she said shyly, still in her black funeral costume.

"So were you," I said sincerely. "I listened to your whole final speech. It's always good. But tonight, it was great."

"You just like it because I'm crying over you."

I smiled. The show might've been good or bad, but there was no doubt she was brilliant.

"You have to forgive me about before the show," she continued. "This has never happened to me before. I have a child and a husband I love. You don't have to worry about me."

"It's OK," I said, still not exactly sure what she was talking about. "Acting plays with a person's head."

"Yeah, I guess." She looked at the floor. Then, as she spoke, she took my ice cream sandwich from my hand, unwrapped it neatly, and gave it back.

"When we were onstage together tonight I could hear your heart beating. It scared me a little bit. It was like I was holding a horse or something. You are so sad sometimes I feel like you are going to implode or pass out, and I want to hold you and tell you that you are doing a beautiful job . . . but I worry that if I do that I'm going to start kissing you." She smiled. "But I won't."

And she walked away, towards her dressing room, her shoes clacking down the long hallway. My lord, she was an incredible woman.

Immediately, Virgil appeared storming in the other direction. He was rushing towards his final appearance in the new king's coronation. He turned to me.

"Do you mind if I give you a small note of encouragement?" He spoke in his proxy pseudo-English accent.

I answered, with dignity, I thought, "You know what, Virgil?

This is my first Shakespeare play ever and I'm on such a learning curve and getting so many notes from J.C. that I'd prefer if you gave any ideas to him and then I can get them all straight from the director. You know what I mean?"

"Yeah," he answered demurely and then proceeded. "Your *t*'s are terrible. You must work on your *t*'s—without *t*'s and *d*'s it sometimes sounds as if you are only speaking with vowels."

"Thank you," I said, "that really helps."

"You'll do fine," he said, and walked away. "Work on your *a*'s, too," he shouted back. "They make Hotspur sound as if he should be fighting Mexicans at the Alamo."

He suddenly stopped and stepped back, fiddling with his sword uncomfortably around his fat belly.

"This text was written by a great poet, it's true, but remember he was also a very fine actor. It's our job to transform literature into an event. We do this with *why* and *how*. *Why* our character speaks and *how* our character speaks. You do well with the *why*, William, that's why you're good on film."

This may sound like a compliment, but it wasn't.

"For you, it's the *how* that needs work. Start with your *t*'s and *d*'s." He finally got his sword situated in a way he liked and looked up at me.

"Oh, don't be a pouty face." He smiled the irrepressible grin of a bouncing sheepdog. "You'd do well with Chekhov—it's a better fit for you. Chekhov gives the actor the leaves—and we must build the tree. But Shakespeare provides the whole tree—only the leaves are ours. Get out of the way. Getting your consonants correct helps 'you' be quiet and lets the character speak." And with that, he bolted down the hallway towards the stage left entrance, dropping his sword as he charged. The metal clamored on the floor and three people struggled to be the first to give it back to him.

NOW THERE ARE few things in life as depressing as a lackluster curtain call, and the first preview of our *Henry* was not for the easily disheartened. The shuffling of hundreds of old people rising from their naps, mixed with the paltry sound of a handful of ambulance chasers (folks that buy tickets for a first preview *want* to see shit go wrong), politely clapping. It was not the embrace we'd been expecting. As we took our last bow, people started standing, and for a moment I thought—*Hold on! Wait, is this a standing ovation?* No. They were just leaving. They were trying to make the 11:40 p.m. New Jersey Transit Trenton local train. Or get their car out of the parking garage before the next hour is charged, who knows? But we couldn't get offstage fast enough. Virgil Smith, our beloved Falstaff, took out his sword and pretended to commit hara-kiri in the steps down to the dressing room. A few people laughed.

"YOU DEPRESSED?" our director asked us. "You should be."

All thirty-nine members of the cast were assembled in the seats of the theater where our audience had sat only twenty minutes earlier. We were patiently waiting for one of the inspirational notes sessions we had come to expect from our director. Most of the company had their jackets on and their feet up on the chairs in front of them, lounging. Everyone's faces looked pale and vulnerable, freshly stripped of their makeup.

"I'm not going to take up too much of your time," our director began. "I know it's late and you're all tired. I just also know I'm too upset to fall asleep tonight without telling you all how disgusted I am." He spoke with a sense of resignation. "To tell you the God's honest truth: watching you all act tonight made me want to quit this profession."

J.C. stood on the stage, staring out at us. He seemed to be in physical pain. His eyes were wet. Slowly we pulled our feet down from the chairs in front of us and assumed a more respectful body language.

"I don't want to be too dramatic here," he said from dead center stage. "As individuals, you were all OK, I guess. But as a company, you failed. I failed." He paused and shuffled his feet some more. "I'm going to focus tonight on the 'tavern scenes.' I'll begin there." He paused and wiped some lint from his jacket. I breathed a sigh of relief; Hotspur makes nary an appearance in the tavern.

"What the fuck happened! What the fuck!" The floorboards shook as he punched one hand into the other. "Where did you all go? Have I been talking to myself for six weeks? You guys want to bring your high school acting coach up here onstage with you and thank her? 'Cause you looked like a bunch of amateurs. 'Gee whiz, everybody, look at me. I'm acting on Broadway! Isn't this fun?' No, it is not. It's expensive and boring. If I'm going to watch people masturbate, I'd rather go home and do it myself."

Falstaff began nervously twitching in his seat.

"Not you, Virgil." J.C. nodded to our white-bearded star. "You were very good. Inspired, in fact, and fully living up to the great actor that everyone on this planet knows you to be. Unfortunately, you were in a high school production of *Henry the Fourth, Parts One and Two,* tonight." He paused, wiped his eyes, collected himself, and said, "I mean . . . *Holy fuck.*" He looked at the rest of us. "I wanted to walk onstage and kick somebody's ass. All of you. Don't you understand that I'm relying on you? We are relying on each other. What happened?" He paused as if one of us might have an explanation. "What happened to all the work we've been doing?"

He looked straight at big Samuel, who was sitting next to me. Samuel's three-hundred-pound body was stuffed into the theater's folding seat. His eyes were stinging with tears. He was biting his lip as he stared at Virgil. Samuel was featured in all the tavern scenes.

The day before, after our invited dress rehearsal, Virgil had gone around to the dressing rooms of everyone in the aforementioned tavern scenes and personally asked them to tone down their business. He felt they were all upstaging him. He claimed he couldn't even hear when he was getting a laugh. He felt strongly that he was being forced to compete for the audience's attention—it was maddening and would they please stop.

"Samuel, I need some kind of explanation," our director asked him directly. Samuel just sat there mute.

"Are you a professional actor?"

"Yes, I am," he said.

"When I looked onstage, do you know what I saw on your face? The same thing I saw on the face of every single person in the tavern scenes . . . Oh my God, I'm onstage with Virgil Smith. I wonder where he keeps his Oscar?

"Yes, we want laughs. Yes, we want to be heard and liked, understood and appreciated—every performer wants that. Every child wants that. But what makes us adults, what makes us professionals, is that it is not *our goal*. Is our goal to get a standing ovation? To sell out the shows? To get a good review? To win the Tony? *No*. The goal is always to play our best. To meet the standards set by ourselves. This world we live in is full of alleged winners, people who appear to be succeeding who are secretly failing and people who appear to be failing who are succeeding. Nothing is as it seems. Virgil got all his laughs. The audience guffawed themselves silly over him and, all the while, in their heads, they were thinking, *I wonder what I did with my parking ticket?; I wonder how long this show is?; I have so much work to do at home.*"

We all sat dumb, like schoolkids in trouble.

"Trust me. If you all take the work we were doing in the rehearsal room and put it on the stage, you will be the best group of actors that I've ever worked with—and that includes you, Samuel. But I need you at your best, and I'm going to push you guys, because we are close." He inhaled deeply into the soles of his feet. "None of that 'acting' shit, OK? Don't do that to Virgil or to me; don't do that to yourself. Remember: It's not how far you throw your voice. It's how far you throw your soul."

I stared at Virgil, the fat fuck. Was he really not going to step forward and admit tonight's disaster was his doing? Would he really let Samuel and the others fall on his sword?

Yes, he would.

"All right," J.C. concluded. "Get some rest and we'll start our work again tomorrow."

I stood up and grabbed my jacket, still anxious to get home to my kids.

"Oh yeah," J.C. added. "Where's Prince Hal?"

"Right here." The Prince stood up, pulling on the sleeves of his overcoat.

"How many fathers do you think Prince Hal has?" J.C. asked.

"I'm sorry, what?"

"There are a lot of people in the world. There are postmen, train conductors, librarians, actors, cops, doctors, soldiers, hairdressers . . . There's a lot of people, right?"

The Prince nodded.

"Well, each one of us only has *one* father. One. Yours dies in Scene Two of Act Five. If it comes off like you are some somnambulistic jerk who, while walking down Ninth Avenue on his way to buy some Camel Lights, notices an old man who just fell over and croaked—I don't even know why I am sitting here paying a hundred and eighty dollars to watch this shit. Do you get it? One father. He's dead. He's *never* coming back. Door closed. You're next. You get it? Work on it. Until you do we may as well not lift the curtain."

"I'm sorry, J.C., it's just that . . ."

"I'm really not interested in why it didn't work. I want it to work."

Prince Hal stood motionless. I felt sorry for him. He was going to cry tonight.

"William, can I talk to you?" J.C. called out to me as people were meandering out.

My body rang with fear, like I'd been hit with a frying pan. He motioned for me to meet him privately by the exit. What could be so bad that it could not be said in front of others?

Underneath the stairwell at the back of the stage, I tried to meet J.C.'s gaze. He was whispering to me, which was terrifying.

"Your performance tonight was damn close to incendiary. It was just as I feel Hotspur should be played. I loved it, but it was also completely unsustainable. If you scream and howl like that every night for a week you will be in a hospital."

I was confused. One part of me was elated that I had received a compliment in the morass of darkness; the other, scared of what he was trying to say. "I need you to take care of yourself. Pay attention to your voice. Listen to it. I've directed this play before and you must beware of Hotspur. It's a lunatic part, and it'll make you mad. You can get close, but don't go all the way in. You understand me?"

I didn't. I was scared.

"I'll be OK," I said.

"Are you OK right now?" he asked.

I nodded. He scoured my face with his eyes.

"My only problem is sometimes I get nervous that I am being outclassed by Prince Hal," I said, smiling, cavalierly pretending I was joking.

"Is it not possible that you both can excel?" he responded. "This is not a movie, William, OK?" This was the cruelest thing he could have said to me, highlighting my lack of training and underscoring my paranoia that I did not deserve to be there in the first place. "Tonight, onstage, it seemed you had gasoline coming from your pores and set yourself on fire. I admit I took secret joy in it, but you will destroy your vocal cords or your back or something. If you keep that up, something inside of you will break."

He paused and observed me again. The silence was terrifying.

"Just know that our hearts are huge," he said, looking at me. "Do you know that? Our hearts are not some small little gizmos. They are fucking big and hang down in the middle of our chests. They're beating and working their asses off but your heart doesn't need your help, you get it? The talent that resides inside each person is not fragile. Your lungs aren't in your chest, they're in your back. Your voice isn't in your throat, it begins in your spine, you get it?"

I didn't understand, but I knew he was trying to bolster my confidence, and that made me feel pathetic and mistrustful of the sincerity of his compliments.

"I'm just saying—we don't know very much. Let go a little bit. It's possible that if you put your anger out onstage in the right relaxed way—releasing it—the stage will take it from you and heal you. That is possible. It's just steady as she goes. Maintain ballast. You understand?"

I nodded.

Then, spontaneously, I asked, "Can I tell you one thing?"

"Yes," my director said, taking a step back to better read all of me.

"That wasn't Samuel's fault or any of the guys', Virgil came to everybody's—" My director cut me off.

"You think I don't know that? You think I'm playing checkers here? I'm not going to stay up all night trying to convince people the sun's coming up. The sun will do that all by itself. Sometimes it doesn't matter who's right or wrong. Samuel fucked up because he didn't believe in himself. Virgil's a genius of the stage, flat out, get used to it. And his own demons are crueler then anything you or I could drum up. He will face those monsters any moment now— the second he's alone. Don't worry," J.C. said, smiling. "That's what I'm trying to say, you're not in charge."

I thanked him and turned to go.

"One more thing." He paused, grabbing my shoulder. "Can you can handle bad reviews?"

"What?"

"The critics," J.C. said simply, "may not respond to your Hotspur the way that I do, but they will be wrong."

I stared blankly.

"They will think you are too modern, too funny, too American, and too angry. Most of them love to quote from W. H. Auden's *Lectures on Shakespeare.* Auden was a great poet, but he misunderstood this play. Now, I can get you good reviews if that's what you want—it's easy. A couple costume changes, omit a few gestures, put your hands in your pockets, and work on your pronunciation of your *a*'s and your *t*'s . . . they are terrible. But, if you do those things, you won't be nearly as fun. So, think about it. If you can't live with *The New York Times* singling you out as the only problem in an otherwise perfect production, then I will give you the tools you need to change. But I hope you will choose to take the bullet for the show, because it's a lot of fun to watch you."

"I don't care about the reviews," I lied.

"Say it again," J.C. said to me.

"I don't care about the reviews."

"Good." He laughed. "My advice? Don't read them. Just, stay alive. Don't do any drugs. Get some sleep. Only smoke indoors while you are drinking something warm. And *do not miss one fucking show.*"

He patted me on the back and walked away.

Scene 3

I waited for the 6 train down underneath Broadway. Slowly, Shakespeare slipped away. I shouldn't have done all that cocaine; that was obvious. It had not helped anything. The aftermath hangover of the coke was catapulting me down into some lower tier of divorcé depression. Stepping off the 6 train and onto the platform, I heard a middle-aged white woman who had been sitting across from me on the subway clearly say out towards me, "The play was terrible, by the way."

I turned around and looked at her. She smiled. The doors closed.

WALKING INTO THE MERCURY, I thought, what had I done with that little bag of coke and the small blue pills that came with it? My mom was watching the kids. She was pissed to miss the first preview but she was the only sitter I had. I didn't want her or the kids to come across the blow. If the hotel cleaning ladies found the baggie, it would be game over. They'd call the cops. The thought petrified me. I imagined the social services taking my kids away. The headline of the *Post:* DRUG DEN DAD.

By the time I got back to my apartment in the Mercury, I felt certain I knew where I had hidden the drugs: inside my guitar case. It was near midnight when I came through the door, so I was sure everyone would be fast asleep. I would find the baggie, flush it down the toilet, get on my knees, ask the theater gods for forgiveness, and go to sleep.

As soon as I stepped inside, I knew something was wrong. The lights were on dimly and romantically. Willie Nelson's "Stardust Memories" was playing, and the place smelled of banana bread. The entire apartment was immaculate, warm, and brimming with a kind of Norman Rockwell peace. My books, which had been spread over the floor in boxes, were alphabetized neatly on the shelves. My records, my papers, my clothes, and the kids' watercolors, army men, Lego—everything was clean and orderly. Still awake with an apron tied around her waist, my mother was busy bustling around the kitchen, doing about seven things simultaneously. My daughter's puppy was sleeping on the leather couch.

I watched her move for a full minute, absorbing just how beautiful the apartment looked. Then I noticed that my guitar was out, nonchalantly placed on top of the piano. It looked good up there, but where was the case?

My mother turned around when she felt my presence.

"Hi, honey, how was the show? Everything's great here. I did some cleaning, as you can see. Hope that's OK? It's just that the little ones conked out so easily and so early. There are only so many emails a person can write in a night before they need to do something productive with their hands, you know?" She smiled at me gently and without needing an answer to any of her questions. She calmly turned around and got back to work.

"Anyway, I made you some vegetarian chili and put it in the fridge so you will always have something healthy and ready to eat. And I made that bean dip you love and some banana bread for the kids. I think that will come in quite handy."

My mother is a beautiful woman. She's only seventeen years older than me and was still in the last days of her forties. People would always tell me how young she looked and I would answer, "She doesn't *look* young, she *is* young."

Tonight, however, she looked younger than usual. There was a scarf around her head hiding the bruising from a face-lift she had about two weeks prior. I found my mother's facial surgery harrowing. It seemed to contradict everything she had ever taught me. She'd spent the last eight years of her life working for the Peace Corps stationed in Port-au-Prince, Haiti. She was managing the largest orphanage in that city and had been successful in enrolling more than three thousand previously unregistered children in school. She was here in New York on a three-pronged mission: (a) to let her scars heal without the kids in Haiti asking too many questions; (b) to fundraise; and (c) to check on me.

I couldn't understand why a woman who was on her way to winning some serious Eleanor Roosevelt–type humanitarian awards would have facial surgery. And while she was still young no less. It floored me. Her skin was so tight, it physically hurt to look at her. Also, there is something about one's mother struggling desperately to hold on to youth that is particularly frightening to the child. You want to believe that aging is going to be OK, that you will handle growing and maturing into adulthood with grace, but when you see your mommy looking like she cut her face in half and stretched it around her ears, it becomes difficult. There was also something "off" about her manic cooking and cleaning. Then the penny dropped.

"Mom," I said, staring at her, "are you on coke?"

She froze. Then slowly, with the canary feathers hanging from her lips, she smiled at me. "I don't know why you're standing there all priest-like. It's *your* blow," she said, winking. Then she turned and went back to the business at hand, pulling the banana bread out of the oven.

"I feel the same about cocaine as I do about eating meat," she said. "It's vile and ultimately morally reprehensible, but as long as I don't pay for it—I find it quite enjoyable."

I sat down in a large leather chair that faces the kitchen and sunk my head into my hands. No wonder I'd become an actor.

"I can't believe you, Mom," I said. "Do you understand what's happening here?" I could barely move. "I let you watch the kids. For the first time in your life you are completely responsible for your grandchildren and I come home and you've got a pound of coke up your nose."

"God, you are impossible! You really are. If you are so above reproach, why don't you try not carrying cocaine around in your guitar case like you're Keith Richards or something?" There was a long silence while my mother washed a bowl. The puppy finally noticed me, woke up, and leapt around the room barking.

"Look, let's move on, OK?" my mother offered brightly. "Can we both just admit, perhaps, that we could have been more responsible; give thanks that everything is actually indeed all right; and talk? Because I've been thinking about you and I don't know why you are acting so torn up about all this divorce nonsense. I don't know why you and Mary are both so upset. This divorce is a wonderful thing. I wrote Mary a letter and told her that, you know? I hope that's OK?"

"What did you say?"

"I explained to her what she doesn't understand: that you are, quite simply, exactly like your father."

"What does that mean?" I asked.

"Look, don't be so hostile," she shouted from the kitchen. "You have such an edge to your voice. I did a tiny bit of *your* cocaine. Which, by the way, you are an absolute royal ass for having in the house. I would not put it past Mary to hire a private detective and smear your name all over kingdom come to make sure she gets custody. She's smart and she's tough, so don't pussyfoot around. You have to pull yourself together." She smiled. "I found your illegal drugs and was going to flush the little baggie down the toilet, but then I thought, *HEY, I'm almost fifty . . . I haven't done any cocaine since 1987, so I'm going to try it.* So I did, and I have been having the best night I've had in a long time and I refuse to let you ruin it. I had a glorious experience cleaning your apartment." She flashed a huge grin as she put the sugar back in the cupboard. "What I did not anticipate was that my thirty-two-year-old, drug-hoarding, depressed, divorcé son was going to get his knickers in such a twist. You'll be glad to know that I finished it. You shouldn't have any anyway—you have to get up early with the small people."

"I don't want any, Mom." I sat, stupefied. "I was going to throw it away."

"Well, good." My mother took off her apron and came out towards me. "Listen, I love you more than anything in the world. You are a wonderful son, but let's face it . . . Mary should crack the champagne. She doesn't need you or any man. You do need a woman. You need a partner and a wife—and that partner is not going to be an internationally touring rock star!" My mother sat down across from me, took some cigarettes out of my jacket pocket, and began looking for matches. "I understand Mary. She's blessed. I realize she doesn't see that she's blessed right now, but she is. She can support herself and doesn't have to spend her life picking up some man's sweaty socks. Do you know how fortunate that is?" My mother found the matches and lit a cigarette, taking tiny little girlish puffs.

"Mary is in an absolutely minuscule percentage of women across this planet who don't have to kiss a man's ass to do the things she wants to do in this life. Mary is a brilliant performer and people respect her. She has a huge gift and if she uses her brain, she can wield that respect, talent, and money to effect real change in this world. Most of us can't move the current, you know? The river just pushes us along and we bounce idly through our lives, but she can push back. If I had her money, I would never bother with a man at all." She patted me on the knee, ashed her cigarette, and leaned back on the couch. "I know my face-lift upsets you. But what you don't understand is I don't give a shit what I look like."

I smirked incredulously.

"I don't, but men do. And I need their attention. Do you know what it's like to sit at a fundraising meeting and watch these rich white guys drift away into their BlackBerries, playing some stupid game, because they are so listless and bored by a fifty-year-old woman talking about how twenty percent of the world consumes eighty percent of the world's resources? That millions of children don't have enough food to eat but then"—she paused for dramatic effect—"when a beautiful young woman walks into the room, *Uh huh hurumph hurumph . . . How can I help, darling? Gee, we must find a creative solution. Let's pull together for the big WIN!* Do you see? I don't want to be 'pretty.' I want to be relevant! It's a superficial world and I'm coping with it." She took a long pause and collected herself. "Just so you know, my face-lift was free. I would never have wasted good money on it."

"What do you mean?" I asked.

"The Haitian Doctor is a big fan of your ex-wife. He has all her CDs and thought that when she sees my great face-lift, she will ask who the doctor is . . . You get it? He worked on me as an investment!" She smiled a big, mischievous smile. "He also happens to respect the work I do."

"What did you mean about me being like my father?" I asked.

She wouldn't answer.

She continued, "You've always done this . . . created a running narrative out of every event in your life. No sooner did something happen to you than you began telling a 'story' about it. And I see you doing that now . . . trying to write the 'story' of your divorce so that you get to be the good guy. But it's not like that . . . Technically, in my relationship with your father, I was the 'Bad Guy.' But look at this coke-snorting bad guy; at least I'm putting my money where my mouth is. I'm getting kids off the street. Putting them in school and saving them from a life of prostitution and crime. One hundred hours a week, I work to end poverty. You work four hours a day, get your picture taken, everyone tells you you're gorgeous, they give you a standing ovation at the end of the night, and all you did is recite a couple hundred rhyming couplets without falling on your ass."

"We didn't get a standing ovation."

"Bad house?" she asked sweetly.

"Terrible."

"I wish I could've been there. Wait till you're fifty years old and nobody wants to hire you 'cause your eyelids hang down over your baby blues. If you weren't so handsome you'd have less than half the friends you have now . . . It's true. You're not that interesting! You'll find a way to sneak your ass into the back of the surgery clinic. Believe me, you'll be getting the hair plugs neatly inserted. You won't be so quick to throw stones then. It's tough to grow old. Deterioration is not for the meek. My mother's dead. My father's dead. It goes so fast. You won't believe it. My mother, my divorce with your father, that's all ancient history to you. To me, it was yesterday. In five seconds, your daughter will be a grown woman with kids holding your hand, taking you to my funeral. I shit you not, Son."

She patted the couch, trying to encourage me to sit next to her. I couldn't do it. The puppy jumped up and cuddled against her.

"Someday you will miss this moment right now. You will miss the night you came home to a clean house, banana bread, and a 'coked-up' mom. You will think it's beautiful and funny. And you will see that the days of that marriage to Mary were nothing to mourn for! They were the painful period. You were deeply uncomfortable. You were twisted up like a pretzel and wondering why your arms hurt. I say, 'Congratulations, my son, you are refusing to live a quiet life of pretzel-like desperation.' Now your kids will know you better and be able to absorb the best from both their mother and their father." My mother smiled. I sat down next to the puppy, and stared out the window at the lights of New York City. There is so much movement, even at 1:00 a.m. My mother stood up, put out her cigarette, walked behind me, and started scratching my back.

"Sometimes don't you just look forward to being dead?" she asked.

"What kind of pep talk is that?"

"Why is looking forward to death not encouraging? I imagine death is wonderful."

She continued scratching, using her nails like she did when I was a kid. "See, for you, death is scary because in death all the 'specialness' of your life will evaporate. Once you're dead, the movies, the magazine covers, the money, the art, the curtain calls—all these things won't matter any more than a fireworks display in 1956. Fun while it lasted, ya know, kid? You enjoy the delusion that you're special and the world supports that delusion, and I understand that would make death frightening. But, you see, I know that you and I are special only in the way that every living thing that fears harm is special."

My mother stopped scratching my back, kissed me on top of the head, and went back into the kitchen to continue cleaning up.

"It's so bizarre," she said, "over all these years and fighting with your dad and hating him and bickering about money and visits and Thanksgiving, and then to watch the thing I love most—you—turn into the thing that has given me the most pain—*him!*

Someday, you will be talking to your daughter and realize that those are Mary's eyes inside her head. See, it's all still happen-ing. Nothing's over. It's all still happen-*ing*." She stepped forward and leaned on the doorway that separated the living room from the kitchen. "I could have ended things better with your father, I guess," my mother said. "Been more mature. That is my only advice: End things well. Be polite and respectful." She stepped back and started washing her hands.

MY PARENTS SPLIT UP around my ninth birthday. My mother and I were living in the suburbs of Atlanta. My father had driven out from Houston to visit, and to try one last time to reconcile. It was the best birthday in the world. At that time, my dad had a wicked-cool '64 convertible Plymouth Barracuda. It was a gorgeous Octo-ber day in Atlanta—a little chilly, but my dad ripped the top down anyway and took my four best friends and me to John's Pizza House and to the movies. An old revival house in Buckhead was playing his favorite movie, *The Man Who Would Be King.*

It was fun to see an old movie and my buddies liked it. The film was about these two best friends that lose their friendship through this bizarre grand adventure in foreign lands. At the end of the story, one of them has been captured and is trapped on a rope bridge and the other guy, Peachy, who is safe, knows it was all his fault. Peachy shouts out to his pal, "Can you ever forgive me for being so bloody stupid and so bleedin' arrogant?" And his friend, who is about to be killed, says, "Peachy, that I can, and that I do!" He smiles, letting his buddy know that he's understood. We're all imperfect. We all screw up. And then *boom,* the rope gets cut, and the friend falls and dies.

I'd never seen a movie with such a bitter, sad ending before and couldn't stop crying. All my friends were looking at me. We were walking through the parking lot towards the Barracuda and one of my friends started teasing me about the snot dripping down my nose. "You really are a mama's boy!" he said.

My dad announced simply, "He's not a mama's boy. If you're not crying, it means you didn't really watch the movie."

My friends shut up.

We drove away and my dad revved the engine at stoplights. He cranked up the music so loud that it annoyed strangers. We got ice cream. We laughed so hard our stomachs cramped. "You boys ever done donuts?" We all shook our heads.

He immediately popped the Plymouth up over the curb and crashed onto the fields by a high school. He started spinning the car round and round at what felt like light speed. The shock absorbers busted into high alert, as all of us began bouncing around the car. We could not believe it. We were terrified and exhilarated. It was the most egregious rule breaking I had ever been a part of. It felt like a bank heist. We didn't even have seat belts. Next he drove fast, bumping and popping and banging all the way across two fields and right up to one of the pitcher's mounds, yanked the wheel hard, and gunned the engine. The car spun in circles. Dirt was flying. We all were howling with joy and fear. We landed back at my mom's, dusty like a band of outlaws. My friends left one by one, all telling me that I had the coolest dad.

He was cool, twenty-seven, with long hair and John Lennon glasses.

His birthday present to me was a slot-car racetrack, and we built it in my room and raced our Formula 1's until it was time for bed. Then we said goodbye. He was driving back to Texas that night, "unless your mom lets me spend the night." He winked hopefully. My mom had an old upright piano and he played Scott Joplin rags, because he knew they were my favorite. As soon as he walked out the front door, I was weeping again. My mom came in to kiss me good night and I told her to leave me alone, and please not tell my dad I was upset. But before I knew it my dad came back into my room—and in the dark, while scratching my back, he said a bunch of tender words designed to make me feel better.

Once I heard the car pull away, I walked out to the living room and asked my mom, "Did you tell him I was crying? Did you? Is that why he came back in to talk to me?"

"Of course," she answered.

"You suck," I said and walked back to my room.

I lay in bed for what felt like hours. Eventually, I heard the Barracuda's cranky old engine return out in front of the house again. I crawled up in bed and saw my dad get out of the car and begin hammering a pair of high-heeled shoes and some lingerie to an old maple tree in our front yard. I opened my window and turned on the light. My dad looked at me across our front yard. Even in the dark, our eyes found each other easily.

Lit only by the headlamps of his car, he shouted, "Peachy, can you ever forgive me for being so bloody stupid and so bleedin' arrogant!"

I tried to answer through my screen window, "That I can, and that I do!" but I didn't say it loud enough for him to hear me. My voice was too emotional. He drove away.

IN MY MERCURY BEDROOM, I began getting undressed, habitually humming to check my voice, running Hotspur's lines in my head, and wondering if I would be able to sleep. I remember thinking, *Is my relationship with my children going to become as complicated as my relationship with my parents?*

Then my mom walked in, dressed in an entirely new outfit.

"Where are you going?" I asked.

"I'm going to go see a friend." She winked.

"It's one in the morning," I said.

"Sorry, Dad, am I not allowed to go out?" she said sarcastically, imitating the voice of a teenager.

"I thought you were going to spend the night here with me and the kids," I said.

"I changed my mind. You don't need me anymore." She smiled. "The kids need alone time with you. Besides, there's no way I'm going to fall asleep. And I lied about the coke being finished."

"Who are you meeting?"

"None of your business," she said with no expression and walked out the door.

AS THE SUN CAME UP on the morning after the first preview, I walked the puppy and bought donuts. I was already panicking again about my voice. The kids were watching cartoons alone. It was freezing outside and the wind didn't help my throat any. My phone rang.

It was my wife. My blood stopped moving. I picked up.

"Hello," I said, fighting the wind.

All I could hear was the sound of the woman I'd promised to love forever uncontrollably sobbing on the other end of the line. She couldn't form a word. She just sobbed, caught her breath, and wailed more.

"I'm so sorry, I'm so sorry, I love you so much," I said. It sounded like she could barely breathe.

I said it again, "I love you so much. I'm so sorry."

She hung up. I called back but she didn't answer. My hands were freezing. I wondered where she was and how she came to find herself awake and wailing at 7:43 a.m.

When she had been pregnant with our first we'd gone camping and woke up to this same kind of freezing autumn air. We watched the sun rise on a small lake in the Adirondacks. Four black bears were on the other side of the lake staring at us: a mother, a father, and two cubs. We could see their breath as they drank and played in the water. Mary and I held hands, warming our stiff fingers. We dubbed ourselves the Animal Family.

BACK IN THE MERCURY I sat by my piano and played Scott Joplin's "Crush Collision March." I thought about my wife's phone call while our son tinkered around with army men at my feet, donut jelly on his hands and face. Our daughter danced along to my poorly pounded rags in the hallway of the hotel with a long black feather boa draped around her shoulders and her nightgown stained with donut icing. That banana bread was crap. My little girl was spinning, round and round in imperfect pirouettes. It struck me that things were very much like they had been when I was little. After my parents' divorce, I would play under my father's piano while he rattled out this exact same song. I remember telling my dad that Scott Joplin was my favorite "singer."

"Someday you'll like your own music," he answered.

"No, I won't," I said.

NOW, ALMOST TWENTY-FIVE YEARS had spun by and all the elements were precisely the same: the divorce, the music, the smell of stale cigarettes, the Native American rug, the empty coffee mugs, beer bottles in the garbage; even the little plastic toy army men were exactly the same. The only real difference was that there were two kids instead of one.

And people say the universe isn't expanding.

Firing the Vainglorious Rocket

Scene 1

W hen the morning of opening arrived, I felt OK, if a snake with a fork through his head feels OK. It was a Thursday. Big-time openings are always on Thursday. That way, the review hits the Friday paper. Apparently, that's the one everybody reads. The night before had been Halloween, and after our final preview I'd walked home. Mary's outfit from the video for "Piss on Your Grave" was the number one costume of the year. I remember hiding my head as I moved through the crowds that last evening of October, passing more than a dozen drunk women wobbling in their heels dressed as my estranged wife. Trash blew across Sixth Avenue as cops took apart the remains of the Halloween parade border structures. One young woman, dressed as my ex, walked straight towards me and stopped me in my tracks. Clearly high, her eyes on the other side of Jupiter, she looked at me, burst out laughing and singing my wife's hit single:

> *I thought you were my next of kin,*
> *But your mind was wrapped in sin,*

You want me to be your slave?
You want me to behave?

She imitated the drum solo, "Boom chicka boom. *I'll piss on your grave.*"

Then as if in a dream she danced her way through fallen candy wrappers, empty cans of Red Bull, and spilled beer.

THE KIDS HAD BEEN with me at the Mercury all week while Mary was in San Francisco for an intimate, sold-out stand at the Fillmore, continuing her sensational press for the new Piss on Your Grave Tour. She was coming back on the red-eye and wanted to meet after I'd dropped the kids off at school. She'd sent an email saying it was imperative we meet. Not from her assistant, from her. It was all very top-secret, mysterious, and exciting. I'd been home from Africa now for six weeks of rehearsal and four weeks of previews, and we had barely spoken since the first few days. There was a rip-tide pulling us apart. My free trial month at the Mercury was over. The rent on the room was now astronomical. Old Bart had played me beautifully. As I dressed the kids that morning, it was hard to tell why my hands were trembling; opening my Shakespeare play on Broadway, or breakfast with my estranged wife.

There was some good news on the horizon: I'd discovered that I'd forgotten to throw out the bag of little blue pills that accompanied Dean's blow. I have no idea what they were—quaalude, Xanax, oxycodone—but I had begun chopping them in half and taking one before each show. They were helping. Short term, anyway. With the pill, I was hurting my voice less and the high-pitched trill of anxiety running up and down my spine calmed to a frequency I could bear. I had two left. When the kids were distracted, I took half a blue pill with a bite of Cheerios and bananas. We dropped my daughter off at kindergarten first and then I walked my son over to his preschool.

"What do you think is cooler, Dad," he asked, holding my hand as we waited for a light to turn, "whistling or snapping?"

"Hmmmm," I said. "I'd have to say whistling is cooler."

"Yeah, I thought you'd say that." He shrugged. "I think snapping is cooler."

There was a long pause as we walked across the street before he confessed, "But I don't really know how to whistle."

"Snapping is cool too," I added.

"Yeah," he said, defeated.

"What do you think is harder," he began again, "to blow a bubble with your gum? Or not swallow it?"

"They're both tough," I answered.

"Do you think policemen have birthdays?"

When we got to his class, I put his lunch box in the fridge and helped him hang up his jean jacket in his cubby. As I hugged him, I said, "So, who do you think is the best dad in New York City?"

"You just want me to say you—but I don't know any other dads," he said flatly.

I looked at him and adopted a British accent, "Ahhh Peachy, can you ever forgive me for being so bloody stupid and so bleedin' arrogant?"

He looked at me confused and then ran away to his friends. I wouldn't see him again until the weekend after next. Saying good-bye to him, and his sister, was like swallowing poison every time. It never got easier. I took the other half of the blue pill at the little kiddie water fountain before I left his classroom. One left.

Near the school was a café named Tea & Sympathy, where I was to meet Mary.

She was coming straight from the airport. What was she going to say? My birthday had come and gone—so that wasn't it. The stage manager and cast had given me a sad little carrot cake at the theater; the nanny had the kids call, but Mary didn't get on the phone. Maybe she felt bad and was going to give me a birthday/opening night present? I didn't know. I just sat in the café and waited.

The longer I looked at my life, the more it appeared like one of those elaborate western film sets, Main Street of Dodge City. At the first glance, it all seems vintage, authentic, full of mystery and possibility. Fresh pine dust, the old wooden swinging doors, the wavy and misshapen glass, the hand-painted signs—all promise adventure. But when you walk inside: it's not a badass saloon with old cowboys playing poker and blushing, tragic whores who secretly love you; it's an empty plywood building. There's a craft service guy next to a space heater fixing up some tomato soup, eating a snatch of gummy bears and handing out vitamin C. Nothing's happening at all, just some people standing around, hoping for a latte.

Mary appeared for our scheduled breakfast meeting at ten past 9:00 a.m. There was no hint of the vulnerability I had heard when she'd sobbed into the phone weeks earlier. She was wearing a long gray fur and wraparound black shades, and wasn't carrying any presents. Her jet-black hair was pulled back in some elaborate number, and her carefully moisturized skin shimmered. She didn't seem to even know that the play hadn't opened, or that my birthday had come and gone. Her driver was waiting outside. She walked in and sat across from me with makeup still left on her skin from the previous night's concert. Looking into her sunglasses while listening to the things she told me, I learned one thing immediately: I was an idiot. We were already a million miles away from one another. I barely recognized her. When had we grown so far apart? I couldn't figure it out. We had been in marriage counseling for more than three years, fighting and bickering, and had been generally miserable with one another—but all the while I still felt we knew one another. We discussed weekends, Thanksgivings, spring breaks, Christmas Eves, all the kids' movements in a very civilized manner. Then we discussed how much money I should be paying her, and a litany of other surgical shit. I'd felt closer to women I'd known an hour. She had a piece of paper with a twenty-point bullet list of things I should go over with my lawyer (whom I still had yet to acquire).

Why wouldn't she take off her sunglasses?

We'd loved each other. We wrote our marriage vows naked in bed. We went apple picking. She had baked me a homemade pie and her hands tasted like brown sugar.

She told me I looked terrible, that the Internet was abuzz with rumors I was a junkie. She ordered me a protein health shake. Eventually, Mary got around to the point of our meeting and why it had been necessary for us to be face-to-face, today. Calmly, she mentioned she was in love with another man. She wanted me to hear it from her first. She'd made it just in time. Apparently, news of their love affair was already on the CNN scroll.

AFTER STUMBLING INTO the theater, still holding my protein, strawberry, banana smoothie, I tried to take a quick nap in my dressing room before Ezekiel arrived. I had a good four hours before our final rehearsal. There was another quote taped to my dressing room door. I sat in the darkness and read it. It was a Huck Finn quote about whippoorwills, leaves, and the sound a ghost makes when it's grieving and can't make itself understood.

———

"ARE YOU NERVOUS?" J.C. asked the company a few hours later in his concluding notes session to the cast. "You should be."

We were all seated, jittery and excited in the house of the Lyceum Theatre. It was our last rehearsal. Opening night curtain would go up in approximately four hours. The cast still had their coats on and some were sipping tea in thermoses. Edward, our King, sat still, quietly reading the paper. Prince Hal was getting his back rubbed by Lady Percy. It didn't bother me. They were friends. The weather had turned cold and winter was on the way. We were expecting an opening night confidence builder— something to drown the butterflies.

"Anything could happen out here tonight," J.C. began. "A forty-pound light could fall from the rafters on your head. Your scene partner could forget her lines. You may forget yours. Your costume could tear and your ass could be exposed for all of New York's finest to mock and relish for the rest of the year. So much could go wrong tonight." He paused. "Anyone have family here tonight?"

About half the cast nodded.

"They may hate the show, you know? Everyone may hate it. We could get terrible notices. What I do know?"

There was a long pause as he mutely asked us all to sit still by staring into our eyes.

"Well, actually, there is one thing I know with absolute certainty." He turned and began to pace across the stage. "And this is it: There is a great deal to be nervous about. So, if you feel hummingbirds banging around in your stomach, or your hands start to sweat and shake; if you accidentally put on two pairs of socks; if you spill tea on your script pages and burn yourself; if anything like that happens—*absolutely nothing is wrong*."

He paused.

Edward was the only actor among us not riveted by our director. The King was still reading the science pages—the rest of us were disciples at the feet of our master. Even Virgil was paying attention.

"You are nervous because you care about what you do and because what we do up here matters. Let your hands shake. Let your mouth be dry."

Nobody knew much about J.C., nobody but Edward. They had been friends for forty years. J.C. had been an assistant director when Edward played Romeo in Stratford. But for the rest of us, J.C. was an incredibly difficult man to get to know. When you were alone with him, he was almost too direct. His eyes were so penetrating you felt he was handling your mind. From the stage, often I could feel him nudging and prodding me—*faster, slower, be patient, stop pushing*. I have no idea what he was like on Christmas morning with his family, sisters and brothers and all his nieces and nephews, maybe very different—but for us, he had cut a very deliberate profile of himself and we only saw what he wanted us to see.

"Tonight, the show is yours," he continued, addressing the cast, pacing back and forth across the proscenium's edge. "Don't push it. Let it go up all by itself. Don't put anything on this stage that isn't felt. Yelling, crying, screaming . . . Those kinds of dynamics are only effective if they are supported by genuine emotion. Real anger. Real laughter. Don't fake it. It doesn't help."

He paused and looked around. The houselights were up and there were still stagehands working all around us. The lighting designer and set designer were having a conference at a makeshift table built over the chairs in the back. Painters were finishing some touch-ups. The stage manager was reviewing safety concerns with the fire engineer.

"I am proud of you all. I feel so lucky each of you chose to be a part of this endeavor and I am grateful to our producers for putting their money where their mouth is and giving us everything we need and not a penny more."

This was pure politicking. Our producers were standing in the back talking to the house manager. They were two men and a woman, and in unison, they nodded to J.C. We didn't know the details but there had been some behind-the-scenes scuffles over the budget. There was a battle scene, the one in which I was so unjustly murdered, for which J.C. had wanted the entire stage to be on fire. They settled on three-quarters on fire.

"And tonight, I give the show to you." J.C. said this and sat down at the edge of the stage. "It's your opening night present. Until now, the show has been, in many ways, mine . . . to tweak and press. We've been partners, yes, but I have been your captain. It's been an honor. Now, it's yours."

He looked around at us.

"Listen to me now: None of you are exempt from the collective. Not you, Edward—or you, Virgil—or any of you. Nobody is alone out there. This is a three-hundred-fifty-horsepower play. Everyone wishes their part were bigger, Ezekiel. Everyone."

Ezekiel, my roommate, was caught momentarily looking down at his phone, unsure why he was singled out. J.C. had directed *Othello* several years earlier in a much-heralded production in Chicago, with Zeke in the titular role. He, like many in our production, was wildly underutilized—but that is what was beginning to make our show feel so exceptional. Everyone on our stage was capable of holding the center spot.

I was sitting in the back, feet up on the seat in front of me, wearing a red lumberjack flannel and my old high school football jersey underneath. Number 13. Lucky. I looked over at our Juilliard-trained Prince Hal. He was no longer getting his back rubbed. He looked at me and smiled. He rode his bike to the theater every day and carried a packed lunch. He had two kids and a social worker wife. They lived in Brooklyn. He read politically relevant books and was a better actor than I was, and no matter what *The New York Times* might end up saying, I already knew that. Under the lights, when he spoke onstage, a gentle cloud would leave his mouth—not some gross spit flying from his mouth like the rest of us, but it looked more like someone misting an orchid. He was in complete control of his voice. He could scream and cry, but never once would it crack or break like mine. He could sword fight for days. I could feel the audience adore him.

"The wind doesn't blow," J.C. said. "You get it? It's wind, what else is it going to do? Rain doesn't fall. It's rain. And you don't act. You are. You get it?"

Lady Percy had on sweatpants and a T-shirt and was now stretching in the aisle, doing yoga poses as she listened to J.C. Her long red hair fell to the small of her back. I was starting to want to fuck her badly. I couldn't help it. It's hard to kiss someone every night, have them touch you tenderly on the stomach, hold their hand, and then just let it go at curtain call. Memorizing lines is easy. Navigating and spending your own emotional currency is difficult. She felt me staring at her ass and glanced over. Her smile revealed just how nervous she was; her mouth didn't move right.

I looked across the house to old man Edward, our King. He smiled straight.

"Let your characters be as interesting and rich as each of you. You are talented and you are prepared. Have confidence. Everything will go up all by itself. I will watch tonight's show, but I will not watch again till we close. So, take care of each other. Take care of your health. Wash your hands. Don't drink too much. Remember, self-pity is the only emotion that doesn't play." He seemed to stare right at me. "Don't give in to it. Not onstage, not in life. Self-pity belongs in the garbage out back. Have I been clear?"

He still held my eyes and paused, and I saw a glint of doubt in his eyes. J.C. was worried. What was he worried about? Was it me? My self-pity?

"That's the truth," whispered a voice behind me. It was Scotty, my understudy. He scared me. His eyes were so blue they were almost white. All during rehearsal, I would catch him writing down my moves. Sometimes I'd hear him running my lines in the hallway. I tried to ignore him, but he was too goddamn gracious. Sometimes Scotty would say, "You have a cold? You sounded a little hoarse out there," and I'd want to wring his neck.

"Now, for my last job as your director." J.C. clapped his hands together. "Rehearsals are over and it's time to stage the curtain call."

"Oh, God no." We all heard Edward groan and look up from his crossword. "Will the tortures never cease?"

"I will have no insubordination, not even from you, Edward. It's time for us to get the damn standing ovation we all deserve."

"Well then, bring out the flags." Edward sighed.

Most directors stage a curtain call before the first preview, but J.C. was old school.

During previews, we did a full company bow in work lights, no fanfare. This was to let the audience, critics, and us know we were still working. We were not allowed to enjoy the fruits of our labor, until our labor was complete. The staging of the curtain call was the final touch for any J.C. Callahan production. He took this shit seriously.

J.C. tore a piece of paper from his assistant's notebook and started calling out names. Stage management walked through the stage left doors with a dozen flags, each carrying one of the various family crests represented in the play. The Percy flag, Hotspur's, had the word "Esperance" embroidered across it. Immediately, it was my favorite.

The final bows began with Prince Hal, the King, Falstaff, and Hotspur walking through the crowd. We were to stride out through the flags, trumpets, and spears, walking side by side. It was strange to do with no one clapping. I was to take my solo bow first, then get offstage through the downstage exit while the Prince took his bow. As we practiced, I bowed and leapt off confidently. Suddenly, J.C. stopped everything.

"William, what the fuck? Do not leap offstage! If you do that everyone will watch you, when they should be watching Prince Hal. But if you walk out with Hal and bow humbly, we, the audience, will feel some offstage healing has happened between you two— the story will be fresh in our imagination and we will cry again at the uncertainty of the universe and leap to our feet clapping with a newfound rigor people usually save for their children! So, stay in the fucking pocket and don't draw attention by leaping offstage as if you're worried nobody realized how awesome you were."

I did as I was told.

"Now," J.C. barked on, "next I want you, Virgil, to come out, step forward, and take your bow. This is the moment when everyone will stand. Take a breath to soak it in, but then, as quickly as possible, you will turn around and see the King right behind you. Gesture to his majesty and get offstage. Let him have the final bow. And, Teddy?" he shouted out to Edward. "Once you come up and get yourself situated firmly at the center mark, I want you to smile. And on that smile . . . Now listen to me, everybody!" J.C. raised his voice, making sure stage management could hear him. "Everything: lights, music, everything will go to black. Curtain. The rest is silence. When this happens, they will shake the roof off this place, begging you for a second final bow. You will, despite your exhaustion, oblige. One final full company bow."

"Ahhh, excuse me," Virgil spoke up. He was still standing center stage, looking uncomfortable. "Ahhhh, Jeez—I don't want to be some kind of giant asshole here but . . . Ahhh . . . I don't know how to say this—"

"Virgil." J.C. stood up and walked down the aisle. "I know and understand fully what you are feeling and what you are considering saying. Don't do it. In vanity productions of *The Henrys,* Falstaff takes the final bow. I know that is very common—and you are well within your rights to expect that. And you are not an asshole for wanting the final bow. You are great at what you do and certainly deserve a final bow. But, the reason that Falstaff often takes the final bow is because usually the whole production is conceived and imagined by some dimwit director who rendered the whole event in service of a star's performance."

J.C. continued, "But in truly magnificent productions of *King Henry the Fourth, Parts One and Two,* it's obvious that the title character, King Henry the Fourth, should take the final bow. And, fortunately for you, you are giving the most remarkable performance of Falstaff New York and possibly all of America has ever seen, *inside* the greatest production of *The Henrys* ever done. So, there may be moments that will be uncomfortable for you—like this one: not taking the final bow. But it is only the discomfort that John Lennon must've felt having to share the stage with Paul McCartney. Imagine how Mick Jagger felt the night he realized how the audience related to Keith Richards. You think he didn't suffer? Paul Robeson and Uta Hagen? Thank God, they carried their burden. It is the discomfort experienced when giants lower their heads in deference to one another—none of them *want* to— and we mortals simply reap the rewards. You understand? If you trust me, and gesture to Edward, and let him have the stage— people will leave here thinking about the play, the greatness of what we achieved as a collective, and not only about you."

"That's what I don't like about it." Virgil half-smiled. The whole company laughed.

"Good. Thank you. Settled." J.C. marched on. "All right, let's run it from the end of the play to Edward's final bow," he shouted back at the stage manager, "and then let's fire this rocket."

And then, just like that, it was done.

Rehearsals were over.

The show was set to run.

It was fight call.

BEFORE EVERY PERFORMANCE, there is "fight call," where the actors run through all the potentially violent moments of the play, making sure the moves are all in our bodies, ensuring that no accidents happen. You don't have to be in costume, but you have your weapons and walk through your more dangerous moves. Next it was half-hour, when we are all supposed to be in our dressing rooms. The monitor is turned on and you can hear the ushers start to file down the aisles, vacuuming the seats, taking the *Playbill*s from their boxes, and pacing around the theater preparing the house. Sitting at our dressing room tables, the whole cast begins their pre-show rituals. Edward, our King, will sit calmly with his door open, doing the crossword. Virgil's door will be shut as he howls his vocal warm-ups. The younger actors are always goofing around, laughing, and running back and forth to the hairdresser's room. The stage manager's assistant will go to all the rooms of the cast members who forgot to sign in. Three dressers will walk down the hall with Virgil's fat suit to help him wriggle into it.

Even with the anticipation of opening night, it was a tranquil moment. Clearly, there was an extra vibration of apprehension in the hallways, but we were all trying to settle it. Flowers were everywhere; most members of our cast had someone—a mom, a girlfriend, a husband, at least an agent—who loved them enough to send roses, irises, lilies, wrapped in plastic. The actresses often would get two or three sets of roses. Virgil's room was a goddamn botanical garden. Ezekiel and I had a few lame vases ourselves. He had one from his wife and one from his girlfriend. I had a bottle of bourbon from my agent and an envelope from my mom. Inside was a picture of Laurence Olivier playing Hotspur. Scribbled on the back was

The Wisdom of the Desert Fathers:
   Abbot Pastor said, "There are only two things a man ought to hate above all, For in hating them, he shall be free."
   A brother asked, "What are these things?"
   "An easy life and vainglory."

Love,
Your vain mother

I taped the image to my mirror next to the other, anonymous quotes I'd been receiving.

The lines of our dressing room were clearly drawn. Ezekiel liked things clean and simple. "There's no dirt in heaven," he'd say. He had his script neatly placed in one corner of his desk, his makeup tidily tucked under the lights of the mirror, a steaming cup of mint tea in front of him, and nothing else. His clothes were meticulously hung in the closet and his chain-mail armor was already on his shoulders. His side of the dressing room reminded me of my grandfather's basement. Grandpa had his hammer, pliers, wrenches, and saws all neatly hung on a pegboard. Then, like a shadow behind each instrument, he had painted the shape of the tool. That way even when you took down the level, it was obvious where to put it back. It was perfect order.

My side was a mess. I liked it that way. Clothes and empty PowerBar wrappers were everywhere. I had the quotes taped up all over the mirror, fan mail sprawled out under my desk, a ventilator for my throat, cough drops, an extremely large poster of Clint Eastwood screamin' his fool head off in *The Outlaw Josey Wales,* and another poster of Derek Jeter making a wicked cross-body throw (those two men were my models for Hotspur). Lots of other papers littered every surface: notes, half-read books, unopened scripts my agent had sent. Cigarettes, matches, my guitar. I had junk everywhere.

Ezekiel said he didn't care what I did with my half, and I believed him. He didn't. I never once breached the divide with my crap. He kept a small scented candle and lit it whenever he thought I smelled. We laughed about it. We got along well and often talked seriously, but at half-hour neither of us would speak, at least not for the first ten minutes. Both of us were never late and the first ten minutes were spent in a kind of unspoken agreement of silent meditation. Then, when we intuited the other was ready, one of us would break the spell with idle chatter.

"My wife's coming tonight," he said when ready. "She's such a piece of work.

"She asked, 'Can I leave after your character dies or do I have to stay for the whole thing?' I was like, 'Listen, woman, don't come at all—I don't care.' She's gonna hate it. *Why are you playing such a small part? Why do you bother? You were better on* Law & Order!' She loathes J.C., calls him David Koresh."

I was still shirtless. My body was twisted and tight like a steel cable. I had these fake scars I'd put all over my chest. There's a scene in the second act when Hotspur is shirtless and I liked the audience to see that this warrior had fought more than once. To that end, I'd drip hot wax across my chest and then I'd paint the wax. It looked tough as hell.

"It's not like she hasn't already seen twenty thousand Shakespeare productions I've done. Back when we were in love she saw me play Caliban in *The Tempest* like eighteen times. She liked Shakespeare back then."

I nodded and smiled as the hot wax dripped down my rib cage.

"She asked me this morning, *'If we didn't have the kids, we'd be split, right?'* And I'm like, 'Are you nuts?' You think I live in this house to enjoy the fruits of our dynamic? You gotta be kidding! Of course, we'd be split. *'What's going to happen when they're grown?'* she asks. Oh God, I'm like . . . 'You're asking me this on opening night? That's like crying 'cause if there wasn't gravity, my feet wouldn't stay on the ground, you know? I mean *obviously,* if there weren't the kids, I would *leave*—but there are the kids and I'm gonna stay. Simple. And only the Lord knows what we'll do when they take off. Things will be different then.'"

Ezekiel took a sip of tea. He occasionally looked at me, but most of the time he was talking to himself in the mirror. I was now taking red and blue powder and brushing it over the wax on my chest to give the scars a bruised and ravaged look.

"Charleze is coming, too." He winked at me and pointed to the cards that came from both sets of flowers that he had tucked into the bottom of his mirror.

"Oh God, this is gonna go great," he moaned sarcastically. "But what am I supposed to do? Charleze *wants* to see the show. She loves me. She believes in me. She picked out this knife for me." He held up a blade he had tucked into a sheath on his belt. "She helped me figure out my whole character biography. We lay in bed and daydreamed about how a black man would have found his way to London and how I came to work for the King." He put the knife away. "She doesn't think I should be rotting away in the back of some TV show. She cares about art, you know? She gets it. We went to the MoMA together. She understands a man needs to aspire to greatness and if he gives up on his hope for excellence, his soul dies. And"—he paused for effect—"she likes it when I twirl my finger in her ass when I fuck her from behind, you know?" He burst out in a big easy grin.

I stood in front of the mirror checking out my scars.

"Do you flex that much when you're onstage? You look like a retarded teenager," he said.

I went into our bathroom, left the door open, turned on the fan, stood on the toilet, and lit a cigarette right up close to the vent. I did this every night at the fifteen-minute mark. Ezekiel didn't mind, but the stage manager lost his marbles if he ever smelled even a hint of smoke.

"Oh God, you know what I said to my wife last night when she asked if Charleze was coming?" Ezekiel shouted to me. "I said, 'Baby, let's just imagine that every Sunday for the past two years, I snuck out of the house and went to Prospect Park collecting this very bizarre form of exquisite caterpillar.' You know?"

"What?" I asked.

"This is what I said to my wife," he told me again, "'Like, let's just say that I loved these rare caterpillars and I would put on gloves and go into the park or wherever and hunt for these little suckers. 'Cause they meant something to me. Maybe they remind of me of a blissful time when I was a kid before I had any responsibilities.'"

His hands were lightly trembling. I stood on the commode listening and smoking. It felt like we were astronauts sitting on top of a rocket about to explode to the moon. Every so often, I would blow my smoke carefully into the fan and watch it disappear.

"'For some reason, when this caterpillar crawls across my hand, I'm like twelve years old again and my heart is beating like a happy bunny—but I know that if I tell everybody that I love caterpillars, people are gonna think I'm childish, right? They will judge me; they'll think I've got some kind of creepy insect fetish going on. So, I keep it to myself. I enjoy these moments to myself. I'm not murdering anybody. I'm not shooting up. It's just that there is joy in this simple pleasure. It doesn't mean I hate my life or I want to get a divorce. It doesn't even mean I want to spend every day with the freakin' caterpillar. I just like to do it sometimes.' And my wife at this point is like, *What the fuck are you talking about?*'"

"I was about to say the same thing," I said, ashing my cigarette into the sink.

"No, come on, listen to me. You're a sophisticated guy. You can understand this." He took a deep breath, giving me a sharp look. "'Baby,' I say to her, 'why can't you look at Charleze like she's just a caterpillar. It's just my weird thing. Something I like, that is personal to me. Why can't I have something that's mine alone? Why does it have to be about you? I'm not hurting you, you are just perceiving it that way.' And she screams, *"Cause you are my HUSBAND and I love you. I don't want to share you with a caterpillar. WHAT HAPPENS WHEN SHE TURNS INTO A BUTTERFLY!'*—and I'm like, 'It's an analogy.'"

"You didn't honestly expect her to be persuaded by all this, did you?" I said, tossing my cigarette into the toilet.

"Would you ever promise some chick that you will absolutely, under no circumstances, laugh at anyone else's jokes?" Ezekiel asked, and then affected a goofy lawyer voice: "I vow to never find anyone else funny." My head was buried in my inhaler. I tried to suck on this vaporizer after every cigarette.

"It's an absurd thing to suggest," Ezekiel continued, "yet people think it's OK to vow to one another that they will never be sexually attracted to any other human again."

"They don't vow not to be attracted; they vow not to act on it," I corrected from my inhaler. I felt like an expert on this commandment.

"So it's OK to find someone funny, you just can't laugh?" When he said that, he noticed his own eyes in the mirror. He hadn't yet put on his eyeliner. Frantically, he reached for his makeup. If a cool customer like Zeke was this nervous I couldn't imagine how the rest of us would make it.

Ezekiel had theories about stage makeup and believed it was important, especially for a black guy, to use this peculiar blue eyeliner. It worked. From ten feet away, it made his eyes look like a panther's. I lay down on the floor and started doing my fifty push-ups. I always do that at the ten-minute mark. Then I put on the rest of my costume. Soon, Samuel would knock and it would be time to dip ourselves in blood.

I started filling my pockets with talismans, small trinkets that would bring me deeper into my imagination. I had a few old prop coins, scraps of paper, a lucky piece of wolf fur—little shit I'd imbued with meaning for my character so that when I was onstage and stuck my hands in my pockets there would be something real there; something that let me know I wasn't wearing a costume.

My real pants were tossed on the floor. I looked at them for a second and wondered what was in my pockets and what did it say about my character.

"FOLKS," the stage manager announced over the loudspeaker. "THEY ARE HAVING A TOUGH TIME OUT THERE GETTING EVERYONE SEATED. SO, IT'S STILL TEN MINUTES. TEN MINUTES TILL CURTAIN."

You could hear the audience. They were extremely loud and impatient over the monitor. Opening night houses are full of people who know each other and it's quite common to start late.

My mind was oddly focused on one thing: Would my wife be in the house? She'd just told me that afternoon that she was in love with someone else, but when I'd called the house later to say good night to the kids, my daughter told me, "Mommy's going out tonight. She's going to a show." And while most likely she was on a date with the fashion mogul, or whatever he was, I still some-how thought, *Maybe she'll be at my opening. Maybe she forgot to tell me she loved me.* What would I say to her if she came backstage? Maybe we'd fuck in the darkness behind the soda machines.

I was good in this play and I looked killer in all this black leather. I imagined banging her with my armor on. What would happen then? Would she move into the Mercury? Fuck no, she detested that place. Would I go home? God, I didn't want to . . . I couldn't breathe in her house—all the nannies and cleaning ladies and hairdressers, that little, loathsome, hairless cat. Oh God. But I did want to fuck her in my chain mail by the soda machines. I could picture it clearly. Her evening gown hiked around her waist. She would look good. She always did.

Ezekiel leapt from his chair and stomped his feet.

"*AHHH,* fuck, I'm nervous. I'm forty-eight goddarn years old. Why am I so nervous?" He took a deep breath and stretched down to touch his toes. Then he said, "Give me one of them cigarettes."

"You don't smoke," I said.

"Fuck you. You don't know anything about me. Give me one of those white boy cigarettes."

I did and he went and stood on the commode. He had trouble lighting the thing. I stood up and switched on the fan for him and lit his cigarette.

My wife wasn't going to come. It was an absurd idea. She hates the theater. She loathes Shakespeare. What was I thinking? But maybe . . . She did love me once.

Suddenly I could not remember my first line.

My stomach flipped. I couldn't even find the breath to check my voice.

"Can I open your script?" I asked Ezekiel. His script was so much better organized than mine.

"Are your hands clean?"

"Yes." I scowled.

"Just wash 'em, will ya? God knows where your hands have been."

"Jesus Christ," I said and walked into the bathroom. I stood underneath him and washed my hands and dried them. He was blowing the smoke straight up into the vent just as I had.

As I flipped the pages of Ezekiel's script, I could see that in the margins of every page, he had written long passages of his "inner monologue"—things he imagined his character was thinking about while other people were talking. Ideas that would lead and inform his next line. I found my first line. *"My liege, I did deny no prisoners."* How could I not remember that?

"Shit, man, I should be playing fucking Falstaff." He jumped off the toilet and flushed his cigarette and started waving the door open and closed to try and dissipate the smoke.

"Did you see the article on Virgil on the cover of *The New York Times Magazine*? 'The Most Underrated Actor in *America*!' The motherfucker is playing Falstaff on Broadway with an Oscar over the fireplace at home, and he's the most underrated actor in America? What am I then, huh? My son reads that article—'Hey, Dad. How come they didn't even mention you or have your picture in the paper? Huh? You must have a really small part.' And then J.C., with his speeches. . . . 'We're all integral!'" He shook his head with an inscrutable expression. "It's hard to be a man. Fuckin' hard." He shut the bathroom door and sat back down. Took his script from my hands and made sure it hadn't been soiled in any way.

"CAN WE FIRE THIS FUCKING ROCKET!" he screamed. *"I can't breathe back here!"* He shouted out so loud his voice boomed through the halls. You could hear an explosion of applause from the rest of the cast inside their dressing rooms.

"I'm serious, bro, I can't goddamn breathe, I'm so nervous," he said quietly to me. "How the hell am I supposed to have the show of my life with those two women out there trying to ruin it?"

"Are they both going to come back here after?" I asked, imagining all of us in this tight space—what we would talk about?

"Let's cross that bridge when we come to it," he said, biting his nails.

"You think the reviews will be good?" I asked.

A silence hit the room.

"Oh God, I hope so. I know I should be beyond it . . . but I need one. My family needs that review. Just one time, if just once *The New York Times* could say—without qualifying—that I can act . . . It'd just help everybody in my family be proud of me and believe that I am living my life in a meaningful way. It would really help." He looked ten years old.

"Can I ask you a favor?" I said. I'd been waiting to bring this up.

"Yeah, man, what's up?"

"I'm not going to read the reviews." The words flowed out of me. "I've promised myself. I just have to not think like they do. I hate myself enough already and there's just been so much crap about me in the papers, on the Internet, and *Entertainment Tonight,* all that shit. I've been finding that the less I know, the better. None of it's real, right? And they're not going to say I'm the reincarnation of Montgomery Clift and that is the only thing that would be good enough. I love this play and this production so much, I just can't bear to think of someone writing anything nasty about it, so I'm just going to live in blissful ignorance, OK? Can you help me? I don't want to talk about them at all, OK? I know it'll be hard at first, but after, like, two shows, it won't matter. So can you help me?"

"Done and done," he said, "but let me say this: The review in my head says Monty Clift couldn't wipe your ass. He was no father. He wasn't half the man you are, or the actor. OK? No shit. This dressing room is pure, one hundred percent rock 'n' roll. Me and you, kid. Our scene out there is flamethrower-hot and everyone knows it."

We did have a good scene just before the Act 3 battle. It was easy and fun, like setting a handful of pine needles on fire. Ezekiel would never let us run lines even though I always wanted to.

"Makes you soft," he would say. "I don't want to know what you're going to do. I want you to surprise me. I don't want the audience to get some reheated performance of something we did great in the dressing room. Go run lines with your drama coach," he would say, swaggering around, pumping himself up. And he was right. Our scene was my favorite five minutes of every day.

"THE MOMENT HAS ARRIVED," the stage manager said finally. "PLACES PLEASE."

Samuel knocked on our door. He held my sword in one hand and his own in the other. "Let's go get bloody." He smiled. And it was on. I slipped the final blue pill in my mouth and swallowed it dry.

When I step onstage I enter a pocket in time where there is nowhere else I want to be. There are no phone calls to be made; no unanswered emails; there's no late fee from the kids' library; the errand left undone is meaningless. All that matters is: Now.

The first act or so was effortless. The play was carrying us all.

ACT 2, SCENE 3, came faster than usual. I was standing on a three-foot-by-three-foot platform about fifty feet up in the air. It was the top of a staircase that rolled onto center stage from the stage right wing. The whole moving piece was made of thick cuts of oak. The wood calmed me. During the previous scene, I had to silently climb up the ladder in the dark. Once there, I was given a torch by Dave, our prop master. He handled all fire code safety issues.

He lit the thing with a blowtorch, gave me a salute, and climbed down. I would stand up, hold the fire, and try to get centered before the stage lights would go entirely black. With the blackout, this giant staircase would be wheeled out, leaving my torch as the only light in the theater. J.C. had managed to sidestep the law to get even the exit signs in the back of the theater blacked out for this scene change. I was shirtless and barefoot, wearing only my scars and black leather pants. Never in my life had I been so goddamn skinny.

This scene was, in many ways, the most difficult I had to do each night. It required a subtlety and restraint that are not my strong suits and was the opposite of almost every other blistering scene in which Hotspur appears. As I rolled onto stage, I would white-knuckle the handle that had been installed for my security. Falling would not be a great way to start the scene. I had assured and reassured J.C. that I felt comfortable up there—but I said that just to be cool. When it moved, the damn thing terrified me.

In Act 2, scene 3, we find Hotspur up in the middle of the night; he can't sleep. He is poring over a letter from a "friend" informing him that this friend finds Hotspur's plans to stage a violent coup foolhardy. The letter is unnerving to Hotspur and he is desperate to understand it or, at least, to toss it off. What makes the scene so precarious to play is that there is a *long* period onstage where he is by himself with no obvious drama. Just a man, a warrior, who can't sleep, reading a letter over and over—quoting it back to himself, trying to decide what to think. Is this a bad omen? Obviously, Hotspur had written this "friend" first, looking for solidarity and more troops. His request is being denied and now he must worry that this once hoped-for accomplice will spill Hotspur's rebellious plans and foil the element of surprise.

No wonder he can't sleep.

Another big hurdle of the scene is that it begins with a monologue where Hotspur is conversing with himself. Often, when a Shakespearean character is alone onstage, the ensuing monologue will be a direct address—but not so with this speech. Hotspur is supposed to be essentially mumbling to himself, and this asks for a level of naturalism that is difficult given the stylized nature of the prose.

But then there is the biggest hurdle of the scene: I must be in front of twelve hundred people shirtless, holding a long piece of parchment paper in one hand and lighting my face with a torch in the other. The problem may not be obvious. But if you hold a piece of paper with one hand in front of twelve hundred people with your shirt off on opening night of a Broadway play it is incredibly fucking difficult for your hand not to shake. The slightest tremor in your fingers gets that paper rattling, and then no one is think-ing, *What a great actor! What an interesting scene! What beautiful dialogue!* They are thinking, *What is that half-naked man so nervous about? Isn't he a professional actor? Why are his hands shaking? Is he the one who fucked that bookshop owner in South Africa and broke Mary Marquis's heart?* And once you start worrying about your hand shaking, the problem grows legs.

You'd think that after my having been a professional actor for fifteen years, this would not be among my top concerns. You'd be wrong. People always ask about "all those lines! Isn't it hard to memorize all those lines?" Memorization only takes time. Using the power of your ensemble's collective imagination to make the audience forget about their sister's chemotherapy and care about the actions of people speaking in verse who lived six hundred years ago—*that* takes something mystical; and if your hands start shak-ing like you're doing a high school oral book report, Dionysus sure as shit ain't going to show up.

There's only one way to beat it. Dive into your imagination. It must *be* the middle of the night; you must feel the hay on your bare feet; you must smell the horses, hear the wood owl, feel the coming morning humidity on your skin. You must picture the face of that cross-eyed, goose-livered *friend* who wrote you this letter. You must remember how much you loathe the King. The patronizing bastard deserves to die. He had your father *killed,* for Christ's sake. You *loved* your father. You must remember exactly the letter you wrote this friend. You must have actually written it. You must fully imagine the conversation you had with your uncle debating the wisdom of approaching this alleged friend in the first place. You were all for it. Your uncle warned you. What's your uncle going to say now? No wonder you can't sleep. You're smart not to sleep. Your hands should be shaking!

And, in some sly way—and this is where it all gets mystic and strange—you can't even pretend you don't notice the audience. This is where the truth lives. They're there; you can even make out a few faces in the front row. You can't ignore them. You must find a way to incorporate these eyes into your understanding of Hotspur's reality. They are the watchful eyes of God.

You walk onstage and say, "Hello, God. I know that you see everything. You hear the meditation of my heart. You make sense of my every gesture."

And you must breathe. Even the big Russian dog himself, Stanislavsky, had to make a friend of his fear; even the Queen's knight, Sir John Gielgud, had to do the same. It's the only way to connect yourself with the shadows swimming around you.

I remember once riding my bike when I was thirteen with my dog leashed to my hand running alongside me. The dog and I were racing down Old Trunk Road towards the train station. The dog saw a squirrel. I, too, saw the squirrel. From the moment of making eye contact with the squirrel, it was probably a mere three seconds later when I stood up with half my face left bloody on the pavement: I flew through the air, cursed my dog, tried to get my hands untangled from the leash, watched the gravel come towards me, and wondered how much it would hurt. It seemed like an hour. Time moves like that onstage. There are moments inside moments.

I gripped the handle tightly as the whole oak apparatus was rolling towards its final mark, my mind attempting to completely submerge itself. Once the massive stairway stopped and I could feel it lock into place, I let go of the handle and pulled the letter out of my pants. My cue light went black and I began my descent. That night, I imagined that Valentino Calvino, the fashion stud who was fucking my wife, wrote the letter. That would get my blood up. That's the trick for me—what I always try to do anyway—just start blurring the lines between the character and me. I read the letter until I stepped off the stairs onto the stage; then I read it again. The silence in the theater was thundering, but I would resist and not speak until I didn't notice the silence at all. J.C. had told me that in rehearsal: "Take all the time in the world. Don't start till you're centered. Wait till you see the whites of their proverbial silence. You have us, just hold us . . ." Then he added with a smile, "Just don't take too long."

"But for mine own part, my lord, I could be well contented to be there, in respect of the love I bear your house."

My voice was strong. Even in a whisper, I could feel the whole house listening. I sucked the air deep into my belly one more time, looked up, and continued talking to myself. They were a good house—I knew it immediately.

"He could be contented? Why is he not, then?"

Boom, a huge laugh. I can't explain what was funny, it wasn't anything I was doing. It's the setup. It's the playwright at work. I could blow the line, for sure, and often would, but when I was in the thick of the play and transmitting correctly, there were so many laughs to be mined. The feeling of making a house laugh with a four-hundred-year-old joke is like skipping a rock seventeen times across a still lake.

"*In respect of the love he bears our house?*" I mocked the numskull that sent me this cowardly letter: "*He shows in this, he loves his own barn better than he loves our house.*" Here, generally, I would pause and shake out my anger. Sometimes, I would freeze as if maybe I heard someone else in the barn and then realize it was just that old wood owl. I tried to let the letter wash over me fresh every night and have no real plan as to how I would approach it other than a few simple fence post ideas to lean on.

First, as I said, I'd start reading out loud only when I was fully composed. Second, I'd set the torch into its holder about five lines in, giving me the opportunity to hold the paper with the other hand just in case the first hand was beginning to shake.

Once the torch was set, I would continue:

"*Let me see some more . . . ,*" I said on opening night, with both hands now firmly, confidently on the paper. " '*The purpose you undertake is dangerous;*'—*why, that's certain!* '*Tis dangerous to take a cold, to sleep, to drink; but I tell you, my lord fool, out of this nettle, danger, we pluck this flower, safety.*' "

Here I would often crumple the letter and throw it. And with that action, sometimes—often, hopefully—I would disappear. Even my breath would no longer be my own. It was drawn from the audience. I could feel them around me like a great cloud of witnesses filling me up. There is a quiet place, a room inside my guts where my head and my heart meet, where bad news is understood before it's spoken, where I am conscious even when I'm asleep, where my dreams are remembered. A room I could access easily in the immense boredom of childhood, staring out the window of my bus going to school; watching the headlights move across my boyhood ceiling late at night as I tried to fall asleep; picking at my food as the adults talked about their jobs. Inside this room in my guts, I imagine a small red-hot fragment of rock. No magic stone unique to me—it's the same thing that's inside a dog, a deer, a porcupine, a maple tree—it goes mostly unobserved— but onstage, if I can breathe right, and the audience will let me, the embers in my gut can swell and spark into a flame. That, to me, is performing. It is a peace I have never felt inside the inertia of daily life.

MY LETTER READING IS interrupted by Lady Percy dressed in a nightgown.

> *O, my good lord, why are you thus alone?*
> *For what offense have I this fortnight been*
> *A banish'd woman from my Harry's bed?*

She is scared and explains that I talk in my sleep of iron wars, bounding steeds, basilisks, cannons, prisoners' ransom. I'm not eating well. She bats her eyelashes, gently caresses the scars on my belly, and tells me I haven't made love to her in weeks. I've given over *"to thick-eyed musing and cursed melancholy."* Goddamn it to hell she's beautiful. I throw her in the hay. She'll get what she's asking for. She laughs, playfully grabs my pecker through the thick black leather, saying she will break my *"little finger"* if I don't tell her the plan and what's in this letter I am hiding. I explain that she cannot reveal what she doesn't know. This secrecy is for her safety. She doesn't like this answer. She gets on her knees and plays with my belt. We get hot and heavy in the hay—until it's too hot, for Hotspur, and I race to the barn door. It's time for war. Besides, women can't be trusted.

I explain to her,

> *Love! I love thee not,*
> *I care not for thee, Kate this is no world*
> *To play with mammets and to tilt with lips.*
> *We must have bloody noses and crack'd crowns.*

She's crushed and answers so quietly. I never knew how she did it. It was like the soft pedal on a concert Steinway. She could speak so quietly and yet her voice could be heard in Connecticut.

> *Do you not love me? Do you not, indeed?*
> *Well, do not then; for since you love me not,*
> *I will not love myself.*

This woman was a magnificent actor. Lady Percy stares back fierce. She is true blue. The best friend I've ever had.

I can't leave her like this. Striking a softer stance,

> *Hark you, Kate.*
> *Whither I go, thither shall you go too;*
> *Today will I set forth, tomorrow you.*

Before I stepped offstage after Act 2, scene 3, on opening night, I stood in the doorway and with a clenched fist blew her a kiss goodbye. I left her waiting; her hair and nightdress sprinkled with hay. The lights faded down to focus on a close-up of her face, then black, and the whole hall shook in applause. My body buzzed as if I had just survived a motorcycle accident. I hid, as I always did, in a dark spot by the ropes on the stage left wall, kneeled and collected myself. Four minutes until my next entrance. During the following scene change I heard soft weeping by the stage left exit. It was my Lady Percy. I stood up and walked over to her.

"You OK?"

She just stumbled forward around all the ropes. "Get the fuck away from me."

"What's going on?"

"You can't do that," she snapped, turning to me, her eyes burning and tears streaming down her face. "You can't grab me like that. I have bruises on my arms. You can't pull me around the stage like that."

"Oh fuck, I'm sorry. I didn't know I was doing that."

"We fucking make out every night. You paw my ass, push me around, and roll me over, and you don't *know* it hurts?"

"I really didn't. And I'm so sorry. I'm just in love with the work we are doing and I thought you were too."

She punched me hard with both fists and pushed me against the wall.

"I'm really sorry," I said. "I love acting with you. I didn't understand. I'll do better."

She pulled me close and jammed her soft wet delicious tongue into my mouth like a woman who hadn't seen her lover in ten years. Wrapping her arms around me, she breathed me in. She slid her hand down over my sweaty leather pants and held my swelling dick with her fragile thin white hand, and whispered, "I'm falling in love with you. I mean, I know it's not you. It's the stupid play, but I worry about you night and day. This always happens to me and I'm too old for this shit. I can't wait till we close and I don't ever have to see you again. But just fuck me one time, will you please? Can we get a hotel room or something so you can let me put your dick in my mouth? I want to feel you come inside me so badly it's like I can't breathe until I do."

My cue light went on.

"Please be safe," she said, pulling her hand away from my pants. And kissed me goodbye.

Completely unsure if we were still acting, or had ever stopped, I charged into battle.

WHAT SEEMED LIKE seconds later, I bellowed, with every bit of vitality I could muster, blood literally spewing from my mouth:

O, Harry, thou hast robb'd me of my youth!

The whole fight had been "off" since the first cue. The fight director had warned us to be extra-slow tonight. He knew everybody's nerves would be both frazzled and jacked for opening. We tried to listen to him, but it didn't matter. When we picked up our blades and charged out, with the cannon fire roaring and ripping in our ears, I leapt up onto an old artillery wagon, spinning my dagger in one hand and my sword in the other. (J.C. thought this an unnecessary show-off move. He was worried one of the blades would fly out of my hands and spear an audience member, but I did it anyway.) I screamed my call to battle:

DIE ALL, DIE MERRILY!

I knew then I was totally out of control. It wasn't Hal's fault; the whole fight was just wrong, and right before I was supposed to get the lance in the gut, I stepped too far forward and the lance gouged me hard in the lower abdomen and then sprang up and forcefully slapped me under the chin. The house gasped. Blood went splattering across the oak planks of the stage and dripped down my armor. Prince Hal recovered and thrust again, this time placing the retractable lance into my chest plate as planned, and we continued. With the pain shooting through my face, the speech finally worked.

"*I better brook the loss of brittle life than those proud titles thou hast won of me; they wound my thoughts worse than sword my flesh,*" I said calmly.

I didn't have to imagine the pain: the whole left side of my face was pummeled and throbbing. I didn't have to fake swallowing blood—I swallowed it. Much better.

"*O, I could prophesy,*" I said with my gloved hands still holding the lance firmly in my belly, my whole body instinctively shaking, like chattering teeth, "*but that the earthy and cold hand of death lies on my tongue.*"

I didn't have to pretend it was difficult to talk. It damn well was difficult. I wasn't sure how bad the wound was, but it felt like I might need to go to the hospital. I gathered my unraveling intestines for the final sentence:

No, Percy, thou art dust, and food for . . .

I gagged and the blood in the back of my throat gurgled and poured out my mouth.

It was freakin' awesome. I actually couldn't finish the line, just as our author had designed.

"*For worms, brave Percy,*" the Prince said, holding me in his arms and finishing my sentence, "*fare thee well, great heart.*"

I lay there trying to breathe slowly, in long even inhales and exhales, so my armor didn't heave up and down. It kills the suspension of disbelief when you see a bunch of dead soldiers sprawled all over the ground, huffing and heaving for breath as the battle ends. Shakespeare has many inherent challenges, and having the dialogue continue around a battalion of "dead" actor-soldiers is one of them.

Damn, I said to myself, *I'll never do that speech that well again.*

"YOU KNOW HOW Olivier played that speech, right?" Edward, our King, asked me later in his dressing room.

I shook my head. I was sitting, still in costume, eating an ice cream sandwich in the right side of my mouth while I iced the left side of my face. Edward was drinking a glass of red wine. His dressing room was wonderful and still. His drink matched his robes. The King's old face was calm and placid. He sat at his dressing table while I hunkered down on his cot in the corner. It was a special privilege granted to me this night to be invited in for his post show glass of wine. The play was still marching on, we could hear Prince Hal's coronation over the monitor, but our roles were done. We were both dead. We were just waiting to take our bow.

"Olivier built the whole character around Hotspur's inability to finish that last word, 'worms.' He gave Hotspur an actual stutter. He went through the text and stuttered on every syllable beginning with *w* or *r*. So, when he got to '*food for w . . . w . . . w . . .*' the audience was right where he wanted them, before he fell down dead . . ." the King trailed off remembering the performance. "Jesus, it was heartbreaking. Truly incredible."

"Fuck, that's brilliant," I said, taking the ice away from my face for a moment.

"It was. Greatest stage death I've ever seen. Only time I ever believed a death. He was astounding that way . . . Even when he exited the stage, you actually could see where his character was going. The power of his imagination was contagious . . . exceptional."

"Why did you wait until now to tell me that?" I asked, pressing the ice back to my mouth, wondering what I could do to make my death more believable.

"Because you would've been tempted to steal the idea. And you mustn't. You must create your own Hotspur."

"Were you in that production?"

"No. I was in Olivier's second *Hamlet*—Laertes. I was terrible. But I wasn't in that production of *Henry*. Gielgud was Hal. Christ, he was even better then Olivier."

"I would've liked to have seen that."

"Yes, but if you had, you'd be old like me. And that is depressing."

Just then my understudy poked his head into Edward's dressing room.

"Great show, boys, really killer."

We both nodded thank you.

"Is your mouth OK?" he asked.

"It's fine," I mumbled.

"You took a shot," he said, and walked on.

"That guy makes my skin crawl," I mumbled.

"Scotty? Really? Why?" the King asked.

"I hear him running my lines in the stairwell. I watch him shadowing me. I feel like he's waiting for me to die."

"He's doing his job. And remember, they are not your lines any more than they were Olivier's."

I nodded and carefully took another bite of my ice cream sandwich. There was a vending machine in the basement and every night, after I died, I collected four quarters from my desk and treated myself. One of the secret blessings of my divorce was I could eat whatever I wanted and still be rail-thin.

"It'll be nice to have this opening behind us," Edward said calmly.

"Do you think it'll go over well?" I asked, carefully chewing the ice cream sandwich with the right side of my mouth.

"The show? The notices? What do you mean?"

"Both, I guess."

The King took a moment and then said slowly, "The show is brilliant. There's no way it won't be beautifully reviewed."

"I like your confidence," I said.

"It's not confidence. It's experience. I have been in bad shows. I've been in controversial shows. This is not one of them."

"J.C. seemed worried tonight," I said, hoping Edward might gossip with me a little.

"Not worried," Edward answered. "Upset. As good as this show is, it could've been better."

"Really?" I asked.

He went on to tell me about the last time he and J.C. had done this play, at the Goodman Theatre in Chicago. The production was far more stylized and radical. Ultimately, the direction of the New York production, Edward said, was far superior. It was just that the Chicago Falstaff had the stuff of legend.

"Better than Virgil Smith?" I asked incredulously. I thought Virgil was a diva—but he was glorious onstage.

"You overvalue celebrity," Edward said to me. "You are impressed by all the ancillary elements: the pizzazz that surrounds Virgil. And there is pizzazz—I'm not saying the sparkle and shine isn't there—I'm just not overly impressed. Glamour is good onstage; it's true. Virgil is a star, but Charlie Maugham of Chicago is Falstaff. He channeled the real pain of being an addict, of being lonely, of being a giant fat person. I loved Charlie's Falstaff, and J.C. loved it more than anyone. Do you know Charlie's work?" Edward asked me.

I didn't.

Over the monitor we heard the Prince, who was now the new King, say to his old friend, Falstaff, *"I know thee not, old man,"* and then the final music of the play began. You could feel the intensity of the betrayal even over the intercom. We had about four minutes till curtain.

"Charlie is the reason J.C. wanted to direct the show in the first place. He built the whole thing around him. But in New York they needed a star. J.C. did everything he could to keep Charlie, but once Virgil expressed interest it was fait accompli."

The King slowly took a sip of his wine. The crossword was his preshow warm-up, "to get the motor running," and the wine was the postshow wind-down, "to be able to sleep."

"I realize," he continued, his diction perfect, "Virgil will win awards for this part and he is a wonderful actor. But Charlie is pure. He wasn't acting onstage; he could live up there—he didn't need a fat suit—he was *fat*—and he had all the discipline of the great theater actors." The King smiled mischievously. "Meaning that he knew the verse so well and the rhythms of this play so intrinsically that it didn't matter how drunk he was—he could still leave the whole house weeping and have the final curtain come down twelve minutes faster than Mister Virgil—Pause—*Aren't I amazing*—Pause—Smith. But the Broadway producers felt they couldn't sell out this expensive a show without a big name, so Charlie was out until tonight."

"What do you mean?"

"Well, the glutton that Charlie is—he bought seats for tonight's show. He's so fat he needs two. He wanted to come to opening night so it could hurt as much as possible. He came this afternoon to the box office to pick up his tickets absolutely stumbling drunk. J.C. happened to be walking through the lobby and Charlie started screaming, *'I KNOW THEE NOT, OLD MAN.'* And charged J.C. After the security guards brought Charlie down to the ground, they couldn't get him out of the building: he weighs a massive three hundred and fifty pounds. Despite a bloody nose, J.C. helped

Charlie up and offered to take him out for a drink. Charlie said, no, that he was leaving, and abruptly walked through the glass doors without opening them. The glass shattered. It was a scene." The King smiled a sad, knowing smile. "As I said, the stuff of legend. So, you see, J.C. had reasons to be upset."

"What happened to Charlie after that?" I asked, finishing my ice cream sandwich.

"He walked away. Simple as that. My bet is, the true Falstaff sits in a drunk tank at this very moment. And the producers spent the afternoon rushing in new glass."

"PLACES FOR CURTAIN CALL," the stage manager announced over the speaker system.

"Let's bow," Edward said with a wink and stood up. "Perhaps you know now why J.C. felt the need to humiliate Virgil by not letting him take the final bow. Ridiculous."

"Well, I think you should bow last," I said. Then, motioning to his beautiful silk flowing gown, I added, "With robes like those, you have to."

"Hmmm." He nodded appreciatively. "They made this costume for me. When I was younger I would've wanted the real thing. Some actual old found fabric from the sixteen hundreds because it would have 'character.' But now that I am old, I like my clothes to be new, because I *have* character."

He smiled and walked out.

I adjusted my armor and followed the King down the hall to our stage left entrance.

"Fame is a 'Black Death,'" Edward whispered to me as we walked the corridor, past the other dressing rooms. "We like to watch people die. So we put them on magazines and fan the flames of their egos until they actually catch fire and explode. The zeitgeist is trying to do it to you right now." He kept walking in long slow strides until we hit the staircase. "And you may mistakenly think that's exciting, or be secretly flattered, or think that it's happening to you because you are important or interesting. But you're not—it's just that you have caught the disease and it's fun to watch you rot." He smiled and we both stepped into the darkness of the backstage area.

"I mean this in the kindest way possible," he continued, whispering even more quietly now. "I believe in you. I think you are doing an excellent job with a very difficult role and that if you were to quit smoking and apply yourself fully to the art of acting, you could have a great life in the theater and make serious art. But there are traps all around you; it doesn't take a psychic to see them. It doesn't take a clairvoyant to see that, most likely, you will die of the Black Death."

He walked very slowly up the stairs to the stage entrance, careful not to trip on his regal robes. "Do not underestimate the disease. I've watched it eat better than you."

Once through the stage doors, the King dropped his voice. Actors and stagehands were hustling in the shadows all around us. Prop men were pulling ropes, curtains were falling and rising, and the music was blaring. Actors were rushing to get in place.

The lights went black.

The show was over. The applause began.

The King and I stood in the darkness of the backstage left entrance and waited our turn to step out. Many people had to bow before our call. Virgil and Prince Hal were stage right. I could make out their shadows across the stage. In his long wine red robes, the King left his arms hanging limp at his sides. The impending opening night curtain call seemed to be making him as apprehensive as waiting for a gas tank to fill up. Our cue arrived and the King and I walked forward, joining Falstaff and Prince Hal against the back wall. The audience still couldn't see us. We were obscured by all the flag antics of the massive cast out in front. My body was strangely vibrating. I'd never opened a play on Broadway before.

The King leaned closer to me. "I have only one real applicable piece of advice for you," he said, his perfect diction piercing through the noise of the crowd. "Have a boring life and make your art thrilling."

The crowd was going bananas, cheering and catcalling. My spine felt liquid. The cannons were firing. Samuel and a few others of our endomorph "soldiers" were waving their banners. It was close now. The company around us stepped back to the periphery of the stage as we, the final four, were revealed. The applause ascended in scale and volume. The wings of my heart lifted in my chest.

I stared out at all the cheering faces. Everyone looked so happy.

Finally, we arrived at the moment where the four of us landed center stage. The rest of our cast turned toward us and humbly kneeled. The roar of the crowd escalated. One by one, I watched twelve hundred people stand up applauding. This was our standing ovation, just as J.C. had promised. The roof of the Lyceum was shaking. There was a wall of sound moving towards us, enveloping us, holding and lifting us.

I remember my first kiss. Michelle Sand. Her breath was sweet. She slipped her angel catlike tongue between my lips and into my mouth. My heart fired like a gun. *Bang.* I couldn't hear anything. I thought I would pass out. Then she pulled away. Looking me straight in my eyes, she smiled. It felt good, like I mattered, like my life was accumulating into something that might have a purpose. Witnessing that standing ovation on my Broadway debut felt like I'd just kissed twelve hundred people for the first time. My knees buckled, my eyes went swimmy with tears. I knew it was pretend, but it was all I had. I stepped forward for my solo bow, leaving the King behind. *Fuck the King,* I thought, *I'm not ready for a boring life.*

> Lord, grant me peace, but not yet.
> I want to be loved. I want to be famous.
> Lord, please grant me the Black Death.

Intermission

The Blue Jean Kid

Scene 2

In the still hot September days before seventh grade, I had this idea: I should wear my blue jean jacket to school every day. That's just what I'd wear. I'd change my undershirt, but every day I'd put on my blue jean jacket and button it straight up. No matter the weather. You could count on it. People would start calling me "The Blue Jean Kid." Some people would say it in a derisive way, but they'd be jealous. I would almost never speak. My coolness would be undeniable. Some guys would hate me and want to fight, but I didn't care. I'd fight if I had to. Girls would like me. They would admire my simplicity. I'd be a lone wolf, wandering through the halls of my colossal high school unafraid, with my jean jacket tightly wrapped around my heart. In my right chest pocket, I'd keep a triple pack of Big Red cinnamon gum and have one stick a day. Only one. I would be a disciplined motherfucker. I'd never give anyone else a stick. But then, at the perfect moment, after months of careful observation, I'd walk up to the most badass, brainy, bitchin' punk rock girl in our class, and say, "You wanna stick?"

And she'd say, pretending she could go either way, "Sure."

And then everybody would know right then and there—we were boyfriend/girlfriend.

Because even a middle schooler knows, the Blue Jean Kid never gives out his gum.

That's what I was thinking about at 12:30 a.m., as I sat alone on my leather couch. There was no music playing and I wasn't smoking. I was just sitting there. It was over. I'd made it. Any second, *The New York Times* would hit the stands; the review was probably available online already. I wasn't going to read it, I'd promised myself. No good could come from that. If it was bad, I'd obsess. If it was good, and it's never good enough, I'd start patting myself on the back like a blowhard asshole, and my performance would crumble. If they didn't mention me at all, horror. Confidence is fragile. So, I just sat there.

The opening night party was still going full throttle, but my nervous system couldn't handle that scene. I'd left after less than an hour. I don't know what I expected. Fire engines! Dancing girls! Guns! Poetry! Fights! Cabaret! I don't know. It all went down at the Tavern on the Green, which was swanky enough. I was just miserable. Every time someone looked at their BlackBerry, I studied their expression, wondering if the reviews were out. I'd been around the block enough to know that if people weren't talking about the newspapers, the news wasn't good. My agent was there. He didn't say anything. The producers were all dressed to the nines. I looked at their faces. Had they read the review? The rest of the cast was duded out with their spouses, getting their pictures taken on the blood-red carpet. Every time I stood for a photo, I imagined that the picture would run in the *New York Post* with the caption LAST KNOWN PHOTO.

Lady Percy was there in an ethereal gown straight off a runway, her long red hair knitted in an intricate pattern. We started kissing over by the bathrooms. It began as a congratulatory hug but went south fast. Her husband was seated alone at their table. That's why I left. Not that she wasn't heart-stopping, I just knew that sucking face with one's married costar at the opening night party was a bad idea. She was drunk and whispered to me she hated her life and sometimes wished she would die in a car accident.

"You going to read the reviews?" I asked her.

"Doesn't matter how good they are, William. Your father still won't love you."

WHEN I WAS A KID and acting in my first movie I remember walking to the set thinking, *This is it, if I do a good job my father will love me.* Sounds absurdly simplistic, but I was not that complicated. Would my father read the *Henry* notices? Did he know about the production? I reassured myself that if my son were in a play I certainly wouldn't love him any less if some theater critic thought he sucked.

Back in my hotel room, sitting there alone, it seemed like it would be years until the sun rose. Not reading the reviews wasn't getting easier. My phone vibrated. I could see immediately it was Big Sam calling to see where I'd disappeared to. He would have read the review. It rang again. He would only call if it was good. Or maybe he was calling to see if I had shot up a lethal dose of heroin after how bad it was?

The phone shook again. I answered it.

Thirty minutes later, Sam and I were playing pool down at a bar called Honky Tonk Angels on the Lower East Side. He couldn't sleep either. He'd hated the party too, mostly because he didn't think he had the right clothes. A cheap JCPenney blazer hung over his giant frame. George Jones's "You're Still on My Mind" was the fifth song we played on the jukebox, and Big Sam still hadn't mentioned the review. It was now 1:30 a.m. I should've gone to bed, but Sam is a persuasive SOB. And God knows, I was never going to sleep anyway. I was having a ginger ale. Since the cocaine episode with Deadwilder, I'd been on the wagon.

"I haven't read the review," he said, slapping the cue ball into the nine. I didn't believe him. His hulking body stretched over the table for his next shot. "I'll look it up on my phone this second if you want. But I think you'll be a whole lot cooler if you don't read it." He missed his shot and began chalking up his stick. I knew him well enough now to know that there was no way he hadn't snuck a peek at the review. He loved me, and if he wasn't telling, that meant it was bad. I shot and missed.

"What the hell does that clown over at the *Times* know about art anyway? Fuck him. He's probably beating off to child porn right now. I want to write a review of his life." Sam laughed. "I will not be kind."

Bang. Sam shot another ball, hard into the corner pocket.

"I don't care what he thinks," I said meekly.

"I don't believe you," Sam said, "but you shouldn't care. Some'll be good; some'll be bad, right? And anybody with a brain in their head knows they should pay an extra twenty bucks to watch you pour turpentine on yourself and light it up every night. You're better than Daffy Duck, man."

"Thanks," I mumbled. Sam was good guy. He took up acting after tearing his ACL junior year of college. He looked at everything through the eyes of sports training and was always a good teammate.

"You know what you should do?" he said, his giant hand wrapped around his drink. "Buy a coffin. Buy a coffin and put it on your bed and sleep in it every night like those crazy monks do. The Trappists, or the Franciscans, one of them—they build their coffins and then they sleep in them to remind them what's really going on, right?" I'd never had the sense that Samuel had ever thought about this shit so deeply. He was a big gangly guy who still seemed more like a defensive lineman than an actor. "The *New York Times* review doesn't mean dog crap. You could get a great review, and on your next movie, they could pay you a zillion bucks, and the whole world would think you were doing really great. But it wouldn't mean you actually *were* doing great. I mean, nobody thinks about me at all, dude. You should be grateful."

He walked to the bar and ordered another Roy Rogers. When I asked him about why he never drank he dropped his big fella persona and for the first time opened up to me, telling me the story of his sobriety.

"When the ambulance arrived I was crying for my mom at Sheridan Square with blood spritzing out of my nose 'cause I was snorting absolutely anything I could carve up into powder. Well, they took me to the hospital, and after I got out of St. Vincent's my buddy Daniel picked me up and told me he and all his drug-crazed buddies were driving out to Nevada for Burning Man. You know what that is? Right?"

I didn't know much but I nodded like I did. I knew it was someplace out in the desert where aspiring hippies congregate and do drugs once a year. The truth is the more he talked the more I began to wish I'd stayed in. I think I'd been hoping we would talk about the review.

"Well, believe it or not, I did the whole drive to the Nevada desert with these clowns not drinking any of their hooch or touching any of their drugs. I mean, you didn't know me back then— but there was no pleasure that I couldn't quickly turn into a pain. Sex. Drugs. My friends called me 'The Elephant.' Once I was there in the desert, I just wandered around and watched all these acid-crazed people having their chemically induced enlightenment experiences ... and I was sober and miserable. I missed this girl I was into at the time. But I knew if I went back to Brooklyn I'd just start using again, and if I did that, I'd end up dead. Then after a day and a half I met this elderly Native American dude. And this is where I may lose you, but this guy was the real deal. For a North Dakota fella like me, there was something about him that was familiar. He felt like family. He was cooking veggie hot dogs on a grill in front of an old Airstream trailer with a Merle Haggard T-shirt on and I struck up a conversation with him. He told me that coming to Burning Man was a strange thing to do to get sober. And we started gabbing and I told him that the truth was that since my mom committed suicide I think I've never, like, moved on . . . I mean, my dad sent me to shrinks and shit, so here I was thirty years old and I thought I'd dealt with it. But I couldn't shake how badly I wanted to see her again all the time. I was already older than she had ever been, you know? My mom drowned herself at twenty-nine. So, this old dude told me he thought that he could probably help me. That I didn't need drugs, what I needed was medicine. And that he could take me on a vision quest to see my mom but that there was a strong possibility that I'd die in the process. Literally die. This old Indian went on to say that the earth's drugs are to be used as agents of healing and not playthings. His bet was that if I took this trip with him, and if I lived through it, I would most surely never abuse drugs again, and if I died, it would only be because I chose to die. Personally, he didn't care if I died, but that I had better choose to live or else things would become very awkward for him with the police. So, he made me promise I would choose life. Obviously, I say I'll do it, right? I mean, how could I refuse?"

I nodded, but frankly, I could think of a million ways to avoid a vision quest. Also, I could already understand that this story was not going to end with him revealing to me that I got a great review in *The New York Times*.

"Turns out that this 'trip' involves smoking the saliva of a certain kind of bullfrog, which is technically poison," Big Sam continued. "I mean, the shit will kill you. But I go inside his little Airstream trailer, which is a very clean and peaceful place to be, and he lit some candles. His daughter starts to sing some old Chiricahua song, and I smoke this shit, right? I mean, frankly I don't care if I live or die—I got nothing to live for—no football, no girlfriend, no mom, but there was something warm and kind about this man. I felt safe. One hit off his pipe full of frog saliva takes my head clean off. I'm not kidding—almost immediately I go into cardiac arrest. I fall down like a fuckin' epileptic. Next thing I know, I'm floating above my body watching these two Indians rubbing my hands and legs. And then I'm floating higher above the Airstream, above Burning Man, and I can see all the people dancing and lighting fires, and then I'm shooting like a star above America and all the electricity, then above the darkness of the Atlantic Ocean, and then the planet is drifting away underneath my feet, and then I'm skyrocketing through the 'howling infinite,' you know? I mean, disappearing into some deep peaceful void of space tucked into the Milky Way and then I hear it . . . this sound of like . . . love. I hear, and feel held, by these voices of love. It's my mom. And she cares for me and it's so arresting, like a cold shower on a hot afternoon. She is fresh. I start laughing, just elated that I am there with her. There are other people too, people I don't remember but recognize, and they think I am amazing and are so happy to see me."

He smiled in the hazy light of the pool hall. We were both just standing there holding our cue sticks at the corner of the table. The place was emptying out.

"I don't *see* them, but I hear and feel them. And then I could feel myself pleasantly begin to evaporate. As if everything I thought of as 'me' was just moisture collected in a cloud and that was about to rain away—my mother's voice—all the voices that identified 'me'—we were all going to rain away and I couldn't wait. I wasn't afraid. Then I heard that old Indian calling me back, begging me, imploring me . . . saying 'you promised!' . . . and he reminded me that there was no hurry. Indeed, I thought, it was wonderful where I was—but it was clear this place wasn't going anywhere, because 'it' was everywhere and everything, it was more real than this bar, you understand? And I did have this life left to live so why not live it? So, in the same way that you can let yourself fall back asleep and almost consciously slip right back into a dream—I returned to that Airstream. Instinctually, I felt there were things I am supposed to learn here right now; there was no good reason to die. There is plenty of time." I was staring at Big Sam's warm brown eyes. People are always all so much more strange than I first imagine.

"And so I returned. And the humorous side effect is: now I don't fear death. Not at all. But even more importantly, I don't fear *life*. I *know* everything will be fine, better than fine. All shall be well. But I also know in my fuckin' core, that there is nothing to 'do' while I am here—but to *live*." He stopped talking and stared at me simply.

I had nothing to offer.

"Abusing drugs is defeating the whole idea of being born. And you know, William, your drug is approval. That's why it's so funny to read all this damning shit about you everywhere, and watch you act every night. You may as well not run from it—no matter what *The New York Times* says—they can't save you. The court of public opinion is in. And you are an adulterous shit and a mediocre actor. You fucked over a Queen. You get it? She's a Pop God, and you're a mortal. So, you better look that square in the eyes. You need to have your own opinion of yourself. You see, I can't think of a person it would bother *more* to have this happen to than you . . . *The New York Times* doesn't know if you are doing a good job or not.

Shit, they don't even know a good actor. If they did they would single my ass out for sure." He laughed.

"How'd you get so smart?"

"'Cause my mother killed herself, and because I tore my ACL and had to give up football, and because I was able to quit drinking."

He looked at me. "You get it? Just 'cause you're in pain doesn't mean anything is wrong."

Just then the door to the bar swung open and a loud female voice yelled, *"Bruce! I lost my keys! Fuck."*

A young woman had barged into the bar, drunk and giggling. She was wearing a blue jumpsuit. She was foxy and keenly aware of it. She enjoyed the whole bar turning towards her.

"Anybody want to get laid tonight?" the girl in the blue jump-suit shouted to the barroom. Sam and I looked up. "'Cause I don't have anywhere to sleep!" Her girlfriend was cackling behind her. Various men began heckling. She ignored them, and walked over to Big Sam and me, confidently picking up a pool cue. She looked straight in my eyes and said, "You boys want to get schooled by a homeless hillbilly slut from Waco, Texas?"

Oh shit, I thought. *Here we go.*

"I'll break," I said.

When the girl in the blue jumpsuit walked in my door at the Mercury, she was instantly in love with my daughter's black and white puppy. They wrestled on the floor while I went to the bath-room, washed my face, stared in the mirror, and wondered if *The New York Times* liked the show.

"Oh my God, does your daughter just love this puppy?" the girl shouted out to me.

I didn't bring this woman home to sleep with her; I just couldn't stand to be alone. Also, I thought it would kind of impress her when she found out that I'd been honest back at the bar, when I had told her she could sleep in my kids' room. I thought it might make me seem trustworthy—at least to myself. It would be something positive "self-image-wise" to build on.

"Yeah, of course she loves the dog . . . It's a puppy. Little girls love puppies," I shouted through the bathroom door.

"What's the troublemaker's name?" she squealed.

"Night Snow."

"Night Snow?" She laughed. "What do you call her?"

"The Blue Jean Kid," I answered.

THE NIGHT BEFORE I'd bathed my two kids together in the same bathtub. My daughter had wanted to bathe the puppy, too, but finally, I drew a line. Two naked kids in a tub was enough for one father.

"Daddy," my daughter asked, "what's the word for when people who get divorced change their mind and get married again?"

"God, I don't know," I said. "I don't think there is a word for that."

"There has to be," she said, "'cause that must happen all the time. I mean, most people don't stay divorced. You and Mommy are the only ones I even know."

"Well, you're only in kindergarten. I think you'll find as you get older, more and more of your classmates will have parents who are divorced."

"Arthur has a friend whose parents are like us," my three-year-old son said.

"Who's Arthur?" I asked.

"A dumb cartoon character, he's not even real," my daughter said.

"Well, in truth, they say about half the people who get married get divorced." I leaned over the tub wringing out a washcloth.

"There's no way that's true, Daddy. That's stupid. Where did you hear that?" she almost shouted, her wet face pink and exasperated.

"I read it in a book."

"Come on, Daddy!" she hollered.

"What?"

"You can't believe everything you read!"

I laughed.

"When did you and Mommy even get divorced?" my daughter asked with her head full of soap. "Because I don't remember when it happened," she continued. "And it just seems like something a person should remember."

"I don't remember either," said her brother.

"Yeah, but you don't remember anything. You're too young!" she snapped at her brother.

"Well," I said, still on my knees, trying to rinse their hair while making sure no one got soap in their eyes. "It's been happening for a while. Your mom and I slowly started growing apart till it seemed like it might be better for everybody if we lived apart."

"It isn't better for me," my daughter quickly added.

"I don't even know if it's better or not," my son said. "I can't remember if we ever all lived together."

"You see!" My daughter stood up in the tub. "He's *impossible*. He doesn't remember anything."

"The truth is, darling," I told my daughter, "this all might be a lot more difficult for you because you *do* remember. It might make it a lot harder."

She climbed out of the tub and sat on the bath towel on the floor and began to sob.

"What is it?" I asked.

Her brother stood up naked and soapy to get a better look.

"What is it?" he asked gently.

She looked at me with fat tears pouring from her eyes as she gently shook her head, confessing, "I don't remember either."

Bathing our oldest as a newborn had felt like a slippery science experiment, she was so tiny and fragile. There was a big plastic doohickey still attached to her healing belly button. When we first brought this creature home I sat down and stared into her deep ocean-like eyes. I loved her effortlessly. And I promised this child—I will be your goddamn guardian-fucking-angel. Not just a father, I will be a winged messenger of heaven floating above you, watching you, laughing when you say something funny, protecting you from danger, helping you remember your hat . . . I will be there with you always. The baby and her mother would sit in that steaming bathtub for hours and I would wash them and love them. Mary and I made the child a chocolate Duncan Hines cake with vanilla icing every Wednesday in honor of the weekly anniversary of her birth. We were beyond happy. Afternoons, evenings we played gin rummy fifty million—a game we made up that never ended. Playing cards was like an occupation in those first days of our daughter's life . . . Bathe, change diapers, make cakes, and play gin were all we did and we loved it. One time I remember laughing so hard at something Mary said, tears streamed down my face and I dropped my hand, playing cards scattering to the floor.

I would get up early with the baby and let Mary sleep. At dawn, with pockets full of freshly bottled breast milk, I would go for a three-hour walk up and down the avenues of the city. Just me and our baby. When I brought her home and put her in Mary's arms—they were both complete. Whole. Watching them together was like living inside the Nature Channel. We were a part of the galaxy. The three of us were tigers walking on ancient stardust into the future. Mary was a great mother. She loved her baby hard. Always stroking her hair, rubbing her skin, keeping her warm.

She never set her child down. Never let her baby cry. She kept her girl meticulously clean—like a mama cat.

"What about this," I told my kids as I dried them off in the Mercury bathroom. "Let's make up a word that means a family who, over time, has healed all of its broken places."

The kids looked at me blankly. They were both wrapped in the fresh white hotel towels.

"What about 'albacyclelion'?" my daughter offered after only a moment.

"Why 'albacyclelion'?" I asked.

"*Alba* is Spanish for morning and mornings are healing. Cycle for bicycles, which make you feel good, and lion for . . . for . . ." She began to stumble.

"For obvious reasons," I offered.

"Yes. Albacyclelion." She smiled.

"You can't do that," my son said. "People can't just make up words!"

"Yes, you can," I said, beginning to put their pajamas on them, "Shakespeare does it all the time."

I STOOD IN THAT same bathroom and listened to the girl in the blue jumpsuit wrestle with the puppy. Taking a deep breath, I looked down at the tiles on the floor and imagined the breath my daughter was inhaling at that instant. I imagined her room at her mother's house and her heavy sleeping limbs. I imagined my son. I pictured his room. I remembered what his hair smells like as he sleeps.

Walking back out into my apartment, I escorted the girl in the blue jumpsuit to my kids' room and showed her the bunk bed.

"My daughter prefers the top bunk, but you can have whichever one you want," I said.

"I have a baby too," the girl said quietly.

I stood silent and looked at her.

"I gave her up for adoption. She lives in Phoenix. At least she did. She's two years old now." She paused. "How old's your daughter?"

"Five," I answered.

"I'll take the bottom bunk," she said sadly.

"OK," I said.

"Do you have any whiskey?" she asked. "I'm not nearly drunk enough to fall asleep."

We went back into my living room and sat like a couple of normal adults, listening to quiet music and drinking whiskey on ice.

"So, what do you do for a living?" I asked, trying to make casual conversation.

She was sassy as all hell; it was hard to be alone with her without thinking about taking off her clothes. She had a kind of rockabilly sneer that was out of place in New York City. Her blue Adidas jumpsuit was zipped up tight, holding back what appeared to be giant heaving breasts.

"Don't ask me that," she said, swirling her ice.

"Why not?" I asked, laughing nervously.

"'Cause I don't want to tell you, and it'll make me feel creepy to lie."

"What, are you a hooker?" I asked.

"No!" She stuck her fingers in her whiskey and flicked the wetness towards my face.

"So, why won't you tell me?"

"'Cause you'll judge me."

"I'll judge *you*!" I laughed. "I already know I like you."

"Yeah, but you're the big-shot, rich movie star." She smiled into her glass.

"Oh yeah, is that what you think?" My material wealth had dropped exponentially since I left my wife—so I was living under this false impression that I had joined the masses and was now among the salt of the earth.

We sat in silence.

"Your wife is crazy hot," she said, obviously pleased with herself for having the guts to broach the subject. "She is, like, so fuckin' sexy. I love her music. You have to tell me about her. She's a legend. The greatest ever—I think. She seems like she's a pretty awesome person too," she said.

"She handles her press beautifully," I said.

"I'm kind of proud of myself that I'm gonna fuck a guy she fucked." She snarled confidently.

"Hmmm," I said, smiling.

"Does that hurt your feelings?" she asked.

"What?" I asked.

"That she doesn't love you anymore—the things people say about you in the press—I saw one program where they were really superhostile towards you—it just seems like that would suck?"

"It's a drag," I said. "I always thought if your aim was true— things would work out for the best," I mumbled, trying to appear cavalier about this news of another disparaging show.

"But what if your aim wasn't true?" she asked sweetly. "What if your heart is a little tiny bit black?"

I looked at her blankly. My blood stopped.

"Even saints have a little spot of black on their heart, don't they?" she asked.

I nodded, some part of me still frozen.

"I think you looked hot on that program—gives you kind of a bad-boy edge, all that nasty press—you know? The more they shit-talked you, the more I wanted to kiss you. Is that weird? You used to be a little squeaky vanilla behind the ears, ya know? I never wanted to fuck you till the lady on the show said she wished there was a prison for men like you."

"What do you do for a living?" I asked again.

"I'm not telling you." She smirked. "What's it like to be rich? What's it like to take a taxi whenever the fuck you want?"

"Are you a model?" I asked.

"Don't be an asshole. I'm not retarded."

Personally, I thought she was gorgeous, but I guess she didn't fit the current model standard. She was only five-two and her teeth were crooked in a sultry way.

"You don't need to lay any lines on me. I'm already here." She poured another slug of whiskey. "You can do whatever you want to me, by the way—I don't care," she said, half-curling her upper lip. "If you can think it up, I'll probably like it." I stared at her, my pants beginning to swell. "Just don't lay on a bunch of corny lines that make me think you think I'm stupid."

She was attractive the way a wild animal is—I just wanted to reach out my hand and touch her.

"Well, what brought you here all the way from Waco, Texas?" I asked.

"It sure as shit wasn't my fuckin' job, you turkey," she said, having a raunchy, private laugh. "And I'm just *from* Waco; I lived in Austin."

"What did you do in Austin?"

"I worked at a place called Sugar's."

Now, I, too, am from Austin, Texas, and I knew Sugar's . . . I passed it anytime we went to the airport. I'd never been in there but I knew what it was.

"So, you're a dancer?" I smiled.

"What are you, Presbyterian?" she asked. "I'm a stripper."

"Prove it," I said.

"Turn off this sad-sack shit music and I will."

I was playing Willie Nelson's "Good Time Charlie's Got the Blues."

"What's your choice?" I asked.

"Do you have any Prince?" she asked, unzipping her blue jumpsuit. She had a white wifebeater on over a black bra. Her breasts were obviously fake. They were perfect and large, much like a drawing on the side of a fighter jet.

"Play whatever music you want," I said.

She walked to the stereo, fiddled with my computer, and put on Prince's "Nothing Compares 2 U."

It's been seven hours and thirteen days,
Since you took your love away . . .

This young woman stepped up onto my coffee table and danced like she was a teenager alone in her room. I was the mirror. The puppy exploded with a flurry of curious barks, circling the coffee table. We both laughed and the girl with the blue jumpsuit slowly removed the blue jumpsuit entirely.

She was a professional dancer, no doubt. She was telling the truth.

At the nape of her neck, she had a tattoo of the head of an emerald green viper spitting out its tongue, the body of which descended, wriggling and writhing, across her shoulders, all the way down her back, swerving up over one hip and then swimming down over the other. The tail swished back and settled erotically in the crack of her ass. When she moved, the snake appeared to slither up her spine.

The muscles of her back looked powerful, but still soft with youth. She moved effortlessly above me, wearing only her white panties and her white see-through Hanes wifebeater. Turning her back to me, pulling her shirt up, she'd let me watch her snake slither. Then she'd pull her shirt down and turn back towards me.

She unfastened her bra and let it fall to the floor without taking off her shirt and slowly slid her panties down with her thumbs. Her pussy was neatly shaved.

Then, she pulled her panties back up again.

She danced. I watched.

As the song ended, she prowled on all fours across the coffee table, and kissed me.

"I want to see where the man of the house sleeps," she said, shuffling barefoot out of the room in search of my bedroom.

"Come here, Blue Jean Kid," she called out.

The puppy took clumsy strides after her.

Here we go. Game day.

I picked up the bottle of whiskey and stood. Turning off the lights, I walked down the hallway. I stopped when I heard her playing with the puppy in the bedroom.

Now, I'd never done anything like this before, but I remember my movements exactly because my throat burned for days afterwards. I took the bottle of Jim Beam that was still more than three-quarters full and drained the whole liter in a matter of seconds. Just hiked the glass bottle above my head and glug, glug, glug, poured the entire thing down into my empty burning belly. As I set the hollow bastard down and stepped towards the bedroom and into the darkness of the hall, I was disappointed to discover that I was still completely lucid.

As I entered the black of my room, my young lover grabbed my face and pulled me down hard into bed. I held her gently and kissed her tenderly—the way I'd kissed every girl since the eighth grade, like a boy who'd been brought up right.

"Oh, Christ." She simpered. "I didn't come here for a back rub.

I came here to get fucked." She bit my ear hard. Ten thousand firecrackers lit up my nervous system.

"If you think the keys to my apartment aren't in my purse, then you're stupider than I thought." She pulled herself up close to my ear, whispering, "You look like an angry young man, but if you want to fuck me, you're gonna have to take this piece of ass. It's gonna hurt. If you have any plans to put your cock in my mouth, or up inside my cunt, you're gonna have to start acting like a man."

She clenched my scalp in her fist and ripped my head back hard. My neck snapped and pain shot through my vertebrae.

I was no longer even remotely concerned about not having a hard prick.

Much of what happened next has disappeared into the void of some Jim Beam–soaked subterranean consciousness. Blurry details visit me from time to time—like how good it felt to hurt her. How much she liked it. The way her breasts spilled out of that sweaty wifebeater. Her arms were so thin. I could feel her heart beating through her wrists. The way she never took off her underwear. It twisted around our clenched fists. She fought hard to keep that cotton underwear on, even while we were fucking. My hands wrapped around her, her voice box vibrating against my palms. There was her smell that marked the room—not just the scent of cum, sweat, and cheap perfume, but also the smell of some kind of terror. How easily she cried, I remember that. She cried all the time. How tightly she hugged me through sloppy tears. "Come on," she snarled in my ear. "Don't pet me like a fucking cat. You think I break?" She'd punch me with her fists; push me away; pull me close. It was dark and I had become shatteringly drunk. The floor had no ballast and was easily confused with the walls or the ceiling. It felt so good not to have to pretend to be nice; to be asked to do things that I had felt guilty for wanting to do. It was as if each time she hit me, I would grow to some other, much greater size. I didn't have to be ashamed of anything.

A slumbering primordial anger in my guts rose like a lizard, stretching and kicking and gnawing and fucking. And this lizard didn't give a shit who he hurt. And this woman was growing too, becoming more and more wicked and treacherous. We brawled all night. Once I thought I'd gone too far and hurt her. But she smacked me in the face and asked me to do it again. "You see, you see, you see . . . I'm not fragile."

I imagined her keening could be heard through the halls of the Mercury.

When I woke, my mouth was swollen and my hair was caked with my own blood. Blood from Prince Hal's opening night smack to the face. Half my rib cage was raw with scratches; that was from the girl in the blue jumpsuit. It was also the first time I'd noticed a small but deep cut in my lower abdomen that must have occurred during the haywire opening night fight with Prince Hal. I looked at the clock and it was four in the afternoon. I'd slept longer than I had at any time since I returned from Cape Town. The girl was naked, cuddled in the fetal position next to me. Her long snake tattoo had lost its menace in the daylight. She looked young and hurt.

On the ceiling of my hotel room was a mural, and I'm not making this up, of Jesus seated next to his scolding disapproving Father surrounded by angels and clouds. It wasn't a great painting; some drug-addled artist had probably done it on a whim twenty or thirty years earlier. I stared at Jesus' face above me.

What are you looking at? I laughed to myself. Somehow, I felt great. I kissed my lover and woke her up. She instantly enveloped me in her sleepy, heavy arms and cried again. I could feel her eyelashes sopping wet on the skin of my neck and felt that somehow everything, absolutely everything—my play, my kids, the scalded earth, the oceans with their disappearing dead plant life, the ozone layer—everything was going to be OK.

The light in the room was green. It was always green in the afternoon. There was so much ivy growing over my bedroom window it washed the whole room in a shivering forest light that shook with the wind outside. Soon, it would be time to go to the theater again.

Now, I realize that I didn't have much to feel good about, but believe it or not, I didn't just feel good; I felt *tremendous*. I was going to make it. I couldn't believe it. I was going to arrive back to the stage alive, rested, and with my mind clean, without having read any goddamn reviews. Not one. I'd made it. Opening night had passed. I'd lived, and even successfully had sexual congress with a woman. Yeah, I'd probably got her pregnant or caught some bizarre STD, but for now, I didn't have one single care about my long-term future. I was so happy to have a rock-hard prick and a strong voice, and not be dead. My body swam in gratitude for the simple things.

"WELL, I DID IT, boys," I said, arriving back at the theater to find big Samuel and the guys sitting on the curb immersed in some desultory conversation and sharing a smoke. I sat down next to Samuel and put a cigarette in my lips. "I haven't read any of the stinky reviews and I feel like a million bucks. Like I passed some test. So, don't anybody tell me nothing. I want to keep my mind clean."

"They were better than you could possibly imagine," Samuel said, winking. "I thought secretly you'd want to know," he added after seeing my expression. "I know you're only not reading them 'cause you're worried they will be bad or that they will affect your performance or something, but they are fucking stupendous and you should know."

I paused and considered how I felt. I was ecstatic.

I knew they'd be great, I thought, but carried on the cavalier charade.

"Well, I don't need some two-bit theater student to tell me how I feel about our fucking show," I boasted.

The guys clapped and lit my cigarette, like I was Steve "Hotspur" McQueen.

"You think my wife will read the review and remember what a stud I am and finally come to the show and beg for me to come home?" I joked, but apparently it didn't come off like a joke 'cause the guys just sat there, blank faced. I guess I came off as edgy and angry.

My understudy, Scotty, looked over at me. "Your wife was making out with that fashion designer dude on the cover of the *Post* yesterday. Did you see that?" He took a deep inhale on his smoke and continued, "She and that creepy rich guy were all over the CNN scrawl. None of us were sure if you knew—and were scared to bring it up."

Big Sam gave him a scolding stare.

I sat there for a long while. The conversation stopped.

"Damn," I said out loud. Somehow it felt humiliating that she was fucking somebody else and that everybody knew it. And I knew I couldn't be justifiably angry with any of it, because this was the same as what I had done to her back when we had the same address.

"Let me ask you guys something," I said. "When I was talking to her the other day, she said I was making a weird noise with my throat and that I did it all the time. Did you guys ever notice that?"

They all burst out laughing.

"What? What? What's so funny?" I asked.

"Dude," Samuel started through his laughter, "you do that *constantly* and it's frickin' spooky and weird!"

"Really?" I asked. I knew I had been doing it, but I didn't know it was obvious to other people.

My eyes stung like I was being made fun of in the schoolyard. "Come on, man," Samuel said. "It's no big deal."

I flicked my cigarette, stood up, and walked into the theater. I couldn't talk to those clowns anymore.

When I got to my dressing room, there was another mysterious note left on the door, again without a name. It was a Henry Miller quote that ended with meeting God, and spitting in His face.

"Got another one," I announced.

Ezekiel was already seated in front of the mirror, on his side of our dressing room. I threw my bag down and tried to casually take off my jacket—all the while holding my breath, so that I didn't make that weird humming noise with my throat.

"Do I make a weird noise with my throat, like all the time?" I asked.

"Does the wild bear shit in the woods?" he asked.

I tried to smile. I was going to cry again.

"To hell with them," Ezekiel began. "They always pick on the movie star."

"Who does?" I asked, sitting down.

"The fucking critics. I hope you're not upset about all that crap they wrote in the papers and can see it for the jealousy that it is."

I stared at him blankly.

"You're brilliant in this show," he continued, "and the whole ensemble knows you carry the first two hours. Those critics just feel like it's too easy to say some good-looking guy like you is also a great actor. Don't take them seriously at all. They're just green-eyed pencil pushers."

I still simply stared at him.

After a long time, I said slowly, "Zeke, I told you I wasn't going to read the reviews. I told you that yesterday. I told you I couldn't bear failing in this play and that to protect myself, I would just make up my own mind and keep marching on. I told you I wasn't going to look at one stupid paper. And you promised me that we wouldn't talk about them in here."

We stared at each other, neither of us moving.

"I know," Ezekiel said with his eyes welling up. "I know, I promised." He took a deep breath, and after a long pause went on. "I told you anyway because I wanted to hurt your feelings."

I looked at him.

"Everybody is so fucking *nice* to you," he began, taking a deep breath. "You get those fan letters you don't even open—and you're bangin' all this beautiful tail—and the only reason these chicks like you at all is 'cause you're famous, and you want everybody to feel sorry for you because your sick-hot rock star wife doesn't love you anymore. And I just don't feel sorry for you. You're rich and you get great roles. You don't even read half the scripts that come in here and it kills me. It literally drives a nail into my heart. So, I told you that you got bad reviews because I wanted you to know that you didn't get good notices and that I did. I was worried you weren't going to read them and you'd never know that I am a fucking world-class actor and you don't have to keep patronizing me."

I stared at him.

"Which I realize you probably don't even do," he continued, sniffling and wiping his eyes. "It's just that it really gives me a tremendous amount of pain, you know . . ." Tears were now flowing down his face in steady streams like rain on a windshield. His voice was raw. "I'm so sorry—" He put his head in his hands. "I have so much work to do on myself. I'm really not a very good person." He looked up. "Please forgive me. Please."

There was a long still silence in the room.

"What the fuck?" I asked. "They were all bad?"

"I don't know, man, I only read a few . . . For the show, they were all great . . ."

"So, it's just me . . ."

I turned and looked for something to do with my hands. I was worried I was going to put my fist through the mirror.

"BEFORE HALF-HOUR, LADIES AND GENTLEMEN," the stage manager announced over the loudspeaker. "IF YOU COULD ALL MEET IN THE GREENROOM, THE PRO-DUCERS WOULD LIKE A BRIEF COMPANY MEETING."

"They said 'company meeting,' Virgil, what are you doing here?" someone shouted from the back of our congregation, and the whole cast exploded in laughter. We were stuffed in the small room where all the coffee, tea, bagels, and throat lozenges are laid out. It's not even a room, more like an alcove in a long hallway. There are couches along the wall for people to nap during the two-show days.

"Ha, ha, ha," Virgil said, as he poured himself a tea.

We were all listening to the head producer speak. Most of us didn't know his name—I didn't anyway. It was disconcerting to be addressed by someone other than J.C., but we all knew J.C. was gone. He was already on a flight to direct an opera in Paris.

"I just want your attention for a second, gang," the nerdy guy began apprehensively, "to say thank you. We had a great night last night and I know we all are supposed to not care about the reviews, but I'm a businessman and I care."

Everyone laughed, but none of us were sure what this little powwow was all about.

"We took a great risk on this show. I've never produced Shake-speare, and you should know that, as great a playwright as he was, his plays have a checkered commercial past on Broadway. Good for the not-for-profit world . . . less so for the capitalist."

None of us knew where this was headed.

"When I asked J.C. why we should invest all this equity into a four-hour Shakespeare play, he said, 'Because I guarantee you the greatest American Shakespeare ever performed' . . . So, when I opened up the *Times* this morning, or I guess I should admit, last night . . ."

Everyone laughed again. I gathered that all my cast mates were weak-minded morons who spent the night online reading about our show. They were not the blue-jumpsuit-fucking Zen monk that I was.

"And when I saw that beautiful photo of you, Virgil"—he gestured to our Falstaff, who falsely blushed—"and read the lede— THE GREATEST AMERICAN SHAKESPEARE EVER—I just had to pinch myself!" He held up the cover of the Arts section.

The whole basement of the theater exploded in applause.

"It really said that?" Virgil said. "Really? Let me see."

The producer and the folks around him nodded and confirmed the news, handing the newspaper around.

"What about my Hamlet?" he asked, and the room roared in more laughter.

"We have had the greatest day of sales in the history of Broadway," the producer shouted, "and I want you all to know that as of 3:56 this afternoon, the entire run is *SOLD OUT*!"

The basement of the Lyceum Theatre shook with cheers and applause. I looked over at Ezekiel. He stared with wide, apologetic eyes back at me. I looked over at our King Edward. He was already quietly and humbly making his way back to his dressing room, as if he'd been called for a false alarm. He wanted no part of all this gloating.

"So this is a long-winded way of saying . . ." The producer

paused, wrapping up. "Book your house seats now. 'Cause they are the *only* seats left!"

Everybody cheered again.

"Thank you," the producer guy closed. "Now, have a great show!"

We all walked back to our rooms to get ready for the show.

Ezekiel pulled me over in the hallway, letting everyone else pass us by. "Listen, man, I first learned about acting in prison. OK? J.C. came to teach a class at the Illinois State penitentiary—nobody knows that, OK? That's how we met, and sometimes I think that just 'cause I kicked drugs and pulled myself outta the shithole I grew up in, that I have an excuse to be an asshole. But if you'll forgive me and give me one more shot to be your friend, I'll never let you down."

I wasn't mad at him. He was a strange guy, I knew that already. I was disappointed that I had personally gotten bad reviews, but that feeling was confused and lost in the excitement that the show had been received so well.

"Done," I said, meekly.

"Thank you," he said, and with that, shook my hand and walked away. We had a long run ahead of us and we were roommates.

I went outside to smoke a cigarette. Big Sam was there. We both should have been at fight call.

"Don't worry about your stupid throat thing," Samuel said. "None of us care."

"It's OK, Sam," I said. "I just don't know how to stop doing it."

"If you ask me," he said quietly, "it's a small price to pay for getting to give such a great performance."

"Thanks, pal," I said.

"Self-pity doesn't play, right?" he said, trying to smile.

I looked over at him. He was down, too. One thing worse than a bad review is not being mentioned.

"Samuel . . ." I didn't want to but I did it. "Do you have the paper?" I asked. I could see it sticking out of his bag.

"Sure, man," he said and gave it to me.

There it was: cover of the Friday Arts page, a full-page color photo of Virgil with the title THE GREATEST AMERICAN SHAKE-SPEARE EVER.

I walked away from Samuel and sat on the curb of Forty-sixth Street, just off Broadway, and read the review by myself. I heard Samuel walk inside and head to fight call. It was indeed a glowing review. No wonder everyone was happy. They wrote that Ezekiel was a "phenomenal talent who appears to actually breathe fire." There were passages about Virgil's towering achievement; Edward was hailed a "national treasure."

Finally, I came to the passage about myself: "Unfortunately, like a great Persian rug that must have one deliberate mistake, J. C. Callahan, the best director working today in the American theater, felt the need to cast a film star, William Harding, as the warrior Hotspur. He is hopelessly outclassed." I imagined Mary reading this with her new lover. Both feeling sorry for me. "Hotspur is a challenging role and the film actor seems incapable of achieving what W. H. Auden called 'the living embodiment of the lost chivalry of the older generation.'"

I stopped there. The black cloud that had been gathering in my chest suddenly receded and rays of the sun broke through. This critic was quoting from that same W. H. Auden essay that J.C. and I had discussed at length and had decided was so obviously, clearly, and hopelessly misguided.

This lily-livered loon from *The New York Times* didn't know what he was talking about. Joy erupted from my heart. I knew more about Hotspur than that cream-faced punk. I looked up and let the pages of the paper scatter as a bus drove by. I didn't care. I go to war for art. The world can think what it wants. They can pronounce you a failure. They can sew a scarlet letter on your chest and call you a cad and a charlatan. Meek voices may murmur derisive whispers behind your back at every turn. They can hate you and blab about it on talk radio with the entire nation listening. And yet, they can all be dead fucking wrong.

A Hell Broth Boil

We were deep in the run now. It was the first Tuesday of the New Year and the kids were headed back to school after winter break. My soon-to-be-ex-wife had just spent the holidays with our children at her new billionaire-boyfriend's palace on the Black Sea. There were pictures of them all over the Internet. Pictures of Valentino teaching my daughter to surf, a lovely shot of the mother of my children frolicking topless on the beach. Extreme macro close-ups of a new diamond ring on her finger. One photo was of the new lovers passionately kissing with my son building a sandcastle in the background. Something from a science fiction film was happening inside my intestines. I was gonzo depressed and had somehow developed an extremely painful boil.

I'm not sure how it all began. I believe the cut came on opening night. Maybe it was from the battle. Maybe it was from the girl in the blue jumpsuit. It was a small slice right below my belly button. After I'd been ignoring it for weeks it became infected from the sweat of my leather costume. Then I started obsessively picking at the infection, until it began to fester. By the time my kids returned from Christmas break, I had a boil protruding from my belly about the size of a shooter marble. With near zero percent body fat (normally fit and trim at 180 pounds, I was now down to 148), this festering ball of pus looked like a small creature trying to climb out of my body. It also hurt.

I picked my kids up from their mother's house the morning they returned from the Balkans. My wife didn't come to the door. The jet-lagged nanny asked me to wait there while she got the kids into their jackets. This was a first. Usually, I was allowed in. Valentino must've been a sleepyhead. I hugged the kids and we cabbed it uptown to take my daughter to her kindergarten.

"So, how was your trip, you guys?" I asked, busy trying to arrange my stomach in a way that could minimize the piercing pain my boil was causing. It felt like someone was pouring hot lead into my belly button.

"Oh, Daddy, it was so fun," my five-year-old daughter said while lounging comfortably by the taxi's window. "Mommy's friend Valentino has all these elves that work for him. So, we didn't have to do anything."

My son was sitting on my other side and said, "They're not real elves with funny ears or anything."

"Valentino just calls them elves 'cause they help him with stuff. He's really funny . . ." My daughter trailed off, blithely spinning her hair in circles around her finger. "He always says things like 'No pun intended,' and we all laugh. Anyway, we played the whole time. The weather was truly *breathtaking*. Very healing," she said in a perfect imitation of her mother's tone.

"They have a gumball machine and movies and a pool and the beach and boats and bananas that you can ride on," my son continued.

"Not real bananas," my daughter corrected, "but this yellow inflatable one that somebody—"

"The elves," my son asserted, "they blow it up for you!"

"It's just so nice there." She paused, taking a more serious tone,

New York City whizzing by outside her taxi window. "And you don't have to pick up your towels or carry your sand toys back inside because the elves will do it."

"And the sand has been *imported* from somewhere really amazing and that's what makes it so special," my son stated.

"It's not like regular sand," my daughter added, "with a stranger's pee on it and stuff." She looked at me curiously, as if to see if I understood what she was saying. I nodded.

"And Valentino bought me a jump rope and taught me how do it. Oh, Daddy, it was so fun. To speak frankly, I just don't know what I would do without Valentino right now. He's really helping me and Mommy through a supertough time."

That's all I remember. The lights went black again.

WHEN I WALKED into the theater that Tuesday night I didn't reveal to anyone the infection under my belt that was now moving and swelling to the size of a golf ball. The pain was fierce. I could barely breathe but went onstage and screamed my fool head off anyway. After I was killed, my voice was so demolished I could barely speak. It'd been getting worse steadily for months, but never this bad. Every sentence coming from my larynx sounded like someone kicking gravel. While I waited for the curtain call, I smoked and bought myself my daily ice cream sandwich from the vending machine backstage.

Once back at the Mercury, I reopened the computer and returned to my online quest, looking for more pictures of my wife and children playing on the beach with that Italian, nickel-rattling, fashion poseur. Then I saw an email from my father.

He apologized for taking so long to write but he was hoping to find a way to contact me without having to reach out to my mother. It was sincere and affectionate. He loved me. He didn't care that I'd ruined my marriage and received bad reviews. He cited some passages from the Bible that might give me courage. He said he understood that I might want to be alone, but he was worried I'd be concerned he was judging me negatively. Well, he wasn't—he was not without sin and he knew from experience that life was unpredictable and that no one gets a free pass. He'd read an interview I'd done in a magazine and it seemed to him like I was in a lot of pain. He'd been praying for me twice a day and just wanted me to know if there was anything he could do to help, to please let him know. He wrote his number and told me to call. I just went to bed. Too little, too late.

THE FOLLOWING DAY was a two-show Wednesday that was pretty much all I'd been looking forward to for the last couple of months. The senior English classes from a dozen New York City public schools were coming to our matinee performance. *The New York Times* could say what they liked, because I was sure that the real folks, the Great Unwashed, the Uncounted Heads, the Salt of the Earth, the Humble of Birth—they would love me. But there was no doubt the daily grind of the run was wearing me down. Even after a night's rest my voice would be hanging on by a thread, and now some kind of poison was bubbling like a witch's brew in my gut.

I could feel my anger pulse from this infected wound in my intestines as I stared at the picture of my brother Jesus Christ on the ceiling. The pain was now so acute I could forget to be worried about my shot vocal cords. The pus was scalding me from the inside. I put some ice in a blue plastic deli bag and lay on the bed, icing my wound all night. After two hours, my sheets were sopping wet from my fever and the melting ice.

Still, the boil grew.

———

BY DAWN, my mattress was like a heavy sponge; my fever was fully spiked; and the boil had grown to the size of a fat Florida orange. I panicked that I might not be able to perform that day. I needed to see a doctor; something was very wrong.

I arrived at Bellevue at 6:23 a.m. and stumbled into the emergency room. My two-show Wednesday had arrived. The 2:00 p.m. matinee performance was the most important for me not to miss. I imagined the students talking to each other when they heard the announcement that my understudy was going on. *Oh, he thinks he's too good for us—he doesn't care. What a spoiled little shit! I knew he wouldn't be here. I hate his movies anyway!*

The ER nurses recognized me from one of my older films and brought me in ahead of some poor, bleeding saps who just stared at me. I got my picture taken with some orderlies. I didn't care; I was glad for the quick attention. The doctor looked at my gut and told me we would go into surgery immediately. He said I was in extreme danger. Apparently, if this ball of pus ruptured into my bloodstream I could get a kind of crazy toxic sepsis, or whatever they called it. I was in a hazy fever and wasn't listening.

"Will I be outta here by one p.m.?" I asked.

"What?"

"I'm doing *The Henrys* on Broadway with a matinee this afternoon and I've got another show tonight."

"Well, you better call somebody and tell them you're not going to make it," he said calmly.

"What do you mean?" I asked, suddenly completely lucid.

"You will not be able to perform today for sure, and probably not tomorrow either."

"No," I said, "I can't miss a show. Can't you just do it quick? I really will pay all the money I have."

"It's not the money." He laughed innocently. "You are going to go under general anesthesia and the hospital will not release you until tomorrow at the earliest. I'm sorry. Them's the rules," he said, affecting a real regular-guy approach.

I couldn't move.

"Can we do it on Monday? On my day off?" I asked quietly.

He looked at me blankly.

"Actually, Sunday evening would be perfect," I went on, "'cause we have a matinee in the afternoon, but then I don't have another show till Tuesday night. That gives me almost forty-eight hours off to recuperate." I felt happy about this possibility.

"If we don't treat this infection right now, you will most likely be dead by Sunday—get it?" The doctor was still smiling. "You could lose your sight even more quickly than that."

"Do you have to use anesthesia?" I looked up, this new idea filling me up with hope.

"Believe me, cowboy, you want me to use anesthesia." He chuckled. "Trust me on this."

"No, I don't," I said gravely. "I'll do anything to go on that stage at two o'clock today. Please."

"Don't you have an understudy?" he asked.

"Today we are doing a matinee for the public schools of Harlem—I can't miss this show. If I miss that show, I'll just be so ashamed of myself . . . Please. The kids, they want to come to see a movie actor, you know? And they will be so disappointed. It means a lot to them. It's important."

"No offense, but I really don't think the kids will give a shit."

"You don't understand—this is my life. Acting in this show is more important to me than real life. My real life sucks. That show goes on without me . . . To me, it's like you leaving a patient on the operating table. Make sense?"

"I guess . . ." He studied me. "But listen, you can barely talk. Is your voice even OK?"

"My voice will be fine . . ." I'd forgotten about that obstacle. "It always sounds this terrible in the morning."

"Well, why don't you take a break? Sometimes our bodies speak to us, and your body is shouting that you need a rest. Spend a couple days in the hospital, get better, and return to the show stronger." The doctor turned and looked at a nurse-type woman standing behind him. She was twenty-five or twenty-six with jet-black hair, black eyes, olive skin, and an Italian name on her little name tag.

"I'll speak to your director," he continued, "or stage manager, or whatever . . . My wife's an actress, so I know about this stuff."

I sat there on the crinkly white paper covering the patient's table and wept in front of the doctor and his uniformed nurse. The only noise in the room was my snorting sobs.

"Please. Please. I beg you. Please. Cut out this infection or whatever and let me go onstage. I have to go on today. I know my body needs rest, and I will rest. But I need to do a good job today more than I need rest. I'll come to the hospital on my day off. Or tonight after the show. Anything. Please. I'll take care of my voice—I just can't miss this performance and I can't walk anymore with this fucking boil-thing stabbing me."

There was a long silence in the room.

The young Italian nurse lifted her lips in a Mona Lisa–like expression at the doctor. She seemed sympathetic. He turned back towards me.

"Look, if you want to do the operation without anesthesia, I'll get somebody to do it." He shrugged his shoulders. "I loved you in that cop film you did. And we'll shoot you up with Novocain, but it will still hurt a lot. This will be extremely painful—the stomach is very sensitive. I'm also going to give you a heavy antibiotic that you *will* take, and I will give you some steroids that should help with your voice. But you have to promise me that you will call me between shows and come back and see me first thing in the morning."

I nodded in gratitude.

"And"—he smiled a big friendly smile—"I need two house seats for February fourteenth"—he winked at the nurse—"for my wife." He turned back to me. "You got it?"

I tried to smile. "Happy Valentine's Day."

They left me alone in my little room for more than an hour. I was shit-crazy. I felt like a wolf waiting in a veterinarian's office. I couldn't stop pacing, touching my stomach, picking things up and playing with them. I was worried the doctor would change his mind. If he did, I decided I would make a run for it.

I forced myself to sit down and think of something else. The room had a poster of the Milky Way with a small red arrow pointing to a tiny blue planet, next to the words YOU ARE HERE.

I could have stared at the poster for a million years. It wasn't going to change the fact that I had no idea where I was, and never had. Next thing I knew, I was asleep on the little patient table and being awoken by a short, elderly female doctor. I checked the time; it was not yet 9:30 a.m.

"Wake up, Mr. Harding." She jostled me. Behind her was the same young Italian nurse and a big, burly bastard in a white robe that I immediately clocked as being the heavy brought in to strap me down. The elderly doctor was like a villain from a James Bond film. Her voice was crackly and hard. Her teeth were small and pointy and stained with coffee and cigarettes.

"So you don't want to go under, huh?" she asked as she was laying out all her instruments. I said nothing.

"It will be no problem—it won't even hurt very much," she continued as she prepared. "I was a field nurse in Vietnam and we did much more invasive surgery than this without so much as a lick of gin."

She held up a syringe displaying the injection I was about to get.

"This will be the worst part, Mr. Harding. Just a few injections into the inflamed area and then your midsection should go numb. You are quite right to refuse sedation. It's ridiculous how overused those drugs are."

Her insistence that this was, in fact, a good idea was terrifying to me. "Lift up your shirt," she asked. "Let me see this thing."

She stared and poked at my boil. Then she prodded the area around the abdomen several times with her finger. I convulsed in agony every time her stubby fingers neared the swelling.

"OK, well, it really is quite enlarged, isn't it? Tender, too." She picked up the syringe. "Don't worry, this will be over in a jiffy. Bruce," she called over to the big son-of-a-bitch, "why don't you hold his arms, and Alyssa, lie down across his legs."

The following eighteen minutes were a kind of physical agony I had never known. I felt I was sliced open with a ragged, rusty blade and then raped in the wound. When the nurse left, I was holding my stomach, with my face and shirt absolutely drenched in sweat, snot, and tears. The infection had been carved out. I had a hole the size of a fist in my stomach and the entire wound was stuffed with some antiseptic gauze.

The young Italian woman, who was the last to exit through the door, turned and said, almost apologetically, "Are you going to be OK?"

"I don't know," I said. "I'm getting a divorce."

"I'm sorry. I read all about that," she said. Then she added, with her hand still on the doorknob, "I'm engaged to be married in May."

"Good luck," I said. She smiled sadly and was gone.

STUMBLING OUT of the hospital, holding my bloody (now boilless) gut with one hand and a bag full of free sample painkillers in the other, I felt all right: I was going to make the show.

That was all that mattered.

On my dressing room door, there was another quote. This one was from Bertolt Brecht, comparing love to letting your naked arm float in the weeds of a nasty pond. I looked around for someone skulking in the hallways. Lady Percy?

When I stepped out onstage, fuckin' A—surprise, surprise—I felt fine. These lights were a holy calling. It was the balm in Gilead, the healing waters of youth, and my springboard into eternity. My stomach was painfully tight, wrapped in bandages, but each breath felt good, the way lifting weights can feel good. It hurt, but it also made me feel awake and alive, like I was gaining in strength.

After my first scene, when I ripped the King a new asshole, I felt even better. My voice was growing stronger with every rhyming couplet. The shot of steroids was doing its thing. Shit, man, I felt like Barry Bonds hammering home runs. As I strode across the stage, I could hear our young public school audience fawning over me, whispering, "There he is!" Titles of my films were being tossed out in hushed voices through the aisles. I like attention. For a second, I thought I saw my wife's black beautiful hair out there in the back row . . . I even thought that perhaps I could make out her shape. Could she have come to a student matinee? Why would she do that? Maybe it was the only one she could make? When I was offstage, I stared through the black scrim at the audience. I couldn't be sure.

Back in my dressing room, I wrapped a leather belt around my wound—I didn't care if it hurt. I had to cover up the incision so that when I took off my shirt, the girls wouldn't be grossed out.

There was something about that performance—maybe it was what I went through to get there, carving out the boil; maybe it was my voice magically healing. It could have also been the fact that the whole house was full of nonpaying students: When they were bored, you knew it. They were not polite. If a scene became dull, you could feel them restlessly checking their phones. But if you moved them emotionally? Oh Lord, *that* is the sweet stuff. Even grouchy old Virgil Smith was having a ball. He was tearing it up. And despite all the laughs adding time to the show, we were still running a few full minutes faster than usual. The pace was clicking and the pistons firing. Where we normally got a polite chuckle, this matinee house exploded in guffaws. When I ripped my sword from its scabbard on an average performance, I'd be met with reserved silence; today: shrieks of terror. Any lewd joke was cause for a full-blown eruption of knee-slapping hilarity. When the girls took their tops off in the tavern scene the teachers had to storm the aisles to quiet everybody down. When I led the charge into battle, I thought the whole senior class might join me.

In the penultimate scene of our first act, when one of my rebel comrades (performed meekly by my understudy, Scotty) rushed in and warned me that the Prince of Wales was coming with his father, the King, to fight me with legions of men *"plumed like estridges,"* I screamed at this little lord, with a voice as powerful as an African drum, *"LET THEM COME!"*

My poor understudy cowered. I wheeled around, my black leather cracking, drew my sword, and hissed, *"They come like sacrifices in their trim"*—this was my favorite part of every show—

"*And to the fire-eyed-maid-of-smoky-war, all hot and bleeding, WILL WE OFFER THEM!*"

Next, I'd walk among my men, jostling their armor, patting them, giving them encouragement. Fear must be killed. What do you kill it with? *COURAGE!*

Finally, in a bit we came up with that everybody loved, I smacked my main man, Big Sam, hard across the face, and—to the surprise of the audience—he would smack me even harder right back. This would launch me out in an explosion of joyful laughter, *I AM ON FIRE!* Sweat flew from my cropped hair.

My men loved this kind of sophomoric frat boy high jinks. I loved it too.

"*Come, let me taste my horse, who shall bear me like a THUNDER-BOLT!*" I took a pause and continued in a mock lisp, while playfully checking my nails, "*against the bosom of the prince of Wales.*"

All my men roared with laughter. It was obvious that the poor prince's puny pecker was a source of outlandish humor when compared to the weight I was wearing.

"*Harry to Harry shall,*" I spoke, striking a more serious tone and playing on the irony that my nemesis has the same first name as I, "*hot horse to horse, meet and ne'er part till one drop down a CORPSE!*"

After that, my handsome men exploded in a raucous cheer. They looked at me with admiring eyes that seemed to say, *Now, there's a stud with some semen in his sack!*

Then one of my other minions ran onstage and tried, in his cowardly fashion, to further caution me that the King's army was now raised to thirty thousand men:

"*Forty, let it be! O gentlemen, the time of life is short! To spend that shortness basely were TOO LONG! IF we LIVE, we live to tread on KINGS!*"

My men responded with the appropriate roars and grunts of affirmation.

"*If die?*" I posed the question as if sincere, then answered it, "*BRAVE DEATH, when princes die with us!*"

With that score settled, I grabbed some lances, maces, axes, and other tools of death and started handing them out to my men.

"*SOUND ALL THE LOFTY INSTRUMENTS OF WAR, and by that music let us all embrace.*"

We all gave each other deep, manly hugs of war as the drums pounded—and, oh man, J.C. was good; these drums beat your soul. This show was not for amateurs. It needed to be precise, and it was. We were an orchestra in perfect tune. These iPhone-addicted, computer-obsessed, tweeting, porn-hooked, theater-hating teen-agers were out there hypnotized. This is who Shakespeare was meant for: not *The New York Times*! Not *intellectuals*. Just plain folks. You play Shakespeare's music right for a real house and that shit goes up all by itself. These kids felt this play like the boom of a spine-cracking orgasm.

I'd rather have gone straight to hell with a broken back than miss this show.

Then, as I wrapped my arms around Big Sam, I said for the entire tristate area to hear, "*For, heaven to earth, some of us never shall a second time do such a courtesy.*" We knew we might die and we were OK with that. Our cause was just, our balls granite, and our hearts? Right as rain.

"*Come, let us take a muster speedily,*" I continued, unsheathing both my blades.

Then it was time for my absolute favorite line. So, without fur-ther ado, I breathed deep—carrying the oxygen down into the base of my feet—and leapt to the top of a collapsed wooden artillery wagon to address my band of ragged rebels. With the teenagers rioting in blustering envy in front of me, spinning a sword in each hand, the cannons firing red blazes behind me, and the orchestra rhythm section pounding beneath the whole city, I roared, *"DOOMSDAY IS NEAR! DIE ALL! DIE MERRILY!"*

Then when the puny prince stabbed me in the guts in that Wednesday matinee in front of all those magnificent "real" people, those public school kids of Harlem, the Bronx, and beyond, when that retractable blade popped me right in its designated spot below my solar plexus, I caught hold of my shadow—just for a second—and it hurt me more than any Italian-stallion-fashion-genius who was fucking my wife and building sandcastles with my kids ever could. It hurt me worse than the *New York Times* theater critic. It hurt me more than the field nurse at Bellevue Hospital. My shadow hurt me with the facts, and indeed—the facts are not always friendly.

The Prince stabbed me in the belly, and to my total and complete disbelief, the audience spontaneously, jubilantly cheered. Before I could even launch into my final *O Harry, thou hast robbed me of my youth* speech, the entire house erupted in a full thirty-seconds-long spontaneous frenzy of applause.

They hated me.

They loved Prince Hal.

They were glad I was dead.

I couldn't believe it. They cheered him through my whole death soliloquy. They didn't listen to a word. They clamored with joy once again when my tearstained, boil-less, bloody body hit the dirt.

I lay on the ground, the steroids still pumping through my vocal cords and my abdomen still strapped tight. The audience adored Prince Hal. They were honoring him for his conquest, lauding his actions, and proud of him for destroying me.

All this time, I'd thought they loved *me*. All this time, I'd been misguided. Suddenly, I could hear how gloriously Prince Hal spoke the text. He was no punk; his voice was eloquent. His gestures were humble. You could intuit from his speech that he was a good person; you could also tell he was a great actor. The guy brought a packed lunch with a banana and a peanut butter sandwich to rehearsal every day, for fuck's sake—*of course* he was the good guy.

Virgil's voice as Falstaff then came into focus above me, and his sound was clear, and ringing. His phrases seemed to corral the audience the way the oldest and strongest whale might sing to a pod of young calves. His voice was a magnet, impossible not to follow. Both funny and touching, Virgil could move you while you were laughing. He wasn't a stuck-up, self-involved diva—he was simply more talented and harder working than any of the rest of the ensemble.

Also, my understudy, Scotty, was speaking above me; he had a short scene with Virgil. He was good. He even got a couple laughs. *Why hadn't I let him go on for me? I'm sick. In more ways than one.*

I lay on floor dead, like a sack of sand.

So, I'm the "BAD GUY," huh? I asked myself. *Holy Great Mother of God! I don't want to be the Bad Guy. I want to be the hero. I would do absolutely anything for these people, but they detest me and applaud my death.*

"Well, now you know!" Edward the King said to me as I walked offstage at the act break.

My cast mates were standing around idle in the halls, watching me shuffle back to my dressing room. Ezekiel stood in our doorway with a heretofore unseen look of warmth and comradeship on his face. Everyone was studying me, wondering how I was taking it. Their sympathy made my experience worse. Scotty seemed to shrug, *I told you so.* The King smiled at me and recited:

> *We would rather be ruined than changed*
> *We would rather die in our dread*

Than climb the cross of the moment
And let our illusions die.

"Know who said that?" he asked.

"No," I answered.

"Mr. W. H. Auden." He smiled. "Not such a dimwit after all, is he?"

WHEN THE SHOW ENDED, my underwear was stained red from the blood oozing from my bandages. I walked onstage for the curtain call and was promptly and joyously booed by my beloved, authentic, salt-of-the-earth public high school friends. It was undeniable, a spontaneous jubilant chorus of "BOOOOOOOOOOOOOOOOOO" rose from the house as I took my bow. My arms hung limp from my sides. I looked over at the shape I had thought might have been my wife, but it was just an English teacher. My head hung low. I was not in danger of upstaging Prince Hal by leaping offstage anymore.

I had seen my shadow and knew my shape.

AS I WAS WALKING OUT of my dressing room after the matinee, hoping to grab a bite and a cigarette, the King signaled to me. "When I did my first play with J.C., we were the only two Americans at the RSC in London. J.C. was assisting the great Sir James Hall and I was playing the male ingénue in *Shrew*," he said, locking his dressing room door behind him. "Anyway, that's not the point—the point is there was a little boy in the show—about eight or nine, and every night at curtain call, he would do this elaborate, intricate, absolutely ridiculous bow." Other actors were streaming out of the theater ahead of us. We only had an hour and a half between shows. Everybody was rushing to get dinner and a nap, but the King moved slowly down the hallway with his deliberate gait.

"Nobody had taught the boy this absurd bow. It was just his childish idea of how an actor should behave. He would doff his cap and curtsy, bending the top of his head almost all the way to the ground, his leg sliding out awkwardly." The King did an arthritic version of the bow. "The first time he did it the audience leapt to their feet with a genuine outpouring of affection. And our director rushed backstage and whispered to the company and the kid's parents to never mention this bow to the boy—to please 'let it be.' It was innocent, magical, and the truest moment we had in the production." We continued out of the theater. "And nobody ever did mention the bow to the boy, and every night, we received a huge boost to our ovation, despite terrible reviews, and an otherwise worthless production. Do you see my point?"

I wasn't sure I wanted to.

We were standing still now, just inside the back door of the theater. The cold street waited for us outside.

"The absolute genius of your Hotspur has been that you've had no inkling that the audience loathes your character. You've obviously never seen the play or read much about it because you attacked this role as if Hotspur was Abraham Lincoln, and it has been glorious fun to watch. You never apologized or tried to be likable. You never even doubted the intrinsic goodness of a bloodthirsty traitor. Granted, much like the boy I mention, it was genius born out of ignorance, but genius nonetheless. And tonight, you will face the real test. Can you continue on despite your education?"

"Great," I answered, still holding my hurting gut. "I can't wait." I opened the door for the King.

"Neither can I." He smiled, and strode into the chaos of Broadway.

IN FRONT OF THE STAGE DOOR, there was a line of students waiting to get on their bus. I promptly turned around and went back inside before one of them could clock me.

I hated those fucking kids.

When did I become the bad guy? When I was a kid everyone liked me. When did I go wrong? Maybe it was one year earlier, on my thirty-second birthday. We were in L.A. My wife was recording an album there and we had temporarily moved the whole family to the West Coast. The recording was a very "demanding" one for my wife—meaning she was taking dance lessons, boxing to get in shape for the video, learning to ride a motorcycle, swimming in a tank with sharks, just a ton of superstar jerk-off crap to get ready for a new record launch. Plus, her manager wanted her in the "best shape of her life," so there was a jockstrap-wearing trainer at the house 24/7, meals being delivered, and masseuses coming by our bedroom. The Polish cinematographer for the videos said she had bags under her eyes, so the kids needed to be kept away from her during the night for her to get more sleep. We had a staff of like twenty-seven nannies to help constantly with the kids, too. If you were an unemployed actor-househusband, it was a home that made you want to take a snub-nosed .38 and blow out the back of your head. I had nothing to do but take care of the kids and there were *real* employees to do that. I was useless and borderline catatonic. I went to the gym, took the kids to the beach when the nannies had lunch, smoked a lot of cigarettes, played the piano, brought the kids to the set for a "mommy power lunch," and went on so-called meetings.

The day of my thirty-second birthday, we had a birthday lunch at the studio with the kids, and then when Mary got off work, we were supposed to go out to dinner with a couple of good friends of mine who were in town from New York. Well, a peculiar thing happened that afternoon. As I went for a walk around the RCA recording studios parking lot, where my wife was overseeing the backing vocals, I saw the most pristine rose red '68 Shelby Cobra I had ever come across—outside of a magazine. Now, anybody who knows me knows this is my dream car. It's a lot like the Mustang Steve McQueen drives in *Bullitt,* but cooler. More horsepower. I went over to check it out. This machine was straight out of the factory. It was hell-bent for leather. I mean the radio, the stitched seats, the cigarette lighter—every detail was cherry. Shit, this baby had a 440 under the hood and only twelve hundred miles on it. It was a work of art, more sexual than Marilyn Monroe in black lace panties holding a bazooka. Then I saw the license plate was from a nearby dealership. This car had been purchased today. The sales slip was on the dash. I walked over to one of the driver guys working on Mary's crew and asked what the story was with this Cobra—was it for a video or what? Quickly, the transpo guy got all squirrelly and strange, saying no, it wasn't for the video, and he didn't know whom it belonged to—he had never seen it before.

That guy was a terrible liar—it was obvious he was hiding something. Why? That's when the thought arrived. *Oh my God, my beautiful, glorious, kind wife KNOWS I want this car more than anything in the world, but that I would never buy it for myself because it's just too damn expensive to enjoy. She's realized what a difficult time I've been having and wanted to do something AMAZING for me, so she bought me this sassy '68 mint-condition Shelby Cobra just to say, "Hey, I get it. You've been making a lot of sacrifices for this family. Thank you, and you are loved. I realize you've felt castrated, so, for your birthday, I symbolically am giving you back your—let's face it— rather large dick."*

I felt so understood. She knew my masculinity had been suffering with how unnecessary I had become; she understood that sometimes a man just has to be a man. And while she shouldn't have spent all that money, it was out of love, so I forgave her. I sat at lunch with the kids, giddy with anticipation. *When is she going to do it? When will she give it to me?* Oh, every time she went to the bathroom or an AD came over to us . . . I thought, *This is the moment. Be cool. Act like you don't know.* But then lunch was over and she hadn't given me the car. Now, I wasn't so sure. Her driver took me and the kids home and my wife said she would see me for dinner around seven.

"Cool," I said.

I ASKED THE DRIVER, Steve, as we left, "Hey, did you see that Shelby Cobra?"

"No," he said, fighting back a grin. His expression was priceless. I knew it. *Fuck,* that car was mine. She was probably going to drive the Cobra home so we could roll out to dinner in style. Seven o'clock spun around and she called: The video shoot was running late. Would I mind if Steve brought me out to set? That way we could leave straight from work and save the time and not be too late meeting our friends for my birthday dinner.

"No problem," I said. I knew what it was . . . I'd been worrying about this: The Cobra was a stick and Mary can't drive stick—so I was sure they were bringing me out there so I could drive the Cobra out to dinner. *This* is *smart of them,* I thought. While I was waiting, I called a buddy and I told him all about my new Cobra. I wanted him to know what a badass, awesome chick Mary was. "I mean, come on," I told him, "that's a great wife!"

"Fuck, I'm so jealous!" my friend screamed into the phone. It felt so good to hear him say that. I just smiled. I wasn't going to gloat; that's not me.

As we pulled into RCA, I tried to relax. I knew it would be

important to Mary that this be a surprise and wanted to fake it well . . . to sell it. When I got there, they were still caught up working and an assistant told me we'd be out of there right away. Everyone seemed to know it was my birthday and they were on high alert to get her out ASAP. I casually looked around for my Cobra. It had been moved. *Hmmm,* I thought, *I wonder how they're going to do this.*

Quickly, she was finished, and hustled to get out of her costume. Then, before I knew it, Steve was driving us to dinner. This part I couldn't figure out. Why was she not giving me the car right away? She wasn't carrying any other presents . . . I still felt very confident that the Cobra was coming, but why this elaborate charade? Then she gave me the clue . . .

"I think Steve should wait for us outside the restaurant and drive us home. He doesn't mind . . . that way we can drink all we want."

"OK, as long as Steve doesn't mind," I said, nodding to good old Steve. Smart. Don't want to drink and drive our first night with the Cobra. Very cagey. Thorough. Sometimes my wife impressed me. The sparkling red rocket would be at home when we arrived. She was probably going to give me the keys at dinner. That was it. That was a great idea. I took a deep breath.

We sat down for our meal and it all collapsed. My wife was speaking with this superior tone she would sometimes get when she'd been in the studio too long or had been interviewed too much—she talked two decibels too loud, as if all of us were trying to write down everything she was saying. She pontificated endlessly, pointing constantly, about the genius of her record producer. She still had on 10 million pounds of makeup and it made her look scary. Then one of my pals, who was Jewish, started talking about his trip to Israel and how meaningful and enlightening it had proved for him and his family. My big-shot, know-it-all wife used this moment as a launchpad for her opinions on Palestinian rights. She prattled on, patronizing my silent friend as if he were a warmongering Zionist. It was beyond exhausting and tense. Never once did the subject of the Cobra come up. They brought out a cake and my friends gave me some presents. I opened them all gratefully. Then, my wife pulled from her purse her present. I listened for the jingle-jangle of keys, but there was only silence.

My gift was an unwrapped, unfinished scarf that she had almost finished knitting. I had been watching her knit the scratchy thing for the past two weeks. She gave it to me and I laughed.

"You're not serious?" I asked. "You're giving me *that* scarf? That's my present?"

THE CAR RIDE HOME was spent in a royal silence. I imagine even Steve felt trapped. As we got closer to our house, I finally confessed, "I thought you bought me a Shelby Cobra I saw on set today, for my birthday. It's stupid and I don't know what's happening to me. I'm just going nuts here in L.A. with nothing to do. You're so busy doing what you love and that's great. But I'm drowning. I thought you noticed and bought me that stupid car to say to me that you understand how hard it's been, and that you don't judge me for the ways I've failed. That you bought it for me to say you see the ways I've tried . . . And, in truth, I'm glad you didn't buy the car, 'cause it really is too much money, for Christ's sake. And, ultimately, I would be just as lost with the cool car—well, maybe not as lost, but you know . . ."

I tried to smile as the zooming L.A. freeway lit up our faces.

"What is a Shelby Cobra?" she asked.

———————

AS I WAS WALKING back down the empty backstage halls, my feet fell silently on the tile floor.

Mary was never coming to see my play. Why would she? I was the bad guy.

Then my imaginary wife, Lady Percy, stepped out of her dressing room. She was on her way to make tea before her between-shows nap. She always did that. On two-show days, she would use the downtime to sleep. Beauty needs rest more than food.

The actor who played Lady Percy was married to someone else, and this was the wrong moment to be left alone in an empty theater with her. I needed to clean my bandages and regroup. Her bare feet gently treaded over the tiles of the greenroom. I glanced and saw her dressed in only a white lace nightgown, with no bra, no underwear, and her back to me.

"Help me make some tea?" she spoke quietly. "Do you mind? I'd love to talk with you for a hot second." She poured steaming water over two jasmine tea bags into two teacups without ever turning around. Instantly, the hallway smelled like it belonged only to her.

Lady Percy was without a doubt the most elegant American actress I'd ever come across. She was like finely blown glass; that's what made her sexuality so particularly bewitching. I was almost afraid of her. She was a year older than me, and I imagined her most physically alluring years still lay ahead of her. There was nothing cheap or passing about her beauty. Her green eyes and bell-like voice were already the makings of a legend. Age was never going to touch her—at least it seemed that way. She had long, light red hair and her skin was paper white. I always felt timid in touching her. It was hard to imagine you were clean enough. In Act 2, scene 3, she wore a translucent gown as we rolled around a pile of hay like farm animals. Eight times a week we did this. The big trouble with actresses, Ezekiel would say, is that they are pretending to be women. I had to avoid Ms. Percy in an extremely delicate way. If I were ever too curt or too distant, it would affect our chemistry onstage. It just would; there was no way to avoid it. Also, truth be told, I admired her and wanted her respect. She had to feel I was avoiding her because I was too attracted to her, and too respectful of her real husband. That was the only way our onstage chemistry could work. It had to be clandestine.

"Are you brave enough to come into my room?" she said coyly and turned, looking at me, "or do you want to continue avoiding being alone with me?"

I knew the dangers of a dressing room. Boredom is a great aphrodisiac.

"I ain't scared of you," I said, affecting a little false swagger. I was in trouble; I could tell from her demeanor. I had been in the doghouse with Lady Percy since New Year's Eve. I had kept her at bay through these weeks and months of rehearsal and performing by flirting and insinuating that we would get together on New Year's Eve. So, by the time December 31 rolled around, she'd put a great deal of effort into arranging things so that we might fall into one another's arms unobserved by her husband, the cast, the hoi polloi, and the paparazzi. Her husband was an up-and-coming hotshot theater director from Montreal. He was taking their child to Canada for the holidays to visit his family, so she would be alone when the clocks struck midnight.

She arranged for the whole cast to be invited to a New Year's gala at the National Arts Club. It was a black-tie affair. She rented a van to pick us up at the stage door; that way everyone could change in their dressing room, and head straight to the party.

There were six bottles of chilled champagne in the van, plus she carried a purse full of ecstasy. A playlist was prepared for the ride downtown. Everything was perfect.

We arrived as a group and had a seriously great time. I wasn't doing any drugs, but I didn't tell her that. The tuxedos, the gowns, the Tiffany glass—all succeeded in transporting us to another time and place: a grander, more perfect New York City. When the New Year struck, Lady Percy winked at me and made a very public gesture of kissing one of her girlfriends, Shannon (an actress featured in the tavern scenes), romantically on the lips.

No one knew of the secret contract between us. We were to surreptitiously exit individually and then rendezvous back at the Mercury. That was our plan, but then out of my mouth, when I was speaking to about half the cast, popped "Hey, why don't we all come back to my place at the Mercury and play guitar, sing some songs, and hang?"

The gang erupted in unanimous approval: that was a grand idea.

She never came. In the splitting up to get into the various cabs, she disappeared. And just like that, I was in the doghouse with my real wife *and* my imaginary one. When I found myself alone with Lady Percy in the dark, candlelit, Chanel No.5–soaked dressing room, she said, "So what's going on with you? What's the matter that you have such a February face?"

I lifted my shirt and showed her my wound.

"Oh my God, William!" she shrieked. "What the hell?" She began rubbing her hand gently around my stomach and studying the wound. "Sit down and take your shirt off."

I did, explaining how I came to have an abdomen stained in blood.

"Lie down," she said softly, nodding as if she understood. "Let me clean you off."

She went into her little bathroom and I could hear her soaking a washcloth with warm water. I lay down on the soft single bed inside her dressing room. I was so tired.

"I know that I scare you, William, and that I came on too strong the other night and that I have been acting a fool ever since we started this run. I want you to know that I understand why you have avoided being alone with me." She was speaking from the bathroom. "And it makes me like you more." When I opened my eyes, I could see only the shadow of her face under her long strawberry hair.

"You're like a deer who runs away if someone comes on too directly. I get it, but I don't want anything from you. And someday, you'll have to learn how to let yourself be loved." She turned around and walked towards me.

I lay there silently as her white hands pressed the warm washcloth over my skin. It felt good. The muscles in my neck eased.

"I know you respect my husband"—which was true, I did. I had had enough exchanges with him to recognize that he was an intellectual heavyweight. "And that, too, makes me like you. I know you don't want to get involved with me. But we *are* involved, you know?" She lifted her wet washcloth and stepped back to the bathroom for more warm water. "I mean, we have been thrust into one another's path for a reason—and, believe me, we are not responsible for what is happening."

What's happening? I asked myself. I closed my eyes and decided that I must try to be stoic; I didn't want to get involved with this married woman. There were only three and a half weeks left to this run. We had another show in an hour and a half, for Christ's sake. I could make it.

"Don't fret, little deer, I'm not going to show up crying at your hotel door," she said from the bathroom. "I love my husband and I will never leave him, nor will I ever let him leave me. He cheats on me and sometimes I do wonder what that must be like." She walked back over to me but didn't immediately continue cleaning my skin. Instead, she held the warm wet cloth in one hand and caressed my hair with the other.

"When my husband and I fell in love it felt like we were one person. In every alley in Montreal, backstage, onstage, we tried to become one—if you know what I mean. And the passion we felt when I was pregnant is an unbreakable titanium bond. We are forever linked. But that doesn't mean rolling around in the hay with you eight times a week is without its challenges. I love my husband and I feel love for you. I watch you free from your marriage and wonder things, things I don't want to wonder. You can understand that, can't you?" she asked, slowly cleaning my belly again, her warmth slowly circling around my wound.

I closed my eyes like a cricket caught in a spider's web. What was coming felt unavoidable.

"I can feel how nervous you are—but see, I think sex is like a prayer. I do. We all understand in some animal way our interconnectedness to everything—that all life is somehow bound together. And sex can be our expression of that bond." She let the warm water drip on my belly. Then wiped me clean. "Yes, of course, it can be something else—something violent or something neurotic." Now she washed me some more, getting so damn close to the most tender area of my belly that I could barely breathe. "But at its finest, it's something healing."

She leaned over me and kissed my forehead. It was a chaste kiss; her lips were wet.

"I know you can feel it when we are onstage. It feels like we are safe underneath a mountain hiding from a storm, doesn't it?" She was whispering. She unbuttoned my pants to ease the pressure around my stomach and brought the washcloth dangerously lower and lower—away from the pain.

"And I know Shakespeare felt it too." She stood up one more time and walked back to the bathroom and rinsed the cloth again. I breathed again. She turned off the bathroom light so her dressing room was black except for the flicker of three small sandalwood candles.

I couldn't think of a damn thing to say or what possible excuse I could use to get out of this room.

"I don't understand when people say actors don't have a real job; that actors' lives are foolish or something . . ." I could feel her shape moving in the darkness near my feet but I could see nothing.

"No, the only true vocation for me is a complete and whole life-long dedication to the performing arts." She began to take off first one of my boots, then the other. My feet slid free.

Next, she grabbed a dry towel and laid it across my naked chest and belly, absorbing the wetness. "Truth?" she whispered. "A few weeks ago I got on my knees in this dressing room and prayed. I did. Prayed for us. I confessed I wanted to devour you. To be wholly devoured by you. And I heard, clearly, a voice ask, *Who will that be helping?* And it was obvious, in that moment, you do not need a lover. You need a friend. I don't need a lover; I have a husband. This feeling we share—this feeling is not love. It's like love, but it's called something else . . ."

I was out of my league and closed my eyes tight. She blew out one candle at a time. The smoky smell of sandalwood filled the room.

"Sex," she whispered. "Is our only healthy vice. Whatever source created me is the same one that created you. And while touching your hair like this"—and in the dark she did exactly as she described—"doesn't bring us necessarily closer to that divine source, it makes us feel not so alone and forsaken, you know?" She was leaning over me, looking at me in the dark. She rested her hand on my solar plexus. My chest lifted and fell. Her hand danced delicately and dangerously close to the red-hot pain that still cooked near my belly. Her lips came out of the darkness and she kissed me full on the mouth for the first time. Just for a moment.

"I know you were hurt when the kids applauded out there this afternoon. I know you were. But don't be so predictable. Go out there and be the bad guy. I like you bad." She ran her finger over my nose and lips.

"I just don't . . . ," I began, half-attempting an effort to talk. She put her hand over my mouth.

"Stop worrying. Let's pray," she said quietly from above me.

I could hear her breathing in the dark for a long time. She didn't move. When I woke up—she was gone. I felt rested for the first time in a dog's age.

ON MY DRESSING ROOM DOOR, the anonymous quotes continued. T. S. Eliot, on the theater, the hollow rumble of wings, the movement of darkness, and the stillness of light.

ONCE MORE with feeling. The evening performance that Wednesday began brilliantly. I was bent on proving to the King that seeing my shadow hadn't scared me. The rose was still in bloom. I was fully capable of playing this role even better than I had before. No good guy, no bad guy, just the truth.

Act 1, scene 3: My first scene with the King. I let 'em have the good stuff, unleashing the same blistering rage, but now with a sprinkle more "You old limp-pricked, saggy-necked motherfucker."

"My liege, I did deny NO prisoners!" I began.

He matched me.

Turning to his knights all around him, he gestured to me and said, *"Yet he doth deny his prisoners but with proviso and exception, that we at our own charge shall ransom straight his brother-in-law, the foolish Mortimer."* He gave a huge burly mocking laugh. *"Shall our coffers, then, be emptied to redeem a traitor home?"*

"Revolted Mortimer!" I asked incredulously. *"He never did fall off, my sovereign liege, but by the CHANCE OF WAR!"* This last bit I hammered home. Asshole.

At this exact moment, the King got up into my grille, as he often did, spraying Shakespeare's verse in my face. *"On the barren mountains, let him STARVE!"* The skin of my face almost peeled off as the old man showed me who had more gravitas.

"Thou dost belie him, Percy, thou dost belie him!" He cursed again. *"Art thou not ashamed? Send me your prisoners, or you shall hear in such a kind from me as will displease you!"*

On this particular night, he was sensing my thrill. I was proving to him that I had lost nothing, and now he, too, was giving it a little extra. His face was crimson, his temper flaring in his nostrils, his eyes purple. He continued, *"My blood hath been too cold and temperate! You tread upon my patience, but be sure I will from henceforth rather be myself."* The King paused for effect and then silenced the theater with the closing phrase, *"Mighty and to be fear'd!"*

The King's eyes rolled into the back of his head, his tongue began to hang too far out of his mouth like that of a dead cow, and then he fell. He fell the way a watermelon falls off the back of a truck—with a loud, broken smack. I stood above him, center stage, staring down at the off-kilter position of his body.

The audience didn't understand that this was not what was supposed to happen. So completely does an audience give themselves over to the reality of the stage that they could witness a man die right in front of them without so much as a wince. They all wore small, blissful smiles. There was a sea of humans in front of me. I looked at them and was stunned. They were loving it. They were perched extra-high in their seats.

I stood motionless, gut-struck. The rest of the cast—the whole ensemble of Act 1, scene 3, the King's Court scene, was standing twenty yards behind me, watching. Mutely I stared at the house for what felt like eternity. One audience member locked eyes with me. He was an Asian man in his forties, very handsome in a sleek suit. I said to him in an extremely muffled voice, as if a sock were over my mouth, "Is there a doctor in the house?"

No one heard me. I remember thinking, *Be careful, William! Don't freak out and blow your voice.* A man was dead at my feet— a friend, a mentor, a fucking saint-hero, a *king*! And instead of crying out for help, I quietly hummed to myself and looked blankly up into the lights, hoping the stage manager would do something. This is the moment I chose for prudence?

"IS THERE A DOCTOR IN THE HOUSE? WE HAVE AN ACTOR DOWN. I THINK HE'S HAVING A HEART ATTACK." Ezekiel stepped forward. And finally, like a dark spell being lifted by the strength of Ezekiel's voice, I too could speak.

"Turn on the houselights," I spoke up to the booth. *"IS THERE A DOCTOR IN THE HOUSE?"* I repeated. With two of us talking directly to them, the audience seemed to wake up from a dream.

The nicely dressed Asian man stepped up onto the stage apprehensively. "Let me see him," the man said softly. "I'm a doctor."

We walked over and looked down at Edward. The houselights came up and the stage manager's voice came over the loudspeaker. "LADIES AND GENTLEMEN, WE ARE TAKING A SHORT BREAK, PLEASE STEP OUTSIDE."

No one moved. It was obvious to me that Edward was dead. His whole color and everything about him was simply wrong. His chest was not moving. His gray tongue lay languid and released on the stage floor.

The prop guy, David, stepped up and started pounding on Edward's chest. I wanted to say, "Stop it! He's dead," but so many people were now crowding around the royal robes in which his body was wrapped that I let myself be pushed back. The ushers were trying to move the audience out the exits, but the crowd of more than a thousand stood listlessly, shifting in place. No one took their eyes off the stage, but the King had left the building.

If Wishes Were Horses

The darkness is not dark to you; the night is bright as the day, for darkness is as light.

—*Psalm 139:12*

My father had written me again and included this biblical quote as the subject heading. I knew it well. I had memorized it for my confirmation. In a strange act of need or anger, I wrote him back. If he was serious about helping me, I told him, I had the kids closing weekend, no babysitter, a four-hour Shakespeare play to do once on Friday, twice on Saturday, and then the closing performance on Sunday at three. If he wanted to come lend a hand, I'd appreciate it. I knew he wouldn't come.

He answered, "I can be there Friday before the show, and cover the two on Saturday, but I'll have to leave Sunday morning. Monday starts a big week for me at work."

And he did it. My father arrived from Houston with my two younger brothers, and they were all committed to the idea of giving me a hand. My fourteen- and twelve-year-old brothers took great care of the kids, while my dad and I felt each other out. We'd seen each other from time to time over the years; this was not our first attempt at reconciliation. He'd visited when the kids were born and on a handful of other occasions, but usually I had angrily demanded apologies or emotionally avoided him. Every encounter had begun with an expectation of healing and ended in an air of quiet disappointment.

"A wrong can be undone," my father, now fifty-one years old, said in his slight southern accent, "but it cannot just develop magically into something good."

We were walking down Sixth Avenue after my last two-show Saturday, and I was smoking a cigarette without even worrying what he thought. I hid my cigarettes from my children now, but not my parents. I had just finished telling my father how much I wished he had seen Edward play the King and not his understudy, and wished he could stay for when the King made his return for closing. Edward had died, but only for seven minutes. Closing night would be his first performance back. He had missed eighteen shows due to that heart attack. The EMTs made their way to center stage, blasted him with electricity, restarted his heart, and rushed him to the hospital, and that evening's performance was canceled. J.C. had been called in, but arrived too late. He sat in the empty wings of the stage softly crying, "Not now, Teddy, not now. The ride isn't over yet. Please not now."

"EVERYTHING DOES NOT always work out for the best. It's not 'all good,'" my father said. We were taking the puppy on her evening walk. It was about midnight but the lights of NYC were still bright and the sidewalks glittered in the taxi's headlights. Dirty Christmas and New Year's decorations still hung from some negligent storefronts.

"Time does not heal anything all by itself. Time can make you forget—but it doesn't right anything just by its passing. You have to go back to the source and heal the break."

My dad had just seen the play, and Shakespeare was making him philosophical.

When he was backstage after the show, he'd enjoyed all the actors in a goofy, fan-like fashion. I don't think he'd seen a play since the twelfth grade. He stood around in the hallways backstage, shaking hands politely and complimenting everyone in his gracious way. It was interesting to see how much respect everyone gave him. I had rarely seen him in relation to anyone but me.

He approached the King's understudy effusively, referencing certain lines: *Sons what things you are!* He turned, looking back at me. Ezekiel and he were fast friends. They ended up hugging when we left.

"Most folks I know in Houston spend all but a few days of their lives totally under this false spell that they are in control of their future. Society supports the delusion . . . But funnily enough, it is when we are wounded and vulnerable that our love gains its real power. Like Christ himself, you understand? Nailed up and bleeding like that."

He looked over at me as I was taking my final inhale of a cigarette. I didn't understand, but I could see that my dad was charming when speaking softly about his religious passion. My whole life, his faith was as real to him as his hands. Whenever he was comfortable, Jesus was all he talked about.

He continued, "The point of staring up and praying at a crucifix is that we don't need to fear being wounded: being wounded is the point of this life. I know it's hard to grasp, but by being wounded, your heart is just breaking open. Let it. That's what I say . . . Let your intellect or your will, whatever you want to call it—your personal agenda—be transformed into faith."

Most grown men I've known take on a posture, an affectation—

a mask of masculinity that becomes their face. It's a way they identify themselves to the world. My father has none. There is an innocence about him that is unaffected and disarming.

"And, remember, when I say 'faith'—it is not *faith* that God exists . . . Faith is simply a way of being completely open to the possible presence of *love*."

There is a bar about ten minutes from the Mercury that is always open late, and lets me bring my puppy inside. My father and I made our way through the doors. Two gay guys in leather jackets were making out heavy in the doorway, saliva wet on their beards. My father passed them by. On the bar in a basket there was some stale candy left over from Halloween.

My father was happy to be out of the cold. He is a Texan. His cheeks were flushed, and his eyes were bright behind his glasses.

We sidled up to the bar.

I introduced the bartender to my dad. They were cordial to one another for a moment while my dad ordered a beer. I had a whiskey and a ginger ale. The barkeep walked away and we moved over and sat at a table in the corner underneath a green dusty neon Budweiser sign.

"I know this is a long way around, but maybe just when you think things are going terribly wrong, something may really be 'righting' itself in you." He smiled a slow, gentle grin and took off his thick glasses. His eyes were instantly much smaller than usual.

This whole period of my life, I was like a burnt-out van, or something people always tried to fill up and fix. Everywhere I went people tried to take care of me—give me advice—put me back together. I always felt a little off balance listening—like I was waiting. Waiting to leave. Waiting for a cigarette. Waiting for someone else . . . In that moment at the bar I realized I'd been waiting for my dad.

"Then again, things may just be getting worse. There's no real way to be sure." He laughed.

I slugged back my whiskey and hailed another. There was a lull between us. Sports highlights continued playing on the two televisions in the corners of the bar. Our puppy licked the remains of French fries at our feet. My dad put his glasses back on and his eyes were large again. A man in his sixties was coming on to a much younger woman across the darkness of the bar over by the restrooms.

"It's freedom," he whispered, "that's the thing I'm talking about. Not freedom *from* anything. That's not important—what you want is freedom *for* something . . . or if you must, you want freedom from your own selfish will, *for* the love for others . . . for reality. I think for some reason we can't understand, it's important for life's most precious realities to remain hidden. Why's there a moon?" He smiled. "*I will speak to you in parables and reveal to you things hidden since the foundation of the world. Matthew* 13:35," he quoted.

The only thing my dad and I usually discussed at this length was the NFL, the Bible, or movies. We both had a great memory for certain football plays or lines from films. It was as if Shakespeare had prompted him, or maybe it was because I seemed so injured and weak that he felt safe to speak freely about anything without fear of a counterattack.

"My divorce from your mother nearly killed me," he said. "I was scared that I would lose you; that I would lose my ability to be with a woman, or to love anything . . ."

He reached out and lightly touched my arm. "See, God is trying, right now, I think, to free you, William, from the false idols you have made of yourself, your relationships, possessions, feelings, behaviors, work, even your own success—all of that. *Unless a grain of wheat falls into the earth and dies, it remains just a single grain.* John 12:24. Freedom is subtraction, you understand? I know you hurt from losing me, for example. And so did I ..."

Aha! I thought. *So here it is, the reason for this little talk.* My father was gearing up to get at his point:

"I don't own you—you're bigger than anything I could create," my dad said. "I couldn't love you right when you were a kid. I was in too much pain. I wasn't grown up. Your mother was extremely ... complicated," he said, carefully choosing a word that was without judgment, "and I failed you." He smiled simply in the dark of the Chelsea bar.

"But I think that, in many ways, you grew in magnificent ways because I couldn't love you properly. I know that might sound like I'm letting myself off the hook, but that's not what I mean. I mean ... I'm not off the hook, but you are. You understand? I've been 'around' a lot more with your brothers and, believe me, they will tell you, you didn't miss much, you know?" He laughed. "And, obviously, the credit of your success is to you. That does not mean that I don't feel shame—Oh boy, I do, and I am so sorry for the ways I've hurt you. For years, I have been trying to go back and find the source of the hurt between us. Where is the moment I need to go back to and heal? It's hard to find the exact place."

I sat, gobsmacked. I'd been waiting for a conversation like this for what felt like a hundred thousand years. Like a dry field hit with rain, I just absorbed everything.

"I don't pray for anything specific anymore ... ," he said, gaining momentum, "*I watch, and am as a sparrow alone on the housetop.* Psalm 102:7. I'm not praying for a healing between you and me; not forgiveness from you; not even for all our health; not for ... nothing. Because I sincerely realize that I don't know even what the right thing to pray for *is*. All I ever pray for is a depth of understanding in regards to love, that's it."

He took a breath. I knew he wanted me to say something, but I was stunned. When the silence became too much, he went on.

"I guess, William, I've been thinking a lot about heaven. What happens to us when we die. I thought a lot about it watching your show tonight. What will we all do in heaven?"

"I don't know, Dad, do you really think heaven is a place?"

"Of course. Where else will we *be* for eternity?"

The puppy found a chicken wing and I had to pull the damn thing from her mouth.

"I think about eternity. And then I think about when you called me when you were eighteen and asked me for money to go to theater school."

"I was seventeen."

"I know I wasn't supportive. And I'm sorry."

"It's OK. Made me work harder, that's all."

"It wasn't that I didn't believe in *you*. I didn't believe in acting, you know?"

"I know."

"But I really just didn't think you could make a living. But then watching all those actors tonight—how wonderful they all were . . . and I started thinking about how I've dedicated my life, the insurance business, ya know . . . It's funny—but there will be no need for insurance in heaven. None at all. And there will be so much need for poetry and songs and jokes. People will value what you've learned. It doesn't matter if you can make a living. Shakespeare will be important. You will be so valuable, William. And I will just sit there listening, realizing how I've misspent my life."

He smiled and we finished our drinks. The puppy was anxious, pulling at my feet.

"I guess maybe we should go," I whispered, "or else I'll have to get drunk."

We paid and started the walk back to the Mercury. I tried to understand who this man walking next to me was . . . He seemed almost like an actor I recognized from the movie of my childhood. Now the makeup was off and I was meeting the real man.

We stepped into the Mercury. Some junkie was sitting on a couch in the lobby, devouring a carton of ice cream. Two young men were bickering about the price of their room with Bart at the front desk.

"You need a hand?" I asked.

"Nope." He smiled.

My father and I were silent in the elevator, rising to the seventh floor.

Once out, we stepped through the shadows of the ancient hallway and found our door. I fumbled through my pockets looking for the key.

We brushed our teeth side by side for the first time in over twenty years.

"I love hotel towels, don't you?" he asked.

"Thanks for coming out and seeing the kids," I said, "and thanks for bringing my brothers, and thanks for coming to the show."

"Oh, Jeez, William. I think"—he looked so sweet and happy, and gestured over to my brothers sleeping on the couch—"this is the best day I've had in a long time. I'm probably going to cry myself to sleep." He laughed a hearty chuckle. "I hope that's OK."

"That's fine." I smiled. "I do it all the time."

We washed our faces, turned out the lights, and got into bed together. I hadn't slept in the same bed as my father in God knows how long.

"I just want to apologize for one more thing," my dad said out towards the darkness.

"For Christ's sake, Dad"—I laughed—"leave something for the morning."

"You remember your ninth birthday, when I drove out to Atlanta?" he asked.

I didn't say anything.

"Well, your mom called me the next day when I got home to Austin and she was really upset and she told me she would take me back. She invited me to move back in with you two. And I couldn't do it." I could hear his voice scratching in pain, beginning to sound like me. "I just couldn't do it. I didn't believe she was serious. I thought she'd hurt me again. And I was too . . . I don't know, fragile." He said the last word as if it were a curse. "I thought that if I tried again and it didn't work, I would break. Like I would die or something. And I'm sorry. I simply wasn't strong enough. I hated myself for a long time because of that weakness."

"Dad," I whispered, "it's not that you weren't strong enough. It's that you were smart. You can feel bad about missing aspects of my childhood if you feel like it, but you were never, never, never going to stay married to my mother. I promise, I know her a lot better than you do."

"I understand you believe that," he said in his emotional raspy voice, "but the truth is, you don't know the same woman that I do."

We were quiet again.

"I'm just glad you're here now, Dad. I really am so glad you came."

We lay next to each other under the sheets, a safe distance between us.

"I'm not saying the right thing to do would've been to run back to your mom," my father added quietly. "I'm just sorry I was afraid."

Adopting a British accent, he added, " 'Peachy, can you ever forgive me for being so bloody stupid and so bleedin' arrogant?' "

" 'Ahhh' "—I smiled with recognition—" 'that I can, and that I do.' "

CLOSING HAD ARRIVED. For some reason, I was suddenly so nervous all over again. I put my dad and my brothers in a taxi for the airport and then hustled off, kids in tow, to the 1 train.

As we were riding the subway uptown to the theater, my son turned to me and said, "Dad, I'm really worried about something." He was seated in my lap, still with his Star Wars pajamas under his overcoat and boots.

"Yeah, bud, what is it?"

"I think I have a drinking problem," he said.

"Really?" I asked.

"Yeah, I've been trying and trying but I just can't stop. I drink in the mornings, in the afternoons. I have way more than two drinks a day."

"What are you drinking?" I asked.

"You know, everything."

"Everything?"

"Orange juice, mostly."

"There's nothing wrong with that," I said.

"There isn't?"

"No."

"On TV, they said if you have more than two drinks a day, you have a problem. And I have way more than that, Dad, I really do."

"They're talking about alcohol." I laughed.

"Oh," he said, pausing for a moment. "What's that?"

"Like beer and wine, stuff like that. Champagne. You can have as much juice and water as you want."

He hugged me. I hugged him back. His sister leaned over next to us wondering what was wrong. We just smiled and hugged her, too.

I wished all my problems could be like that, some giant misunderstanding.

When we arrived at the theater with fully charged iPads, stuffed animals, and colored pencils, the last quote was on the dressing room door. It was a Dostoyevsky quote about the joys of breaking things.

I pulled the small paper off, brought it inside, and taped it to the mirror with all the others. There were a shit ton by now. This secret admirer of mine had left close to thirty of these kinds of quotes. I still had no idea who it was; neither Ezekiel nor I had ever seen anyone loitering suspiciously. They were clearly for me, as each was taped to the door with masking tape marked in black ink "To W—"

For a while, I thought it was Lady Percy who had left the notes, but I confronted her and it wasn't her. Then I thought it was King Edward, but they continued to arrive even when he was in the hospital. Then I got worried that maybe they were from my understudy, Scotty, but the penmanship didn't seem to fit.

The stage manager welcomed Edward back over the intercom.

For more than two weeks we'd done the show without our King. His understudy was quite capable. In several scenes, we missed Edward—but in others it was possible to say the understudy played the role a little better. There was no denying that the understudy was funnier. He got a lot of laughs that Edward had let go. Edward was the greatest, wisest actor I had ever worked with—and in some ways, the show was better without him. I just couldn't wrap my mind around the idea. With Edward, the show had more depth, more sensitivity, more sadness; but with Jerome, the show ran six minutes faster, was unquestionably angrier and more humorous. We got standing ovations on all eighteen shows Edward missed. It was as if nothing had changed. I preferred *Henry IV* with Edward, but I know many audience members considered themselves lucky to have caught the show with this "undiscovered gem." All this worked to unravel me. For if Edward was replaceable . . .

A few days after the heart attack, the stage manager told me King Edward had asked to see me. When I went to him in the hospital, he welcomed me immediately.

"Well, now my tutelage is complete," he announced as I stepped into the white antiseptic room.

"What do you mean?"

"I taught you to say the most famous line in the theater!" he said.

I looked at him blankly.

"Is there a doctor in the house! Now you're prepared for anything." He laughed. "Yes, I'm back from the dead, for a moment or two."

The space of his hospital room was constant and even, and the air was perfectly still, just like his dressing room.

"Well, thank you," I said.

"Your voice sounds terrible."

"What am I going to do about it?" I scratched out to him. "It's just been getting worse and worse."

"First, you have to stop talking so much." He gestured that I should sit down.

"I get so scared I'm going to miss a show," I whispered. "Even now I wake up in the morning and the first thing I think is what if I lose my voice and won't be able to do the last show with you."

He stared at me blankly.

"Are you familiar with the violinist Michael Rabin?" the King asked.

I shook my head no.

"He developed a peculiar phobia of performing. He worried that he would drop his bow. He worried so much that he would drop his bow that he almost could think of nothing else. Constantly drying his hands before each show, he began to be distracted and lose his focus. Nervously obsessing about the temperature in whatever hall he was playing in, he became difficult to work with . . ." The King paused and looked me up and down. "He couldn't enjoy his playing anymore. All he could think about was what would happen if he dropped his bow. He imagined the audience would gasp in horror. People would see he was not as in control as he had presented himself . . . they might ridicule him with laughter. The critics would call him an amateur. If he let it slip and fall, would he even be able to go on? He couldn't see past the fear of it. His tour progressed and his hands began to sweat more and more profusely. The bow began to be uneasy in his grip like it never had before. He would wake up each morning before a concert in an absolute crisis of anxiety. So, one performance, at the finest hall in Vienna, he told his accompanying musicians that he was going to deliberately drop his bow after a certain section was played. He would let it fall and pick it up and they would start again. On their sheets, they all marked the spot. He did it. He dropped it. The audience gasped. He picked up his bow and played on . . . And everything was fine. Some even wrote that it was his finest concert. Do you understand? None of them even mentioned the dropped bow."

I shook my head; I did not understand.

"You are so scared of losing your voice that every night you go out there and try to blow it. Your phobia is creating the reality."

He leaned forward and whispered in his ancient silky voice, "There is nothing to be afraid of. If you miss a show the world will recover . . . and so will you. You are letting your fear win. You are not essential to this production. Neither am I. Neither is Virgil. At our best we are contributing significantly but none of us alone are essential. I have seen the understudy rehearsals. Scotty in particular is excellent."

He took a sip of Gatorade. "He's not you. But he is a very good Hotspur. Would you like some?" he asked, gesturing to the pitcher of red Gatorade.

I nodded.

"What's it been like?" I asked. It felt like I was visiting the dead and getting to ask the only real question.

"What do you mean? Missing shows?"

I nodded and took a sip. The liquid soothed the tattered corners of my throat.

"Drop the bow, and next time take a show or two off."

He looked at me and knew how hard that would be for me to ever do.

"You can't be present at your destination, if you are not present while you're traveling. You understand?" The King smiled. "Fear is the problem, not your voice."

I nodded although I did not understand. Then I asked as quietly as possible, "Fear of what?"

"I can't be sure; you probably fear that you are not as strong as you would like us all to believe." He smirked. "But guess what? We already know."

I sat unmoving.

"I always imagine myself as an eagle," the King continued. "Sounds silly, but I don't picture eagles beating themselves up, you know? I try not to twist the present into something it is not. Accept it on its own irrefutable terms."

He smiled at me.

"Don't be deceived, nothing else is as exciting as what *is*. The next moment is not greater than the present one. This one right now. All the moments of our life are indestructible. You understand? 'To be or not to be' is not whether to kill yourself or not—it's asking the question, Are you going to be awake and present for your life? Can you see that today is not a bridge to anywhere else?"

We sat as the King just looked at me. The hospital was noisy with phones ringing, wheelchairs squeaking by, announcements through the intercom.

"This is why, for me, acting in the theater is such a noble profession. In the attempt to be present onstage we have the opportunity to cultivate our ability to be present in life. Be free of all the illusions and distractions and live in the lucid present. Our lives are composed of the moment-to-moment struggles to be present. We grow in proportion to our ability to live in a true reality. The stage is our platform to develop."

I smiled.

"I know you feel your heart is breaking, you've lost your voice, your wife, your family, and you feel you can't handle it. But don't worry, our hearts are so resilient. I've had two heart attacks. My heart has been smashed to pieces and yet here I am." He smiled and tried to feel his own pulse. "As our playwright reminds us, 'Live and love thy misery!'"

He asked me to run lines with him, and we did for over an hour. I had strict orders to go back to the theater and let everyone know that he was not brain damaged and that he was capable of finishing the run. He was only going to return for the final show—he wanted to let Jerome go on as much as possible so that people stopped "feeling happy for him and started missing me."

"Never let your understudy go on for only one show. If you miss one, you must miss at least three," he told me from his hospital bed. "The first performance, every understudy is 'brilliant.' They are running on pure adrenaline—and everyone is so grateful the alternate didn't completely blow it. No, you must let them burn out and become ordinary—then you return to reclaim your role."

We split some more Gatorade. He asked me how my marriage was sorting itself out.

"Ya know, OK," I answered. "I don't know why but I'm still kind of hopeful that somehow all this might work out for the best."

"Well, you know what I say to that?" Edward laughed. "If wishes were horses, beggars would ride." He burst out laughing.

"If I hadn't lost James," he continued, "my life would be unblemished. I've had two divorces, but ultimately those relationships don't haunt me . . ." A darkness moved through his body. "James. That's a mess." He took a sip of the bright red drink from his white Styrofoam cup, wiped his chin, and kept his eyes looking straight out the twelfth-story window of Lenox Hill Hospital.

He told me James, his only son, had committed suicide at the age of twenty-three. Maybe he was manic-depressive. Maybe he was gay and scared to come out. Maybe Edward had been away too much. He didn't know the answer.

"I swore to myself when he died," Edward added, "I would not let this tragedy define me. And I'm proud of that. I've moved on. I picked up my feet. I'm not saying I don't miss him. I'm not saying I don't shoulder a good part of the blame and carry it around with me daily, but I console myself with the fact that there are certainly worse fathers than me. There have been terrible fathers who didn't have a son commit suicide."

An orderly came in to check his vitals. The King paid no attention as his blood pressure and IV were all noted.

"I should have cared for James better than I did—that's true, but I can't do anything about that now. Except try to tell you that the decisions we make matter." He turned and looked straight at me, his blue eyes deadly clear in the hospital light.

"Every decision matters. Sometimes time slips by and pages of the calendar just rip off and you can trick yourself into thinking that none of the minutiae, the business of each day, is of any real consequence . . . or that it's all predetermined. It's not. Our actions are the ground we walk on. If you practice Hamlet's speech to the players, if you practice that speech a lot—when the time comes, you'll deliver that speech well. If you don't practice—you will not. Luck is the residue of design. A man makes being there for his son a priority—chances are good that boy'll turn out safe. You understand me?" He looked at me head-on, the white hospital light hitting his age-spotted face directly. "What I'm saying is, being in a healthy marriage takes two. Being a good father . . . all that takes is you."

WE WERE CALLED to stage early that final Sunday, half an hour before fight call, to walk through the King's more intricate scenes and make sure Edward was comfortable with the blocking. He remembered it all effortlessly and joked through the whole affair. But before he went on for that final performance, I could see he was shaking. He was drinking tea with lemon and sucking on lozenges. His fragility made me love him even more. When he first stepped onstage, his voice was wobbly in a delicate, almost broken, teenage way—then he fell into stride and hit the text as robustly as he always had. By the end, he was magnificent.

I remembered why I liked his performance so much—he made all of us better. He wasn't funny the way Jerome was funny—he was the King and let us get the silly jokes. Laughs that I thought were mine, I now realized were ours. The audience was not laughing at my expert delivery, but more at his sideways glance reaction. The entire eighteen performances that he had been gone, I did not get my exit applause at the end of our first scene—I couldn't figure out why. Then, upon his return, the spontaneous round when

Hotspur left the stage happened again. I'm still not sure how he got that for me.

THE LAST SHOW, for me, began in poor form. At fight call, after keeping my temper cool for six months—I lost it. The fight call for Henry IV was long and involved. For a three o'clock matinee, fight call was 2:00 p.m. I never missed one. Lots of guys got casual about it, but I never did, and Prince Hal never did either. Of course, Edward never missed except when he was in the hospital. But Falstaff came only one time, the last. His understudy had walked through fight call for him every performance, and his deliberate absence made me apoplectic. He didn't give a tinker's damn about the company.

On the last day, he showed up in only his jockstrap, leather boots, sword belt, and a Santa hat. Everyone erupted in cascades of friendly, jocular laughter. He looked deliberately preposterous with his giant Santa Claus beard, roly-poly belly, and hairy legs.

"I'm ready for fight call," he announced, swinging his sword around dangerously from his groin. And I broke.

"Listen, motherfucker," I started out, "I don't care if you think you're such a monster-great actor that you don't ever once have to practice with the rest of us—but don't mock us. We all found the time to come here eight shows a week. We are the reason nobody got hurt on this show."

I held up my knife. "Every night, I thought about sticking this blade right through your fat gut just so I could say, 'Sorry, old man, if you'd come to fight call *once* . . . maybe this could have been avoided.'"

Nobody moved. I was sweating.

"You're a fucking leech sucking off our professionalism." I was proud of that line. I said it to myself a million times.

"I don't care that you have made no effort to be friends with any of us. I realize you think God loves you best, but guess what? *I DON'T LOVE YOU BEST. I THINK YOU ARE A SELF-CENTERED BLOWHARD.* I think you're a ham and that you take too many pauses, and have no idea how to work *with* another human being—and frankly, I think you are the worst kind of actor. One who makes others worse."

The entire theater was quiet as a mouse.

Then Virgil very sheepishly said, "I feel like you're mad at me?"

And the whole ensemble burst out laughing again. I dropped my sword and missed my first fight call.

I went back to my dressing room and tried to cool down. My kids were in the wardrobe room. The ladies in there were gracious and let my kids goof around, organizing buttons and playing with the sewing machines. Why had I blown up like that? I didn't understand myself. I tried to be still. Why was I so mad at Virgil? A lot of it had to do with a stupid article in the *Times* about what a genius he was. He was on the cover of the Arts section again for closing night and they cited his performance as Falstaff as one of the greatest of the century. It made us all feel a little worthless.

Ezekiel walked in. He gave me an avuncular pat on the shoulder. In a few more minutes, I thought, I would calm down and apologize. But before I could quiet myself, there was a knock at our door. It was Virgil. He peeked his head in and said with a twinkle, "Are you still a grouchy bear?"

"Get the fuck outta here," I yelled. "You don't make me laugh."

He shut the door. Then from the hallway, he delivered a rousing version of Mercutio's "Queen Mab" speech.

> *O, then, I see Queen Mab hath been with you.*
> *She is the fairies' midwife, and she comes*

In shape no bigger than an agate-stone,
On the fore-finger of an alderman . . .

He went on and on, running up and down the halls. When he was finished, the entire backstage area filled with applause. Such was life with Virgil Smith. Ezekiel just looked at me and shrugged. Finally, I laughed.

"You know what he's doing every night when we're at fight call? He's warming up his voice like a madman. Think about it, killer. Let's not waste time being jealous of him. Let's learn something. It's possible that if you spent a little more time taking care of your voice, and less time trying to be everyone's buddy, you'd stop clicking your throat like a lunatic and then someday you could have a private dressing room, just like Falstaff."

"I like having a roommate," I said.

"I'm just saying, think about it."

ON THE MIRROR, next to all my anonymous quotes and the opening night card from my mother, there was a letter from J.C. It'd come in the middle of the run. I read it before every performance.

To my tabloid sensation Hotspur,

I know you're learning. Keep doing it. It's obvious you get sleepy every time I mention the Iambic, but the fundamental principle of the iambic pentameter is best expressed in the opening bar of Beethoven's Fifth—which is not in four beats as generally supposed, but in two sets of two beats starting with a rest. This creates the five-beat line, which is, simply put, the perfect length to be spoken in one breath. I don't know why. It just is. Listen to Beethoven's Fifth before every performance.

Music is constructed in notes. Language in words. Both are communicating. Music is a language of feeling, the heart. Words are the music of the mind. Theater is their marriage. That's our job, to make ideas and experience *feel* like music. A reader can see a question mark: "?" The audience must hear the question mark. Words like "and," "what," "but," "or," "if" are essential. Nothing is to be thrown away. There is a world of difference between ". . . ff t'were done, when tis done." And, "*if* it t'were done . . ."

When we hear the *if*—we know we are dealing with the concept of choice.

Shakespeare could do anything with words. You are not more intelligent than he—so don't try to fix his writing. Try to understand it. If the language is clumsy or contradictory—consider why? Every word was deliberately chosen. Trust me.

There are no accidents. Every *t* and *d* is essential. Each vowel has a different feeling. Verse or prose? Never a whimsical decision. Consider the climax of *Hamlet,* not acrobatic verse but humble prose—

"We defy augury.

"There is special providence in the fall of a sparrow. If it be now, 'tis not to come, if it be not to come, it will be *now*. If it be not now, yet it *will* come, the readiness is all. Let be."

Have a great run,

J.C.

I loved the letter. Everything but the bit about the *t*'s and *d*'s.

CLOSING NIGHT, as we prepared, Zeke offered up some more of his dime-store philosophy, "Chicks make you feel like—especially as a black dude, let me tell you—chicks make you feel like if you don't give 'em the best lay of their life, that you are somehow less of a man. Then they also act, simultaneously, as though if you take your cocksmanship to some other lady, that you have somehow failed your better, higher self. They always want it both ways"—he exhaled, as if it was difficult to hold all the world's most important knowledge in his head alone—"if you let them hold the reins of your life, you wind up in the mud."

I was putting on my scars as always.

"And if you listen to popular culture or society," Ezekiel continued regally from his dressing room chair, "they are all talking about how great one kind of man is—what kind? The rich kind. That's a woman's voice right there. They want their men obsessed with wealth. That way we don't notice we're stuck in a gerbil cage spinning the wheel to keep the lights on—ya know? Yet we all know that most of the rich people we see are miserable, right?"

"I hate to give you the news, but I think a lot of rich people are actually pretty happy, buddy," I said, out of breath on the ground starting my preshow push-ups.

Zeke leaned over me. "That creep who was the lead of the unmentionable TV show I was on for those years," he continued, not worried at all about the closing performance, "well, that Archie Bunker mo-fo was a sad, sick prick. Was he richer than God? Fuck yeah. But he was miserable as a dead spider."

"FIVE MINUTES," the stage manager announced over the monitor.

I finished my push-ups, stood, and let the blood in my body settle. When we began this run, Ezekiel and I hardly spoke before each show. Now we chatted like old biddies in a hair salon.

"I'm confused," I said. "Are women the problem or is money?"

"Wait till you hit forty, smarty-pants. You'll see"—he continued with a sigh—"life's not a straight trajectory, slowly ascending, where you gain in knowledge and talent little by little until you arrive at some Buddha-like enlightenment. It's a fuckin' morass—it's a slog. Fighting all the way. Sometimes up, sometimes down, sometimes twisting in place." Ezekiel sat back down, completely placid, casually sipping his tea, looking at himself in the mirror and talking nonstop.

"What I'm saying is, there's this thing out there that nobody wants to say—which is that the goddamn womenfolk are so good at running things they're even able to hide the fact they're running the show. The sadist controls the masochist, ya know?"

Putting on my costume for the last time, I asked, "So who's the sadist and the masochist with my wife and me? We both seem to think we are the one getting hurt."

"Neither one of you are victims!" Ezekiel's voice lifted now that I was engaging him. "You know what you have to do? This is the big trick—listen to me now, 'cause this is some real shit—the straight dope—I'm not joking around now. You must use your heart as a spear. You actually have to fight with your tenderness, your perceived weaknesses, your vulnerability, with love, with warmth. That's the trick: There's no trick. Be completely open and absorb the world's contradictions—like for example, the best thing that ever happened to me was being born a black male in America and the worst thing that ever happened to me was being born a black male in America. Those are both true statements. Absorb the contradiction with an open, loving, tender heart. Do you understand?"

My son and daughter entered the room and I barely had enough time to set up the iPad and plug in some headphones for them before I went out for my last show.

BEFORE THE FINAL PERFORMANCE, I did the same thing I had done each of the previous eighty-two shows. I stood behind the stage left black scrims and stared out at the audience, looking for my wife.

My mad hopefulness was part of my illness. My outlook was so consistently off kilter, like when you are smashed by an ocean wave and don't know which direction to find the sky and wind up lifting your head into the sandy bottom of the sea. I believed that if Mary came to the show, I could do it—I could give our marriage one more try. I felt near certain that our union was doomed to painful failure—but *still:* I did not want to get divorced. I missed my kids badly when they were gone and could not shake the feeling that my balance had been permanently injured. It seemed the fluid in my inner ears was not level and that the separation from Mary was the cause. I felt sure she would come to the play, see how hard I was working, see that I was a part of something of worth, and remember the man she fell in love with—though I hardly resembled him. From the wings, I searched the twelve hundred faces in the house—looked at every pair of eyes. She wasn't there.

Not yet.

There were two empty seats right front and center—and if she were to come, she would certainly have great seats and be late—so maybe. The facts were lining up against me, however. I just kept hoping I was wrong, like maybe the earth could spin in a different direction, or dogs could talk, or flowers could bloom in a blizzard; anything so that the discomfort of a long drawn-out divorce could be dodged. Starting over seems so impossible when you don't know how far back you need to travel.

THE LAST PERFORMANCE of *Henry IV* went by like a pack of ravenous coyotes chasing a jackrabbit. Fast. Daily exchanges that had seemed ordinary became full of power because you knew that you would never be able to perform this simple action again. Scurrying through the ropes and curtains across the back shadows of the stage, rushing to make an entrance on time, picking up our weapons together from the giant barrels—all the mundane aspects of our performance, the tiny beats that held up the flashy ones. They were where it felt possible to touch and hold the magic; just for a second.

After the King spurns me, and leaves the stage, I turn to my uncle and say:

> *He said he would not ransom Mortimer,*
> *Forbade my tongue to speak of Mortimer,*
> *But I will find him when he lies asleep,*
> *And whisper in his ear: MORTIMER!*

That always got a big laugh. I'd never get that laugh again. I'd worked hard on the timing of that joke, but now it was gone. I wondered how long it would be before I couldn't even remember the lines.

Lady Percy and I had so much fun with one another onstage. There was trust in our eyes. I was finally comfortable touching her body, and letting her touch me. In front of all these people, she allowed me the confidence to gently cup her bottom as I exited and said,

> *Come, wilt thou see me ride?*
> *And when I am on horseback,*
> *I will swear I love thee infinitely*

She grabbed my package with one hand and then blew me a kiss with the other.

Why is it so easy to tell someone you love them when you are leaving?

After Hotspur died and I had my cigarette and ice cream sandwich, I went and found my kids and gave them each an ice cream. My daughter was getting her hair braided in the makeup room and my son was slaying video–game dragons with Big Sam and the guys in the boys' company dressing room. I decided to sneak out into the back of the house and watch the final act. I stood in the shadows behind the audience and watched Virgil play the "Chimes at Midnight" scene.

The lighting was a morning blue somewhere between dog and wolf. It made my eyes well up with tears. The set was exquisite in its minimalism. There was no set. Somehow, the way it was built lifted your eye into the actor. It was as if there was nothing else in the world but Virgil Smith and his friend, grave Master Shallow.

"We have heard the chimes at midnight, Master Shallow," Falstaff said.

"That we have . . . That we have . . ."

The iambic rhythm was as natural to Virgil's language as the tick is for a clock, inexorably marking the present and discarding the past; or like the beating of a heart, because it gave energy. He controlled the pace inside my chest, he had his hands on the heart of everyone in the auditorium.

Watching Virgil Smith playing Falstaff on the last night of our production was like watching one of legend's great rock concerts; the time Jimi Hendrix surprised everyone and played a set in the rain for only two hundred people at a park in St. Louis . . . only more sorrowful, more funny, and more magnificent. Simply put, the writing was better. It was healthy and intoxicating, like red wine with Thanksgiving dinner, like St. Joan leading you into battle, a walk-off home run; it felt good like that.

But watching Virgil had a melancholy sting to it as well. Jealousy always spun threateningly close. It was hard to reckon with just how much better he was than the rest of us: *Why him, Lord?*

At my final curtain call, as I bowed for the last time, I saw the two seats where I had hoped my wife would have sat, still empty. My wife was never going to see the show. It was over. I don't know why I ever thought she would come. She probably didn't show up for the same reason I couldn't ever reach out to her. We both were letting go. We had loved each other madly, like many other young lovers. We wrote poetry. We looked at the stars. We held each other all night long without sleeping. We watched a baby grow in her belly and were so transfixed by the magic, power, and pulse of the universe calling this child into the world that we immediately did it again. And then just like another parallel line of lovers squabbling and bickering, daily life had now given us gripes and grievances that we couldn't walk around. *Why didn't you do this for me? How could you? You promised! I thought things would be different! I tried! NO, you didn't! You lied!* I was beginning to feel about my marriage just as I was feeling about the play: some of it was elegiac, some of it was torture, I was glad I did it, and I was glad it was over. I couldn't understand how all those things could be true simultaneously, but they were.

After the final bows, there was lots of hugging and shouting in the hallways backstage. Champagne corks were being popped. Costumes were being tossed. I walked into my dressing room and both my children were on the floor watching *Annie* on my daughter's little iPad. She looked up from the film with tears in her eyes. Taking off her headphones, she jumped into my arms.

"What is it?" I asked, holding her sweet little frame.

"Oh, Dadda, I just want to be inside that song."

"What song, honey? What do you mean?"

"That song Annie sings about missing her mommy and daddy. I want to be inside that song." She squeezed me as hard as she could.

"What do you mean?" I asked, holding her up and considering her wet blue eyes.

"I don't know. Don't you ever feel that way—that you love a song so much you want to be inside it?" She looked at me imploringly.

"Yes, I do," I said, "I know exactly what you mean. And there is a way," I added conspiratorially. "If you still want to when you're older—I'll show you how."

I leaned down to kiss my son.

He looked up and said, "Is it over?"

"Yeah, all done," I said.

"Can I play with your sword?"

Before we went home I took my kids out into the now empty theater to have one last look at the set. I couldn't believe it. It wasn't yet an hour since the play had closed and already there was a crew of construction workers ripping up the floorboards. The back doors to the stage were open and cold air was drifting in, along with a smattering of snow flurries. Somebody in the costume department had given my kids blue and green glow sticks, and they were running through the empty aisles laughing and swinging the neon light sticks. Hammers, snow, people partying in the lobby shouting and drinking, children laughing—it was all almost too much to take in.

Ezekiel was sitting in the middle of the empty theater and called me over. I sat next to him.

"Hurts, don't it." He smiled.

I nodded.

The workers were now rather violently tearing apart the wooden slab that held my artillery wagon, where every night for months I would step up, spin my swords, and shout Hotspur's anthem, *"DIE ALL, DIE MERRILY!"*

It was done. Never again. There was literally the sweat of thirty-nine actors spread over that stage, every piece of wood was scratched up with someone's mark, and it was all headed for a dumpster. Our names would be ripped from the seams of our costumes, which would be sent back to the shop to dress some other actor at some later date.

I BROUGHT my small people home to the Mercury Hotel. We sat in the back of the cab, my son on my lap and my daughter still playing with her fading glow stick.

My son stared at his fingers and said, "Do you ever notice that your thumbprint looks a lot like the rings on the inside of a tree?"

"No, the inside of a tree looks like the tracks of planets going around the sun," my daughter corrected.

"No, the inside of your eyeball looks like stars and galaxies and stuff, not trees."

"Supernovas look like jellyfish," she noted.

"That's true, but they also look like eyeballs."

"Sometimes, your heart and veins and stuff, when it's not inside your body, looks like a jellyfish."

"Dad, do you think we all have a jellyfish inside of us?" my son asked.

"Or a supernova?" my daughter pressed.

Looking at them both, I said, "What happened to 'Why is the sky blue?'"

I paid the fare and stepped out in front of the Mercury. It was now a full-blown snowstorm. My son turned his face up towards the falling snow and let the giant fat flakes fall into his mouth. Then, once inside the heat of the lobby, with his face all flushed and his cheeks red, he said, sighing, "Snow would be perfect, if only it was warm."

I put the kids to bed. My voice felt assured reading to them that night and they fell asleep quickly. Once they were down, I paid one of the hotel cleaning ladies a handful of cash to sit in my living room and watch TV until I got back from the cast party. She was a cool old lady. The kids liked her and often sold strawberry lemonade in the lobby with her help. She had my phone number, so I wasn't concerned.

In the cab to the bar, I checked my messages and, to my surprise, there was one from J.C. He said he was in New York but wasn't coming to the party; he didn't like drunk people, and he didn't like the fact that when things went well, as they had with our production, people tended to think the director was responsible for how it all evolved. He wanted to thank me for not missing a show. He told me that in the six times he'd directed the play, he'd never had a Hotspur make it all the way through.

"Lastly," he said, "I will never cast you again until you quit smoking. If you look at the history of artists, self-sabotage is more responsible for the collapse of our dreams than the whips and scorns of time. So, get to work, take care of yourself, and good night." He hung up.

I sat in the quiet of the cab and considered J.C.'s message. It was important to him that I hadn't missed a show. I compared his words with King Edward's advice about letting things go and being willing to see yourself as replaceable. I wondered who was right. What would they say to each other?

The party was somehow dismal. The show was over and there was nothing to talk about. All the guys were hammered except for Big Sam, and everyone just sloppily told each other they loved one another. Bumping my way through all the drunken people at the old Broadway hangout Joe Allen's, I tried to avoid Lady Percy, because she was with her husband and I didn't want any strange goodbyes. It was not a problem; she was avoiding me. I was looking for Virgil because I wanted to tell him what a goddamn revelation he was—as well as apologize for my earlier outburst. He wasn't there and I swelled with anger all over again. Why couldn't he just show up and be a regular guy—just once?

Zeke said wisely, "Dude, he's not a regular guy—why should he pretend?"

Then, standing in front of me was an actress I didn't know well. She was one of the "tavern girls" and played largely only in those scenes, but I didn't share any stage time with her and hadn't had much contact with her throughout the run. Act 3, scene 1, opened with her naked, looking at herself in the mirror while Falstaff talks and tries to find his pecker. It was a good scene, and she was brave and funny in it. But truth be told, she had a sketchy, dangerous vibe. Now she stood drunk in front of me and slid a note into my hand.

Immediately, I could tell from the handwriting and by the expression on the young woman's face that she had been my secret admirer.

"Somebody gives you secret notes every day and you're not even curious who they are?" she asked contemptuously. Her eyes exposed heartbreak, not by me, but by the finality of closing night.

I started to give a lame answer, but she cut me off.

"Somebody thinks about you, sees that you're in pain, reaches out, but you don't even want to say thank you—or notice them?"

"Thank you," I offered.

"I guess you're just used to everyone noticing you."

"I loved the quotes you gave me," I said sincerely. "I loved every one of them."

"Well, fuck you," she said, snarling. People began to turn and stare. "I worked so hard and I really cared about this show and about you. I was worried sick about you. You were so thin and sad. And you don't even know my name, do you?"

There was an awkward silence. Then, praise Jesus, without a thought it came out of my mouth: "Shannon. Shannon McQuarrie. You are great in the tavern scenes."

"I *was* great, past tense." She turned and spoke to the people staring at us. "And now we're all just supposed to walk away, forget everything, and be polite. But I don't want to be polite. I don't want to forget. And J.C. can't even show up? Virgil, I didn't expect—that fat fuck. But I got naked for you all every night. We went through something together— And I don't want to pretend we didn't. I'm going to miss this show; I'm going to miss it badly"—she turned back to me—"but I hate you for being so fucking cavalier. I guess you're off to some other job, got a film to shoot in Timbuktu or something? I don't have another job and I'm going to wake up tomorrow and want to talk to everyone . . ." She started huffing back her sobs. "I just hate this fucking show. And I hate you . . ."

"It's just a dumb play," Big Sam offered.

"It's better than my dumb life."

She burst into tears and hit Big Sam on the chest. He grabbed her gently and several of her friends held her and told her to calm down.

"I DON'T WANT TO CALM DOWN!" she screamed and ran to the back of the bar towards the bathrooms. Big Sam chased her the whole way. In the confusion, I slipped out into the snow still holding her final slip of paper.

Shannon McQuarrie
28 Scott Ave.
Grovers Mill, New Jersey
08550
(It's my parents' house—but they will live there forever.
Please stay in touch.)

I wished I would write her, but knew I wouldn't. Planning on having a smoke and going back in, I felt the cold on my face, and I realized it was over. I wanted to say goodbye to Big Sam, and Zeke, but didn't. Looking down at the snowy sidewalk and then up at the whirling lights of the yellow taxis moving all around me, I took one step, then another.

Back at the Mercury, I went upstairs and let the cleaning lady go. The kids were fast asleep but the puppy still needed to pee, so I risked one quick stroll in the snow. Still buzzy from the drinks, I hummed to myself and checked my voice for what might have been the last time. I'd made it. My nervous tic was leaving me as mysteriously as it arrived. When I looked up, the falling snow seemed to be dropping like stars in a meteor shower. The ice was hitting the sparkling sidewalk and the whole universe around me shimmered in prayer. Wind numbed my cheeks. I felt like I was walking through outer space. Either that, or I was strolling along the bottom of the cold ocean, where every sound is muted and safe.

Memories of other winters and previous snowstorms seemed to sift together. I could see my future as a divorcé. Angry, uncomfortable parent-teacher conferences; trading the kids at airports on Thanksgiving; being seated at different tables at my son's wedding—I could see it all lined up in my future. I could even intuit that I would fall in love again and how someday I would be happy. I walked through this storm. For a second, I could see my whole life, what was left of it, ahead of me. And it was not going to be all that much different than the days behind.

All these last months, as my marriage collapsed, I'd believed that if I loved my wife, I would need to stay with her. But walking in the lightness of the new snow, I could tell that I did love her and I was going to leave her. She was a woman unlike any other. I was smart to have let myself commit to her and to have had these children. They were wonderful and I was lucky to be their father.

It was also obvious, however, that being married had for some reason tangled me up, and I needed to straighten out. There was no real choice involved. I had taken such pride in my marriage, in our love, like a peacock strutting around, thinking he was responsible for his feathers.

I looked around me and absorbed the peace of a sprawling bustling city stopped dead, socked in snow. My puppy jumped and barked, twisting and sliding. I was instantly wildly grateful just to be awake and witness all this stillness. *I don't ever want to die,* I thought, *I want to live forever.* New York seemed like a toy replica of a city—silent and unreal. We are told the snowflakes falling around us are each unique—but they are also all falling, all have six points, and all melt in your hand. Are they so different?

When I walked back into the Mercury, the lobby was empty. Nothing was moving.

Even old sleepy Bart was nowhere to be seen. I stood in silence waiting for the elevator. When the bell chimed and the doors opened, I felt compelled not to enter. Instead, I stepped away and let the doors close. The dog and I decided to take the stairs.

The back staircase of the Mercury Hotel is like a small enchanted castle stair. It smells ancient and sweet. The steps are narrow and made of a dull white marble. Somehow it still feels grand, like it has been, and will be, there forever. In the center of each heavy stone you can see a slight indentation where, over the years, feet have worn a path moving ever-upwards. At first, the wear is obvious. As you ascend, it grows subtler. Walking up, step after step, you feel yourself following a well-worn line. The higher you rise, the narrower and the steeper the steps become. The tread path is less obvious and more difficult to see. The floors no longer have numbers. When you breathlessly arrive at a landing, somewhere in the middle, the trail disappears completely. All you see is another staircase.

Acknowledgments

I would like to thank every actor I've ever worked with for the inspiration and friendship. I'd also like to thank Eric Simonoff, Jordan Pavlin, and Mark Richard. I owe a joyous debt of gratitude to my first reader, best friend, business partner, co-parent, wife, and final reader, Ryan Hawke. Lastly, I need to express gratitude to my whole family, especially,

```
        M         L
      R A Y     G R E E N
        Y         V
        A         O
                  N
```

ALSO BY

Ethan Hawke

ASH WEDNESDAY

Jimmy is AWOL from the army, but—with characteristic fierceness and terror—he's about to embark on the biggest commitment of his life. Christy is pregnant with Jimmy's child, and she's determined to head home, with or without Jimmy, to face up to her past and prepare for the future. Somehow, barreling across America in a souped-up Chevy Nova, Christy and Jimmy are transformed from passionate but conflicted lovers into a young family on a magnificent journey. *Ash Wednesday* is a novel of blazing emotion and remarkable grace, a tale that captures the intensity—the excitement, fear, and joy—of being on the threshold of the mysterious country of marriage and parenthood.

Fiction

VINTAGE CONTEMPORARIES
Available wherever books are sold.
www.vintagebooks.com